GATEKEEPERS
JOURNEY

Jody Brady

WESTBOW
PRESS®
A DIVISION OF THOMAS NELSON
& ZONDERVAN

THE HOLY BIBLE, NEW INTERNATIONAL VERSION®, NIV® Copyright © 1973,
1978, 1984, 2011 by Biblica, Inc.® Used by permission. All rights reserved worldwide.

WestBow Press books may be ordered through booksellers or by contacting:

WestBow Press
A Division of Thomas Nelson & Zondervan
1663 Liberty Drive
Bloomington, IN 47403
www.westbowpress.com
1 (866) 928-1240

ISBN: 978-1-5127-9704-6 (sc)
ISBN: 978-1-5127-9705-3 (e)

Library of Congress Control Number: 2017911540

Print information available on the last page.

WestBow Press rev. date: 08/18/2017

CHAPTER ONE

WESTERN WYOMING
PRESENT DAY

The ridge was very narrow, a rocky spine extending out from the shoulders of an even higher pinnacle to the north that thrust upward over a thousand feet above the timberline. The air smelled of smoke as a strengthening wind pushed upward from the deep drainage below.

"Juliet Division, this is Mankato Lookout," a radio broke the stillness.

A lone sentinel stepped from the shadows beneath the sub alpine fir into a small mountain meadow covered with lush grass and blue and red flowers.

"This is Juliet. Go ahead Mankato Lookout," the man responded to the call on his own radio situated diagonally across his chest in its harness over his yellow, nomex fire shirt.

He removed his hardhat and wiped his forehead with a moistened bandana. The day was hot, the humidity low. He had to be careful to drink plenty of water because dehydration could occur easily in such weather.

"Be advised Juliet. I am picking up two smokes low in Mill Creek drainage."

"Copy that Mankato. I'll take a look," Juliet Division Supervisor answered, peering into the sun down through the expanse below him.

There was static over the radio and the faceless lookout spoke again, "Be advised that the RH has dropped to 8%, winds out of the south at 14, gusting to 20."

"Copy that Mankato. Thanks for the heads up. Juliet clear."

"Mankato clear."

From his vantage point high on the ridge, Juliet could see most of the drainage below him, possibly five hundred acres of thick fir with scattered aspen, except along Mill Creek itself that meandered through a wide, flat bottom choked with willows. He glimpsed several ponds of glistening water, most likely caused by the abundant beaver that made Mill Creek their home. But otherwise the stream was hidden by the thick undergrowth and lush grass. Mill Creek lay below him to the east. The main fire burned through several drainages to the west of his position.

Several days before the Beaver Fire had made a violent run across the face of the mountain, exploding along the ridge that he now stood on at several locations. The fire had scorched much of the timber below him, leaving behind a blackened graveyard. Other places the fire had only crept through the timber, burning the understory, torching an occasional fir, but leaving much of the timber only slightly damaged. There seemed to be no pattern to its destruction.

The aircraft had stopped the forward progression of this flank of the fire, painting the ridge with their pink slurry that stuck to everything and would leave an unnatural pink hue across the landscape until the winter snows. The fire had slowed, but it was still very much alive, gaining strength with every passing day of no rain, the ever present afternoon winds and low humidity as the ground crews fought desperately against time to construct control lines around the perimeter and destroy its last strongholds of heat before the fire regained its strength to make another run.

The main fire had spawned two small spot fires in Mill Creek itself that had slept hidden beneath the dark canopy until now. Juliet Division was a geographical line of defense designated by the planning section of the fire's overhead team the day before the fire had threatened the ridgeline. The division stretched over two miles from a large meadow at the base of the mountain to the great expanse of broken rock above the timberline. The plan was to build a fire line along the black from the meadow to the rockslide and then kill any fire that lay along the ridge that could threaten the line. The two spot fires were on the wrong side of the line. If they awoke and made a run, they could threaten the crews working along the ridgeline above.

The Juliet Division Supervisor, known as Tom Mackenzie, walked to the edge of the meadow from where he could better see the two smokes. It was customary for the division supervisor to take on the name of the division itself during fire control operations when talking on the radio. All other firemen used their last names, at times including their rank or position as well. Tom was thirty-five years old, a product of Virginia Tech's forestry school who had eleven years experience with the US Forest Service.

The two spot fires produced twin wisps of gray smoke that floated harmlessly upward into the blue sky. They originated deep in the drainage just above the creek itself among the thick beetle killed timber. The timber above Mill Creek was in poor shape, overcrowded, the ground littered with the skeletal remains of the trees that had previously died. Now that the beetles had attacked the stand, entire sections were covered with dead snags, intermixed with dying trees with their characteristic red crowns.

The Forest Service, foreseeing the future threat of beetles and decline, had proposed a thinning several years before to reduce the stocking level and enhance growth of the stand, but the timber sale had been blocked by environmentalists. Now the stand was dying, a powder keg ready to explode.

With fire in the drainage, conditions were right for the entire slope to explode into a fiery storm. And the crews were building line along the narrow ridgeline above.

Not a good place to be if the two fires gained momentum, Tom thought as he plotted the approximate location of the two smokes on his topographical map. The two smokes were just below the mid point on the slope below a saddle in the mountain that was readily visible on the map as indicated by the curved topographical lines.

He insured his radio was tuned in on the tactical frequency for his division. He had three, twenty person crews, one from North Carolina and two from New Mexico. Also a four man felling crew from Oregon and a strike team leader from Georgia were under his command. The strike team leader had direct supervisory control of the crews. Juliet was responsible for the overall operation of the entire division.

He keyed the mike, "Davis, this is Juliet."

"Go ahead Tom," the radio answered with a slow South Georgia accent.

"You hear the traffic from Mankato Lookout?"

"Yea, I can barely make out the smokes below us. The canopy is real thick. We could be in a bad way if it makes a run, but it actually appears to be a little up drainage from us."

"What's your location John?"

"About a hundred yards from where we ate lunch. The saw crew is a little ahead of us snagging the burned out area."

Tom Mackenzie studied his map carefully. He was used to working with topographic maps. The slopes back home in western North Carolina where he worked as a forester for the US Forest Service were just as steep, but the mountains out west just kept going he mused.

His men were somewhat exposed if the new fires made a run toward them, but they were working close to a previously designated safety zone, a meadow approximately ten acres in size. The meadows were still green and did not burn, a condition that would change later in the year. He, on the other hand, stood about a mile from the meadow among thick timber where the previous fire had only meandered through with only the narrow meadow around him as a possible safety zone.

He looked around him. Too small! If the fire made a major run, it would blow right over his position. He didn't yet know how far it was to the end of the division at the rockslide along the base of the higher mountain. That would be another safe zone, but to reach it, he would have to climb through the thick unburned timber. Not a good choice either, but at this point, he wasn't extremely concerned. Maybe this was the chance that he had secretly wished for, he thought.

He pushed that thought away. Right now he had a job to do.

The safety of his crews was the most important thing. The only attack option he presently had to control the two fires was to order a helicopter for water drops. The sekorsky, a heavy helicopter was available earlier in the morning. He called back to Davis on the division tactical channel.

"Okay Davis, I'll order a heavy to work the smokes until Ops can get a crew in there to work the spots. I'll make sure that Mankato Lookout lets us know if anything changes. If it makes a run, you high tail it back to the meadow."

The smokes darkened a bit and grew wider. Heavier fuel had been consumed and the fires appeared to be slowly spreading.

"Copy that Tom," Davis answered, the buzz of a chainsaw in the background. He must have approached the felling crew.

Tom switched to the command frequency and immediately he could hear other command overhead personnel talking. The fire appeared to be gaining strength in other sectors as well. Resources would quickly become scarce because of the increased fire activity over several different divisions.

"Ops Dumbar, this is Juliet."

"Go ahead Juliet," the reply was weak and broken with static.

"I am requesting a heavy to work two small spots in Mill Creek drainage."

"Did you say Mill Creek?" Ops asked after a moment, the voice now stronger. He must have changed his batteries, Tom thought.

"Affirmative. Two spots on the east side of my division, low in the drainage."

There was a longer pause as Tom waited for a reply. A monkey wrench had been thrown in the plan, Tom thought and Ops was most likely studying his own map and hopefully coming up with the same conclusions. If the spots could not be quickly killed, Juliet Division would be lost.

Ops finally answered, "I'll get you a ship right away. It will be 7-Sierra-Hotel. He'll call you on air to ground. You got coordinates?"

"Not exactly, but I have a visual. The spots are too far down the drainage to send someone, so I'll be the contact. I can lead him to the location."

"Copy that Tom. Let me know how it goes. Right now all other air assets are busy on other fires, but I may be able to get a bomber if we need to."

"Copy that Joe, Juliet clear."

"Ops clear."

The heavy was a Sekorsky operated by a private contractor from Montana. From the meadow, Tom could see far down below the drainage to the wide valley below. To the north lay the rugged Wind River Range, a land of hundreds of high elevation lakes and mountain streams. Farther west, he could barely make out the Grand Tetons, their snow covered peaks a distant shadow on the horizon. Closer in lay the wide open rolling plains of western Wyoming, the slopes tinted purple in places by thick sage and then a low ridge heavy with timber, dotted with scattered homes. Below the ridge lay Horse Creek where the helibase was situated on a flat meadow next to the Forest Service guard station beneath a broken ledge of red rock that extended several miles across the face of the slope.

He saw three helicopters situated in the field, the Sekorsky and two smaller ships. A white supply tent sat beside a gray communications trailer next to Horse Creek Road. Across the road, among the white barked aspen, several small tents were scattered randomly near the creek. These were home away from home for the air operations personnel.

One of the smaller helicopters rose above the ground, a long line attached to its belly carrying a cargo net filled with supplies for one of the crews working somewhere across the fire that was now approximately 15,000 acres in size. The helicopters had been supporting Charlie and Delta Divisions all morning with both water drops and cargo drops. Because the fire was still progressing at a constant pace toward a mountain subdivision, these two divisions were priority. Juliet had only been a small blip on the radar screen until now. If the two spot fires made a run, that would all change.

The Sekorsky helicopter, painted black with a bright red stripe, sat closest to the communications trailer. A refueling truck pulled away as the crew ran across the field to their ship. Even though he was several miles away, Tom could faintly hear the engine come to life.

Tom looked back to the smokes. They appeared to have grown wider, the smoke itself a brownish-gray now, with occasional puffs of black. The fire had reached the beetle-killed timber. Were the fires spreading? That was harder to tell from this distance. The orange ribbon that he had previously tied around two dead snags along the proposed fire line whipped about as the wind increased.

Something was happening. Tom could sense it. He could feel the subtle changes that warned of increased fire behavior. All veteran firefighters knew instinctively when a fire was beginning to birth or grow. The trick was to pay attention to the clues that your environment gave you, to be prepared for the coming change. Fire was very unforgiving to those who did not respond to its subtle warnings. It was a monster that grew unpredictably. A master of trickery, a diabolical monster of intrigue, a dragon, but it always provided hints to what it was thinking to those who knew what to look for. Fire was a formidable opponent, one to be respected, but not necessarily one to be feared.

"You want to come out of there, don't you," Tom spoke in a low voice. He addressed the two smokes as if they were living creatures.

As if responding to his inquiry, a sudden puff of dense, black smoke came up through the trees. The red, burning tentacles along the forest floor had found new fuel to consume.

CHAPTER TWO

BEAVER FIRE
PRESENT DAY

Jack Darnell had flown Chinooks in the Gulf War for the army and then again in Somalia in 1993. He had seen the body bags of nineteen rangers and deltas laid out side by side in the hanger, angered at a Commander in Chief that tied his hands and made his job difficult, but his time was near. Two years later he retired from the military and moved back to Kalispell, Montana with Heather, his wife of twenty-two years. Now he worked six to eight months a year flying contract helicopters for the US Forest Service. He and his wife had never had children, so she traveled with him everywhere that he went. They had a small home several miles from Kalispell near the reservation, but they were only there during the winter months. The rest of the year, they traveled from fire to fire across the entire west, nomads living in a small trailer pulled behind their late model four-wheel drive pickup. The truck had scars to show its mileage. The red paint was rusted in places, but the truck was paid for. The pay was great and all expenses were paid. They were together and Jack loved what he did. Life couldn't be any better.

Jack had been eating a late lunch when the call had come in. Juliet Division requested water drops on several spots that were over the line. Leaning over the table, he kissed Heather lightly on the cheek and ran out the door. Their trailer was situated close to the tents of the other firefighters across the road from the helibase.

The crew chief, David Myers, was already at the ship, doing the last minute inspections required before each takeoff. They had been flying before lunch dropping water for Division Delta near several homes that were threatened by the slow progression of the fire. Jack had to quickly look at the operations map stapled to the bulletin board at the supply tent to find Juliet Division that lay across the fire from where he had been working.

The day's shift plan identified the division supervisor for Juliet Division as Tom Mackenzie, a forester from North Carolina. Good firefighters, those Carolina boys, Jack thought, although they had limited experience working with the larger helicopters. They preferred the smaller Hueys.

"Everything is ready to go Jack," Myers had completed his check and was climbing up into the back of the aircraft. He would help the pilot with the water drops. Jack climbed up into the pilot seat and strapped himself in, positioning his helmet and earphones and toggling the communication switches.

"Copy me okay David." Jack checked to see if the helicopter's on board radio worked properly.

"Got you loud and clear," the crew chief answered.

The helibase manager stood several hundred feet in front of the ship. He was responsible for all of the air traffic that flew in and out of the helibase and assured that all was ready on the ground each time a ship flew out or landed. The smaller helicopter that had flown out earlier hovered a safe distance away, only the long line hanging below, waiting for the larger helicopter to leave so it could land. A ground crew feverishly prepared another cargo load in several nets to be hooked up to the long line as soon as the big Sekorsky left the helibase.

The manager gave the okay sign and Jack fired up the engine. The ship immediately came alive, shuttering as the blades turned above. Inside the ship, the sound was deafening, but with his earphones on, Jack only heard a low rumble.

"7-Sierra-Hotel, you are clear for take off," Jack heard the manager over his radio, "Winds are out of the south at 10 miles per hour."

Jack pulled back the throttle and the great ship strained upward. They were at 8000 feet elevation, which hindered helicopter operations, somewhat, but the powerful engine took hold and the ship climbed upward. The helicopter climbed quickly above the meadow. Below the personnel turned their backs to the ship, leaning down, and holding their hard hats, as the rotor wash swirled around them. The winds caused by the blades bent the grass below and several of the smaller trees across the road. As the ground quickly fell below him, Jack could see the smaller helicopter turning for its own landing. He also spotted his wife. She stood by the trailer as she always did, looking up toward him, shielding her eyes from the sun's glare. She blew him a kiss, and he turned the ship toward the north.

From his vantage point above the fire, Jack could see across the entire range. The main smoke column pushed over 8000 feet into the air and extended for several miles along the western perimeter where Delta and Charlie divisions were located. The other divisions were all manned as crews worked the flanks and rear of the "beast" as Jack thought of the fire. Small smokes could be seen across the entire fire area as smaller sections continued to burn.

Juliet had been quiet ever since the wind shift that had pushed the fire away from Mill Creek, but now as he looked to the east, he could see twin smokes that appeared to be gaining strength.

Their water source was Horse Creek itself. Jack lowered the aircraft over the water and David guided him directly over the deep pool, where he lowered the ship until the bucket was totally submerged. He then yanked back on the stick and the engines whined as the aircraft pulled upward, the bucket full. Now they could head for the target.

"Juliet Division, this is 7-Sierra-Hotel."

"Go ahead 7-Sierra-Hotel, this is Juliet."

"I'm about one minute out. I see two smokes low in the drainage. Can you confirm that those are the targets?"

"That's the ones. I see you now. Continue at your 12 o'clock and you'll fly right over the targets."

"Copy That Juliet. Do you have any one on the ground down there?"

"Negative. All personnel are working the fire perimeter on the ridge directly above the smokes. No one should be anywhere near the target. You are free to work as you see fit. Can you give me a recon before you begin?"

"Copy recon, I'll get back to you," Jack switched to the ship frequency, "David give me a good look over before we begin dropping."

Jack's pilot seat sat high over the crew area of the ship. Although he had a great field of view all around him, he could not see the ground directly underneath him very well unless he turned the aircraft on its side. The crew chief however could see well below and would help with water placement when they began their drops. The bucket hung directly below the ship and carried 500 gallons of water.

As the ship circled the two fires, David searched the ground first for any personnel and then at the fire itself.

"Okay Jack, I've got two separate spots, each about one acre in size. The flames are beginning to increase and there appears to be a lot of fuel just upslope. If we're not careful, these things are going to blow up on us. By the look of the timber down there, the fires will make a run all the way to the top of the mountain."

"Copy that," Jack switched over to air to ground and relayed the information to Juliet.

"Appreciate the info. I'll inform my crews," Tom answered and immediately switched to his divisions frequency.

John Davis had been monitoring the radio traffic and knew already. His crews were working along the portion of the ridge that had been scorched, therefore there was no vegetation left to burn, a condition known as "good black" and they were safe. Davis assured him that they would not continue past the blackened area until the two spots had been dealt wish. They would "shade up", a term for taking a break preferably in the shade out of the sun, and wait it out if there was any chance of the fires making a run on their position. With the black next to them, they could just peel back into the drainage or back to the meadow if they felt threatened.

"Sounds good John. I'll stay here where I can see the smokes. I'm in a small meadow and should be fine. Mankato Lookout will inform us if conditions change," Tom answered

The meadow was too small for a proper safety zone if a fire torched out and a firestorm swept through the timber below him. But his crew was safe for the moment. The lookout could see better than he what the fires would do and when they would make their run. If the helicopters crushed the fires, that would be great. If not, then maybe this was indeed the time. He had been battling that possibility for several months. It would not be such a bad thing, he reasoned. At least his family would be taken care of. The way things were now he sure couldn't do it.

Tom was a depressed man, the failures of his life bearing heavily on his soul, the lies of deception strongly embedded in his mind. He had a wife and three kids that he loved dearly, but the struggles of the past few years had finally broken him. He had cried out to a God that he had served for most of his life and there had been no answer. Instead things had only gotten worse. Now he sat on a secluded meadow and pondered the possibility of his own death. The note had explained it all. Hopefully his wife, Nicole, would understand.

She would be better off after all. With the insurance and the firefighter's death benefits paid out by the federal government, all of their bills would be paid, the kids would get free college educations and Nicole would have enough money to live on for the rest of her life. He had made sure of that before he had left for his first tour of duty fighting the western fires. This was his second and final trip of the year. If it were to happen, now would be the perfect chance.

He watched as the helicopter made its first drop on one of the fires below him. The wind was increasing, the humidity lowered and all of the signs told him that the monster was coming alive. He knew the signs. He knew what he needed to do to be safe, but at this point, he had made his decision. He pulled out his canteen and drank the last of the water, placing the empty container back into its pouch by his side. Taking off his firefighter pack, he placed it against a lone pine that stood in the middle of the meadow and leaned back against it. He had a beautiful view below him.

There were eighteen Watch Out Situations that all wildland firefighters were required to know. The eighteenth situation was taking a nap near the fire line. Tom had not forgotten it; he just did not care. If he fell asleep, that was okay. At least the pain of failure would finally be over.

CHAPTER THREE

MOUNTAINS OF NORTH CAROLINA
PRESENT DAY

The stone house sat back against the base of the mountain, partially hidden from the road by several large oak trees that provided much needed shade on a day where the summer sun baked the drought stricken earth below. A slight breeze offered some relief. All of the windows were open throughout the two-story farmhouse, several rotary fans helping to circulate the air, but it was still hot.

The mountain rose sharply behind the house, rocky slopes covered with large white pine, the understory thick with mountain laurel and rhododendron along the lower slopes. A small mountain stream cascaded down from the steep drainage and crossed the open valley near the home through usually lush hay fields in better times. The drought had reduced the grass to yellowed, overgrazed pasture, the stream to a small trickle of water. It had been five weeks since rain had come with no relief in sight.

A winding, single lane gravel road left the highway and passed four newer homes before ending just past the stone house next to an old barn that was only now used to store hay when there was hay to store, The house had been built just after the great depression by the landowner who at that time owned the entire valley that covered over two hundred acres. The structure was one of the few granite rock houses anywhere around, the rock quarried from the river ten miles upstream. The locals told stories of old man Jenkins back when he was young, hauling the rock on wagons and building the house for his bride. Seventy-five years later and two generations past and all that was left of the original farm were the house and two acres immediately around it. The rest had been broken up and sold over the years by family members, characteristic of the many mountain farms and timberland tracts. Times were changing.

A small, red pickup turned off of the state road and immediately was lost in a swirl of dust, the yellow blinking light sitting high on the roof above the driver. It was the mailman. The truck stopped at each of the four houses before reaching the last mailbox. Luckily the stone house was far enough from the road not to be effected by the dust cloud.

A small girl dressed in shorts and a tee shirt ran from behind the oaks, her older brother just behind. They had been playing under the shade of the trees.

"Mommy, the mail!" the girl hollered excitedly. She was three years old, small for her size with long blond hair and sky blue eyes.

"Megan, stop!" her mother shouted after emerging from behind the same tree where she had been working in a flowerbed, one of the few things in life that gave her pleasure as of late.

The girl, Megan, quickly stopped as told causing her brother to pile into her. They both fell among yellowed grass, their legs entangled in a heap of laughing children. The mailman stepped out from his truck with a large package and several letters that were too large for the mailbox.

"Good afternoon Mrs. Mackenzie," the mailmen greeted as Nicole Mackenzie untangled her two children and sent them on their way back to the shade of the trees.

Nicole stood just over five feet tall. She was dressed in jean shorts and a tank top, her hands dirty from the garden, her face streaked with sweat and dirt, her eyes blue like her daughters and her hair blond, hanging just below her shoulders. Today it was tied up in a ponytail that made her appear even younger than usual. She was a beautiful woman who appeared to be in her early twenties, even though she was thirty-four with three children.

"Have you heard from Tom?" the mailman asked. He was a volunteer fireman and had heard that several local Forest Service employees, including Tom Mackenzie, had been recently dispatched to help with the growing number of western fires that were spreading like a deadly cancer across the western forests and grasslands.

Nicole took the packages in her arms, "No, he has been gone for three days. Usually it takes at least that long before we receive something from him."

She glanced through the letters and noticed a postcard, "Well it looks like I got something here."

The mailman tipped his cap, "That's great. You have a wonderful day."

"You too Jim," Nicole turned and called to her kids as the mailman climbed back into his truck, turned around in the driveway headed back down the road to the highway.

Before long, the fires would start here as well, he thought to himself. If rain didn't come soon the summer and fall would be very busy for the firefighters. He waited for a log truck loaded with pine logs to pass and then pulled out onto the highway. He still had another hour before quitting time. Boy that Tom was a lucky one, he thought. Nicole Mackenzie was one fine woman. He dismissed that thought. Tom was a friend of his and besides, he was married, although his wife didn't look nearly that good.

On the front of the post card was a picture of the Grand Tetons. Nicole flipped the card over as Megan and her older brother Seth ran up to her.

Back at the Mackenzie home, Nicole called to her children, "Look guys, Daddy sent us a post card!"

On the front of the post card that Nicole held in her hands was a picture of the Grand Tetons covered in snow. Nicole flipped the card over as Megan and her older brother Seth ran up.

Nicole read the note to her children.

"I miss you all already. We landed in Jackson Hole at night. I'm in a hotel room now. I'm not sure where I'll be going tomorrow, but they said the fire was 80 miles from here on the national forest. Nicole I love you, sorry about the mess. Kids you be good for mom. Take care of each other. Love ya."

"Can I see the card?" Seth asked excitedly.

"No me first!" Megan pleaded.

"You both can see the card," Nicole stated and bent down to show the picture to both of them.

"Is that where Daddy is staying?" Seth asked, "Has he seen Indians this time?"

"I'm sure he has," Nicole answered, "Now you two go back and play. In a little bit, we have to get baths. We have church tonight."

Nicole looked back at the note.

"Sorry about the mess," Tom had written.

She clutched the card next to her, looking away toward the distant mountain range. She missed Tom so much every time he left. When they had first married, she couldn't function when he was away. Her whole life was wrapped up in him to the point that when he left for trips on his job, she would stay in the house the entire time, only leaving when she absolutely had to. That had been years ago back when the panic attacks came at her often. Counseling and medication had helped her to finally overcome the dependence on her husband. Now she could function apart from him, but the old feelings lay dormant deep within her soul. At times she could feel them there, ever ready to awaken, and claim her mind. She fought them off and it was easier over time, but the last six months had been extremely difficult and the anxious feelings were returning.

She watched as her two younger children played under the trees in the front yard of their home. They had lived there ten years. She could still remember the day that they pulled into the yard to see a large banner tied to the front porch. It had read, "Welcome home!"

Tom's parents along with his entire family had come to help unpack. They were starting a new life. The day was a joyous occasion as all of their family unloaded the truck and worked around the old home to prepare it for the new family. Nathan, their oldest boy, had only been three and Tom had recently been hired as a forester for the U.S. Forest Service. Both Tom and Nicole had high expectations. Not only the new job, but also the couple was starting a youth ministry at a church in town. Great things were in store for them and everyone was excited and happy.

Nicole lowered her head, saddened at all that had transpired over the last few years. What had begun with such high expectations had fallen into the abyss of the failures of life, she thought. But there were things that were working out. She had three beautiful children and was very close to finishing college. She loved her church and she and Tom were still together, but there had been unexpected pressures and their relationship was strained.

"Come on kids, Let's go inside."

The children whined, but reluctantly followed their mom into the house.

"Sorry for the mess," Nicole read the note again.

She placed the mail next to a growing stack of bills that came each and every month, a constant reminder of the peril that they were in. It had not always been that way. Tom was able to take care of them well for several years. Nicole went to school part time, worked odd jobs at times and cared for the growing family. The youth ministry was expanding and the couple worked closely together. They were impacting the lives of hundreds of teenagers, but under the surface of their own lives, the troubles stirred.

Tom had difficulty being a proper steward of the finances and their financial situation began to suffer, and Nicole was unaware of the growing problem. Several poor investment decisions had drained their savings and then the medical bills began.

During this time, Nicoles's nightmares came, shattering her very existence with violent reminders of a horrid childhood of abuse and pain that she had hidden in the recesses of her mind for years. Although, Tom was aware of his wife's difficult childhood, he was not prepared for the exposure of the dark secrets that even Nicole had somehow hidden over the years from herself. Hidden that is until the memories returned in unsettling dreams that would leave her crying and clinging to her pillow, curled up in the corner of their bedroom. The "voices" followed along with headaches and memory losses and prolonged sicknesses. Nicole had to drop out of the ministry as well as school as the couple searched for an answer.

They prayed earnestly for God to heal her, but she slipped deeper into the world of insanity. Nicole was diagnosed as Bipolar at first and began to take medication that seemed to help, but only for a while. Counselor after counselor worked with her as her condition worsened and their finances slipped even deeper into debt.

But they continued to pray and Tom continued to work in the youth ministry and their debts continued to grow. And Tom hid from his wife the fact that they were slowly losing control of their financial situation to the point that all would be taken away.

And then suddenly, two years before, God healed Nicole and the voices stopped, the personalities melted away as Nicole through counseling confronted each of them and her dark childhood as well.

Tom had always been there for her, she knew. He had stood beside her as she confronted her past, held her close as she cried, stayed with her throughout the night when she had tried to commit suicide, and countless other nights when she was sick, but something had changed within him. He loved her still, she knew, but somehow at first he didn't trust her after she began to recover. He always worried that she would fall back into the deep pit of depression therefore he continued to hide the truth from her, but he could not hide it forever.

The final blow came when Tom, realizing correctly that he could no longer function as a youth pastor, resigned from the church and they moved to a new one, but to him he had failed once more. He could not pay all of his bills even after getting a second job and God suddenly appeared to be a million miles away. Nicole on the other had begun to shine as she became active in the new church by the river. She started back in school and became very active in ministering to youth again through her college, but everything the family now did was chained under the growing weight of financial ruin.

Nicole pushed the pile of letters angrily away. How had everything gone so wrong? There were such great possibilities ahead for them, but because of that stack of papers, it all seemed to be hopeless. She could cry just thinking about it. In fact, for the past few weeks, she did cry almost every night after Tom fell asleep. She prayed for God to help them, but deep within her heart she knew that until Tom changed, God's hands were tied.

At times she became so angry with him. How could he get them into this mess? They seemed to argue all the time about their situation lately up until several weeks before after Tom returned from his last trip out west. He was working the extra tour of duty to gain extra income to pay some of their bills, but while he was gone the last time, the house of financial cards that he had built tumbled down around her while he was away. The phone and electricity had been cut off and they had received a notice of foreclosure on the home. The money from the first trip helped to settle the problem only temporarily, but Tom suddenly became silent on the subject, almost calmed. It was one thing to be calm in the storms of life with the knowledge that God was in control, but this was not the case. Something dark was growing in his mind, but Nicole could not completely understand what was going on.

Nicole pondered that and began to worry even more about her husband. She knew him enough to know that he had come to some kind of decision, and that scared her. The last year, her husband had difficulty making any kind of decision, as his relationship with God seemed to weaken. He had lost the zeal for ministry and for the first time in their life began to succumb to the seductive lies of depression himself. Nicole knew all about depression. After all she had battled that problem for years. Depression still haunted her sanity, but she was now able to control it by the grace of God. Tom on the other hand seemed to be slowly giving way to its deception.

Nicole's thoughts were interrupted by the sudden cry from Megan. "Mommy, Seth hit me!"

She quickly placed the post card next to the mail and proceeded down the hall and into the living room. Seth was nowhere to be seen. Nicole picked her daughter up. Usually when Seth hit her, she had done something to him first.

"What did you do Megan for Seth to hit you?" she asked.

"Nuthin," the child whispered as she looked away.

"Well you seem to be fine. Now go get ready for a bath. I'll start you some water."

She placed Megan down on the couch and went into the extra room that was used as a recreation room, office and laundry room to find clean clothes for the children. Un knowing to her, a presence hovered over her. As she walked by her husband's desk, the Guardian named Raham, an angel that had been with Nicole for her entire life whispered in her ear and Nicole stopped and turned to look more closely at the desk.

A ministering spirit created by God, Raham chose to reveal herself in the form of a woman to her kind, but she could just as well have been a brilliant streak of a silver comet or the sparkling mist of morning fog over a mountain pond. She was a spirit being that was not restrained by the laws of the physical world. Thick locks of golden hair hung just below her shoulders. At times she would braid her hair and adorn it with flowers, but now a single leather band tamed it in one thick main. Her eyes were blue like the sky or at times green as the emeralds that adorned the gates before the portal to Eden. In battle, they turned silver, glowing intensively with a passion for Holiness. Her face was small, childlike in appearance with slightly slanted eyes, small ears and full red lips similar in some ways to Nicole herself. Her body was lithe and athletic, but very feminine and graceful as well with long slender legs and narrow waist.

Raham stood now beside her charge, her hands on Nicole's shoulders to comfort her. To Nicole she was a deep comfort, a small still voice, a warm memory brought forward in her mind, a soft suggestion, or an inward strength at times when her own strength was gone. Raham had fought along with the spirit of this dear woman when the spirits of depression and suicide had battled to destroy her. The Guardian had been there to comfort the girl Nicole when she had been terribly abused as a small child, restrained by the beasts of lust and hate, but only for a season. This brave woman had come far, but she still battled depression. What she was about to find would be a hard blow, but it was imperative that she find it so that the Gatekeepers could begin their work. Her prayers and Tom's had been heard and the plan to reconcile them was beginning.

For the first time, Nicole saw an envelope with her name written on the front. It lay on a pile of Tom's work papers at the corner of his desk partially hidden by one of his forest management reports. She opened the envelope and began to read the letter inside. Raham spoke words of comfort and strength to her as Nicole collapsed in the chair, visibly shaken.

"Oh!" she whispered, " Oh Tom, no."

Raham summoned the Messenger nearby. The battle was joined.

CHAPTER FOUR

WESTERN WYOMING
PRESENT DAY

The Beaver Fire continued to burn in a physical realm filled with men. The mountains were aglow with fire, thick, acrid smoke billowing upward into the heavens. There were over seven hundred men and women fighting the blaze scattered over 15,000 acres who were assigned to ten divisions, one base camp, two staging areas and one helibase. They all worked hard each day from early morning to after the sun finally melted away over the wide-open Wyoming plains.

The firefighters were not the only beings that worked and fought each and every day. There were others, although they lived in a different realm, a spiritual realm that mirrored the physical one that was separate yet linked through the spirits of men themselves and the God that created them. For every firefighter present here, there were many of another race, warriors fighting their own eternal battle, a battle for the souls of men.

The two spot fires began to take advantage of the increased fuel, growing stronger as they continued to consume the dead wood around them with red tentacles of death. The forest fire was very similar to the ones that burned in the spiritual realm, dark fires of depression and grief, condemnation and hopelessness.

The helicopter slowed the fire's progress somewhat by cooling the fire's heat, but the two spots continued to spread until they joined in an unholy union with destruction as their ultimate goal. They became one fire and with their combined strength, began to grow faster than the helicopter could fight. The pilot was an experienced one, having battled the western fires each season for almost ten years and knew that his helicopter would need help for the new fire to be defeated. He would make the request.

Time worked differently in the spiritual realm. The warriors were tied to time just like their human counterparts in the physical realm, but they were also outside of time just as God is outside of time. The spiritual beings operated outside of the boundaries of time in a way that only the Creator of time could understand. There was a lot at stake. A battle was being fought for the lives of two individuals whose days had been intertwined since birth, soul mates ordained by God who were now standing at the precipice of the abyss of destruction.

A streak of brilliant light flashed across the treetops and through the dark smoke of the main fire, a red glow just behind it. Both lights swirled through the helicopter itself and another blaze of red shot upward from the ground and intercepted the silver light. All three materialized into warriors, one bright as the sun, holding a golden sword and the other two, dark beings, swinging double bladed axes.

The helicopter turned back toward the river for another pickup, the blades cutting through all of the figures like they were air. There was a sudden explosion of gold and one dark figure disappeared and the second retreated back over the mountain, trailing red smoke behind that mingled with the gray smoke below. The sword disappeared and the form changed again into a streak of silver. It floated slowly downward before disappearing near the meadow above the fire, changing into a silver mist glistening beneath the grove of aspen until the shape of a man materialized. Only the trees knew of his existence in the physical. The brush parted slightly with the man's coming, but no one noticed the movement. To a human it would have looked like the wind or the fluttering caused by a bird.

The man stepped out into the meadow and searched over the forest opening for one of his kind. He was small, athletic with strong legs of an Olympic runner, a body made for speed and stealth, although he could fight if needed as well.

One of the firefighters sat next to the tree below him, watching the growing fire and the helicopter in the drainage below. A dark shadow floated over his head and shoulders, sickly black tentacles of depression and hopelessness messaging the firefighters shoulders.

"I'm over here," a voice whispered from behind a broken tumble of rocks. The man turned to his left and saw another of his race step out into the clearing. He took two steps and faced the man, bowing in greeting. The other bowed in return.

"You are Kapar, Guardian of the firefighter below us?"

"Yes, I have been with Tom Mackenzie the whole time. Hopefully you have news for me?" Kapar asked hopefully, staring at the growing black mass that enveloped his charge.

He was a tall warrior, standing over six feet. Unlike many other Guardians, he preferred his hair short similar to a soldier he had once served many years before. His eyes were very dark, almost black that sparkled when he laughed.

He could keep the thing at bay, but could not totally destroy it until Tom himself willed it to be gone. Then his sword would slash the ugly tormentor to pieces.

The Messenger spoke, "Raham sends her greetings. She says that the note has been found."

"Has the prayer begun?"

"As you know, Nicole rages her own battle against depression, but Raham is confident that the Spirit will lead her to do what she must."

Kapar smiled. He had known of Raham's courage and confidence in the Spirit. He knew that Raham understood as well as he the war that had been fought in both the physical and spiritual realms for the souls of Tom and Nicole. Since childhood they had been selected as soul mates with a great destiny in store for both of them, but the journey had been a long one, the battles hard, the wounds deep.

Kapar hoped that what Raham thought would be true. He knew that the two loved each other dearly, but over the last few years their relationship had been strained to the breaking point. Past hurts and failures, poor choices and personal tragedies had left their spirits scarred. Yes their love held them together by a weakened strand of hope, but unless a break through happened soon, that hope would shatter and all would be lost. Even now, Tom had made the decision, a decision conceived earlier in the year. The stress was so great, the self-condemnation too strong, the quilt overbearing his desire for life. But the note that Nicole had found held the key to the beginning of recovery. God could move mightily if the two could just hold out a little longer.

The Messenger pointed to the firefighter, " I don't understand. He was a youth pastor. He was called of God at an early age. He has a great destiny before him. How can he choose this way? How can any of them choose this way?"

The Messenger had never worked directly with the human race. His job was to send the messages from one warrior to another over the expanse of the battlefield of men's souls. Although he was a warrior himself, always vigilant to protect the message, fighting side by side with the Guardians who worked directly with the human race, he did not have relationships with the humans themselves. He could not understand the personal battles that humans fought each day of their lives.

Kapar attempted to answer the Messenger's question, his own heart heavy with empathy, " He can't see the harm that his decision will do. He has allowed the spirits of depression and guilt to cloud his judgment. The Spirit speaks to him, but he can't hear the Voice at times."

"You say that he loves her. Raham says the same thing. But how can they be the way they are now if they truly love one another. He can't love Nicole and do the thing that he is prepared to do at this time."

"Have you read the note, my friend?"

"No."

"Tom is doing this because he does love his wife. That thing," Kapar pointed to the black swarming mass of tentacles that completely covered the firefighters head and shoulders, "has perverted his mind, clouded his judgment and prevented him from hearing the Spirit, but one thing that the note does show is how much he truly does love his wife. And that will come out when she reads it. Then she will see that she can trust him again and will pray. Now he is trapped in this dark thinking, this blackness, until she does. He may be wrong, but the note is very clear that he is prepared to give his life for her because of his deep love for Nicole."

"You try to justify his decision. Try to make it sound honorable," the Messenger countered.

"No. He is very wrong because he no longer can stand the weight of condemnation for his past mistakes and he sees this as a way to make up to Nicole for all of the trouble that he has caused. But she has felt and feels the same. Her past sickness placed a great strain on their relationship. Her bouts with depression and attempted suicide have left Tom's spirit beaten as well. They have both cared for each other through terrible times. but the stress built up over the years had to come out some time. Now that it has, recovery and reconciliation can begin and the two can again travel the road that God has placed ahead of them to travel."

"Were they once on the true path our Lord placed for them?"

"Yes, in fact they still are to a certain extent. It used to not be this way. Their journey has been a difficult one, but they have been able to overcome much in their lives. You must see to fully appreciate the decision that has been made." Kapar stepped closer to the firefighter and the black, withering mass retreated a short distance in fear of the warrior who brandished a double-edged broadsword.

"Your time will come very soon" the Guardian warned, holding the demon at bay, trying to allow a bit of freedom for his charge, but several tentacles remained embedded in Tom's brain.

The fire below continued to gain strength as the helicopter worked to suppress it. In the spiritual realm the fires of deceit wrapped their way around the firefighter, but in this case he could not read the signs.

Kapar turned back to face the Messenger, prepared to release him, "You have done well."

Then he noticed that the Messenger had been wounded.

"You have been hurt?" the Guardian questioned, concerned, "When did this happen?"

The Messenger looked down and noticed for the first time himself, the gash through his abdomen.

"Ah, It is nothing. Several of the enemy tried to stop me on my journey, but I will be fine."

"You should rest a while. I can do nothing until Nicole reaches out for her husband or until Tom himself breaks free, which he shows no signs of doing. You spoke of wanting to understand. Sit here, by the rock as we wait and see. Their story will hopefully show you why we are all here this day."

Kapar helped the weakened Messenger back into the grove of aspen. He had been wounded more than he had thought, but he was a Messenger and would not stay once his message was delivered, "I'll be fine. The Rivergate may yet need me, therefore I must return. Others will soon join you. One is on the way as I speak."

The Messenger saluted the Guardian and disappeared back over the mountain. Kapar watched as the Messenger flew past several of the enemy before disappearing beyond past the highest peaks of the surrounding mountains. A strange breed, he thought to himself and then returned to his charge. Kapar would stand guard as he had always done and hold back the mass that held his charge captive. He knew that others would soon come to finish the deed. Hopefully the prayers would rise upward and other warriors would be summoned to his assistance. He did not always understand the Lord's plan, but he knew that he must be ready when the time came to fulfill it.

"There is a portal nearby Kapar," a voice spoke from the shadows of the large pines.

Kapar turned sharply, sword in hand and then took a step back. Another man stood among the pines, his sword sheathed, his purple cloak fluttering softly in the light breeze. He looked vaguely familiar to Kapar. The man pointed to a jumble of broken rock along the narrow spine of ridge above the meadow.

Kapar turned his head questioning the man. They all knew that the world, when it was created in perfection was filled with portals between this ball of life called earth and the heavens of eternity or other dimensions outside time and space, the greatest being the door to Eden itself. But when sin entered the world, the world itself began to break down and the portals as well. Over the eons of the earth's existence, many eroded and when they did, doors opened that humans were not meant to walk through.

But over the years many have. The enemy always searched for portals that had fallen to the curse of sin, hoping to use them to once again gain entrance to Eden. Kapar's kind were sworn to prevent that from happening, therefore all portals were protected by Guardians of their own to prevent the enemy from using their power. Their battle was hard and never ending. They were called the Gatekeepers, feared warriors who fought to themselves, always protecting their territory until the time when the Lord calls them home.

Kapar knew a few of them, had seen the devastation caused on humans when the portals fell into enemy hands, but he had also seen the wonders when humans were allowed to briefly see through one by the Gatekeeper themselves. He had been present when Enoch was called upward through a portal, the first since Adam. He had also been present many times since then when the people of God realized that the windows of heaven were open above them and the blessings poured down, when angels walked on ladders of pure gold between Heaven and Earth. He remembered the story of Jacob's ladder as well, although he had not been there to see that particular portal.

There were places all across the world where portals existed. They were placed here after Eden to be used by God's people themselves in the spiritual realm, but the decaying presence of sin itself on the earth had transformed many into the gray world between the physical and spiritual dimension.

Kapar focused his attention again on the battle he knew was coming.

The earthly fire began to gain strength under the mountain below the two warriors and their charge. In the realm of the angels, a dark cloud materialized over the horizon. Kapar prepared for the coming battle. If help did not arrive soon, all could be lost. The portal may just be his answer to prayer.

"How did you know the portal is there?" Kapar asked, knowing that the Gatekeepers hid the openings well even from others of their kind. They were very secretive.

The man smiled, "You guessed right Kapar when you thought that the portal may be of assistance. This particular one is damaged and is now a part of the netherworld between dimensions and time. It leads to many other places and time, but it can be a place of safety. And I have come from a perfectly functioning one, one that holds great power. The Gatekeepers there are strong and growing stronger each day, but in Tom's case they need more time to work. The note has been found, but it will be a while before the forces come. You and I are all that stands between that," he pointed to the growing blackness swelling up from behind the dark smoke of the fire, "and Tom."

"What you propose may possibly be dangerous. Certainly it will be confusing to Tom himself." Kapar countered the suggestion voiced by the man, one that he, too, was entertaining.

"But it will give us time. Your charge has decided to end it here not knowing that in so doing, he made a way for the Lord to help."

"Are you sure that the portal you speak of is strong?" Kapar asked.

He had seen the gate that the man spoke of, but because he was Guardian to Tom, who for the past year had been unable to yield to the Spirit's pull in his life, Kapar had not himself been able to fully glimpse the powers that were building by the river back home. His sight was limited by the spiritual blindness of his charge.

"Yes, I know for a fact that the Gatekeepers there have the power to intercede on your behalf, given time. I was there in the beginning when the gate was first established. I was there through the ages while the gate lay dormant. And I saw when the gate finally opened wide. It is growing daily."

"You are a Gatekeeper then?"

"Yes Kapar, I was the first assigned at that portal, but now the true Gatekeepers have taken control and I was released to work for our

Lord in other ways. What is happening here in this time actually has its beginnings a very long time ago."

Kapar had not known that the man was of such a strong contingent of angels. The man tightened the sash around his garments, pulling the sword from its scabbard, testing the sharpness with his finger.

He smiled, " Kapar we have a long fight coming, but first I must seek a certain Gatekeeper. He must be near, perhaps somewhere among the rocks just on the other side. If we are to use the opening, we must be assured that Tom will be safe until help arrives. The Gatekeeper here can tell us this"

"You have a name, Gatekeeper?"

"Sarat, Captain of the Rivergate."

And the fire rushed forward.

CHAPTER FIVE

THE MOUNTIANS OF NORTH CAROLINA
DAY ONE AFTER EDEN

A golden ball hung just above the hazy blue mountain range, casting the deep ravines into the shadows of the approaching night. The mountains formed a semicircle around three sides of a wide valley of heavily timbered slopes and scattered meadows. A meandering ribbon of sparkling water gained strength from hundreds of high mountain streams to form a mighty river that flowed through the center of the valley among the scattered lowland grasslands and thick stands of pine and hardwood.

The day before, the valley lay in pristine glory the way that it had been created, but now a foreboding darkness flooded across the land that originated when the decay of sin entered the world through the fall of man.

As the sun melted away behind the pale blue-gray mountains, casting the scattered wispy clouds in pink and lavender hues, the shadows marched across the landscape in unrelenting waves. The light of the physical day gave way to the darkness of another night. In the spirit realm, the darkness spread across the land as well.

There was no moon, the night sky filled only with untold stars. A breeze stirred, swirling playfully through the valley, caressing the new leaves, budding forth with spring. They had been soft and deep green, but now curled brown at the edges and covered with the spots of death.

The perfection that had once been present was now marred by the sin of mankind. The portal to Eden was shut, the perfect world gone until it's future time of redemption. Black shadows hovered over the dark forest, whispering to the breeze, swirling across the landscape, searching.

A single star fell from the sky above and disappeared, followed by several more, bright comets streaking toward earth. One of the black shadows moved, twin red eyes searching toward the heavens, but too late to have seen the small lights. The smell of decay lingered along the riverbank that lay covered in a ghostly mist. The breeze had finally stilled with the total disappearance of the sun. Along the riverbank stretched a meadow covered in lush grass and wildflowers.

The black shadow stood among the thick alders by the meadow searching for any sign of movement. It was a watcher that stood silently, waiting for an enemy that hid somewhere nearby beneath the pines or among the thickets across the meadow. The watcher was a product of the darkness itself, spawned by death and decay that had infected the creation. He was at one with the darkness in which he now hid and could see just as well in the dark as in the day. Something was out there hiding, waiting as he waited, but he could not see it. He could only feel the presence.

The victory of Eden had been a day before, although time in this realm mattered little. He as well as his enemy lived outside of time just as easy as they operated within its constraints. When sin entered the world, causing death to fall upon the creation itself, his master had sent countless numbers of his kind across the whole world in waves of darkness searching for another entrance to Eden. They had felt the hand of destruction and could be used for the master's purpose if control could be won.

The shadow shifted as another watcher floated down through the treetops and descended quietly among the alders. The first one said nothing as the second stepped forward to the very edge of the meadow. Both were spiritual beings, their race having rebelled against their Creator. Because of their rebellion, their race was disfigured, although they could take various forms depending on their particular assignment or rank The ones sent forth after the portals were warriors in their truest sense, with only two passions, the destruction of mankind and capture of the portals.

The watchers were black apparitions that could blend in with their earthly environment just as easily as they could at times masquerade as Spirits of the Light. But only mankind was fooled by this masquerade, therefore when dealing with the Creator's army, they used stealth as their weapon, hiding in the darkness, until called forth to fight by their commanders.

"The gate has to be near," a raspy voice broke the silence of the night.

"If it is here, do we have the forces to hold it from them?" the first watcher asked.

He had guarded the valley since the beginning of the rebellion, waiting for the gate to show itself, but there had been nothing. Now with the fall of man and the closing of Eden to all, fighting had sprung up all across the land as the forces fought for control of the land, but there had been no action here. No enemy presence had materialized until just recently.

That presence was very strong, even though they could not locate its source. It cast a foreboding doom over both of them.

"I believe so when the others arrive," the second turned nervously, "but now it is but you and I. We must stay hidden and watch closely. The gate will appear in time and we must be ready to take it when it does."

The watchers knew the importance of their mission. If the portals could be taken and destroyed, God's future plans for mankind would be hindered. They did not fully understand the plan of God to redeem man and the world back to him, but they knew the importance of the portals. And now with the world's decay, many of the portals were also decaying, changing their structure, opening avenues into different dimensions both in the physical and in the spiritual realm.

A sudden explosion of silver shot forward from the river itself and the first watcher vanished in a red vapor that floated to the ground and disappeared. The second watcher drew his sword and turned toward the light.

"There's only one now." A voice spoke from the darkness.

The watcher backed up nervously into the meadow, his own sword drawn, his eyes casting an eerie red glow over the dark water. He had seen the other watcher disappear in the flash of light and red smoke and expected to be attacked by the Creator's Guardians for they alone had such power. Still he saw nothing.

The river flowed toward the east below him past the thin line of alders, the riverbank 20 to 30 feet high at this point. His orders were to locate the gate that was somewhere nearby and wait for reinforcements to take control of it, but what could he do alone. It was a cool night, but he began to sweat, the cold, clammy sweat of fear. He stepped back again, holding his sword before him with both hands.

Where were they? He had heard the voice from the river itself. He wiped the perspiration from his brow. If he retreated, his master would most likely destroy him, but if he stayed, he could join his comrade in the netherworld of the abyss. The attack had come suddenly from the water itself. How could he defend himself from such an attack?

He backed a few feet further into the meadow to give him more space in which to defend himself.

There was a flutter of commotion among the thickets to his right and he turned quickly to face the threat. The red glow of his eyes washed the foliage with its pale light, revealing a deer, wet up to her neck from swimming the river standing in the meadow, her eyes looking past him. She could sense his presence and appeared confused. The deer took two tentative steps out into the meadow and then suddenly turned on her back legs and with one leap disappeared back into the thicket. What had she seen that frightened her?

The watcher swirled quickly around, realizing suddenly the presence of his foe too late, swinging his sword as he did to parry the blow that was coming. Red steel struck against silver, spraying the ground with sparks of blue light. The blow was crushing, knocking his sword down into the thick grass where it disappeared.

All was lost. The watcher turned to fly to safety but met another sword that flashed out of the darkness, cutting his body in half before he too vanished in a puff of red smoke, leaving only the smell of sulfur behind.

Three warriors emerged from the water and sheathed their swords, climbing the bank with ease and stepped through the brush to where two others stood. The one who had vanquished the last watcher knelt down and taking a hand full of grass, he cleaned his weapon before sheathing it in the scabbard by his side.

"There were only two. Undoubtedly a scouting party searching for the portal, but we hid it well as soon as we got the warning that Eden had fallen," the warrior spoke as he sheathed the sword.

He was a tall warrior, with long black hair that hung down to his shoulders, curly and unruly that he held in check with a purple headband. His partner was almost as tall with short blond hair. Both wore the tunic of a Gatekeeper, Guardians of the portals of Heaven.

The three who had emerged from the river also wore the tunic. Their leader bowed slightly in greeting to the two who had dispatched the two watchers. There were now five warriors standing among the alders by the river.

"I am Anah, this is Koah and Nakar, fresh from the throne room of our Lord. We have come to assist in protecting the gate. It must be a very important one for the five of us to be dispatched to guard it. We seek Sarat who is to be our Captain."

The tall warrior eyed the three suspiciously at first and then smiled briefly at his comrade, " Well you have found him and this is your new lieutenant, Nasag."

The blond warrior bowed in greeting.

Sarat continued, "We have seen the fighting across the mountains, but our Lord commanded that we hide the gate and remain here to protect it. The portal is pure and should remain so. It is a regional portal and will require all of us to protect it until the Redeemed ones claim it for themselves."

Anah looked around the meadow, "You have hidden it well Captain."

"You are in the middle of it. The portal is very large. One day after the work of redemption a great place of worship will cover this entire area and thousands will believe because of what is done here. Until that time, we must guard it well and help Guardians of the faithful to find and then open it."

He turned toward the ridge across the meadow, "We have established a small camp just under the ridge among the rocks. From there we can watch the entire valley. We must persevere gentlemen. No matter what we see, we must never forget the reason we have all been chosen for this specific mission. The forces of darkness are assembling. I feel that they intend to take the entire valley, but as long as we hold this sacred ground until the appointed time, then we will have won. That is the way of the Gatekeepers. That is why our Lord gives us this sacred trust. We must not fail him."

The forces of darkness were gathering. Ahead of them, a single scout sat on a log that floated slowly down the river. He had seen enough. With a short hop, the small scout shot upward and disappeared over the ridgeline. The reinforcements were too late, but at least they would know that the portal was indeed located by the river.

CHAPTER SIX

WYOMING
PRESENT DAY

The ridgeline above the meadow was crowned with a broken tumble of jagged rocks jutting up between the thick firs. The lee side of the mountain was extremely steep, falling a thousand feet down into the drainage, the slopes covered with the dark green foliage of the alpine fir forest. Here for some reason the Beaver Fire had only crept through the understory randomly, leaving large areas of unburned fuel in the trees above the smoky, blackened forest floor. The rocks and trees along the ridge were painted with light pink hue, residue of the retardant dropped by the water bombers several days before.

Sarat left the Guardian Kapar by his charge and climbed the short distance to the rock outcrop. He knew that somewhere among the rocks, a portal was hidden. He could sense the presence of the portals, both spiritual and physical in nature.

Somewhere among the rocks lay the opening that was decaying along with the rest of the world because of the fall of Eden. It had broken through the spiritual dimension and now flowed through both realms, violating the natural laws of physics, time and space. Mankind very rarely found one, but over their time since the fall of Eden, a few had stumbled into the openings and traveled into the netherworld between dimensions and time, most of them forever suspended between the realms, lost to the world from which they had come. Only a few had returned with strange stories to tell. They spoke of places where time seemed to stand still or of openings hidden in the fog where one would become easily disoriented, as directions seemed to reverse themselves and compasses gave false readings. They never, however knew how they had managed to return, their experiences shrouded in their memory like fading dreams in the morning.

Sarat could see the split in the fabric of space, a place where the rock face was set apart from the rest of its form. The increased wind bent the grass in front of the rock and for a moment the grass disappeared into the rock itself. He tapped the rock lightly with his sword until the sword was swallowed up by the rock. If the gate was protected by his kind, he would have been challenged, but this gate had no protector. It had decayed to the point where it no longer could be used to access Heaven itself, but Gatekeepers still monitored the activities around all of the portals.

Sarat stepped through the portal and on through the rock to the other side. Because he was pure spirit, the gate had no effect on him, but he knew that if a human were to step through the portal, he would immediately be flung into the space and transported to the other end of the tunnel which could be anywhere in the universe and outside of the confines of time as man understood it.

Sarat stood by the door for a brief moment. He could see Kapar take a step away from him, drawing his sword. The battle was soon to come.

A streak of light flashed before him, trailing a ghostly trail of silver particles behind and a sword struck lightly against his own before the Gatekeeper changed form and materialized.

"Captain, what brings you here of all places?"

It was the Gatekeeper called Nasag.

"It is good to see you again, Nasag," Sarat greeted, "I had heard that after our victory at the Rivergate you had been sent to patrol the broken portals."

"Yes, I have been here since that time. Is it true that the Rivergate is now in the hands of the Redeemed and growing daily?"

Sarat nodded.

"There are many portals throughout this land that have decayed. Most have fallen in on themselves, but there are a few that leads to far places in the universe. For many days, only a few humans found them, but this last day, there have been many that search for them on purpose. The enemy has increased their activities along the portals as well."

"Since the victory at the cross, the enemy knows that their time is near. They seek any way to break through to Eden once more." Sarat answered.

"Why have you come Captain?" Nasag asked lowering his sword before him.

Sarat sheathed his sword and pointed out of the gate to where Kapar stood, his back to them, "We must hide a human here for a small time until help arrives. Is the gate safe for a human to access?"

"This portal leads to another physical area a thousand miles from here, but time is altered. Others have used the gate many times on the other end, but that was before I came. The last person who found the opening did so over 400 earth years ago. The man is still trapped there. To him, he has only been there a few days."

"Okay. The forest fire that could kill the human, as well as a full troop of the enemy that is after his soul will soon overwhelm this area around us. If Kapar can break the hold that the spirit of hopelessness has on him for a moment, he will react to the situation that he faces and we can lead him to the opening. Can you ensure his safe journey into and at the appropriate time back out of the portal to this time and place? We will defend against the coming attack until help arrives."

"It is an honor to serve with you again Captain."

"And you as well Nasag, Godspeed. Be strong in the Lord Nasag. I am not sure the strength of the enemy attack or to what depths God will allow the man's soul to endure."

"I will stand with him Sarat. My sword will carry him through. That is our way."

Sarat clasped his friend's hand, turned and stepped back out of the opening. Although he could not see the Gatekeeper, Sarat knew he was still visible to Nasag. Before moving away from the portal, he smiled and gave the Gatekeeper a thumbs up sign of encouragement. Nasag was a strong one, Sarat thought, a lone guard who often battled the enemy who searched for a way to Eden alone with his sword and the everlasting faith that God was his strength.

Kapar pointed to the fire below and then to the helicopter that was fighting valiantly to slow the spread of the fire. Soon it would be a lost cause. With the strong winds that grew stronger because of the approaching troop of demons, the fire would soon explode up the drainage. Sarat was immediately at the Guardian's side.

"Will the portal be safe for Tom? " Kapar asked.

"Yes. We can hide him there as long as needed to escape the coming fire."

"The helicopter may be in trouble. There are no Guardians with them so they are not redeemed ones. If Tom hears their call for help, he will respond. That's the kind of man my charge is," Kapar said with a measure of pride. "Then that thing's hold on him can be broken long enough for me to vanquish it to the abyss and we can get him to safety."

Both of them suddenly knew what was about to happen as the Lord gave them a brief view of the next few moments in time. There would only be two humans through the gate. The third would unfortunately pass through a final portal, the portal of death itself.

CHAPTER SEVEN

WESTERN WYOMING
PRESENT DAY

J ack Darnell had enough experience to know when a fire had
beaten him. He was not going to keep the new spot from spreading
up the mountain above Mill Creek.

"David, I don't think we're going to do any good here," He spoke
to his crew chief over the ship's radio.

"I'll agree to that. This thing is fixing to blow up on us. You better
alert Division."

Jack switched over to air to ground, "Juliet, this is 7-Sierra Hotel."

Tom had dozed off under the tree, something uncharacteristic of
him, but he had made a decision, however wrong it had been. The call
awakened him from the gray world of half sleep. Had someone called
him? He listened now for another call.

"Juliet, this is 7-Sierra Hotel," the radio at his chest called again.

He was now fully awake. How long had he dozed? He looked at
his watch. It had only been a few minutes. He bent his head forward
and raised the radio from its resting place.

"Go ahead 7-Sierra Hotel, this is Juliet," Tom answered.

He could see the helicopter circling the column of smoke. The
wind was blowing stronger than expected, with violent unexpected
down drafts as the air current swirled though the rugged mountains.
The smoke column turned to match the gust, temporarily hiding the
helicopter from view.

"Juliet, we have lost this fire. You better get your people to safety zones. With the increased winds, this thing is going to blow out the top of the ridge."

"Copy that. Could you notify Ops? I'll tell my people. We should all be safe no matter what it does," Tom lied. He knew that he was definitely not in a safe position if the fire turned toward him.

"Davis, Juliet,"

"I copied direct Tom, We're all in good black." Tom referred to the area where the fire had already burned, leaving behind nothing but scorched earth and ghostly, blackened trees.

"Sounds good John. I guess we'll just ride this thing out. It ought to be a Kodak moment."

"Copy that Tom," the strike team leader answered calmly which assured Tom that they were indeed in a good safety zone.

He, on the other hand, had made a fateful decision that he would have to now live with, or rather die with. The fire would indeed blow out the top of the ridge and from the slanting smoke column below, he lay directly in its path with no place to go. A growing fear welled up deep within him. If only he could had remained asleep, then his death would have come quickly, possible even while he slept. But now, he would feel the full brunt of the fire's attack. He suddenly did not want to die! What had he been thinking?

Tom grabbed his pack and pulled the harness over his shoulders, attaching the buckle across the front of his chest. He had the fire shelter, but he placed little comfort in its ability to save him. The meadow was too small. If the fire didn't kill him, he would still be burned even if he deployed the shelter. The fire intensity would be too great. He was going to die!

The withering mass wrapped around his head spoke softly to his spirit, "That's right. You are going to die. That's what you wanted. Just breath the smoke in as the fire comes. You'll be dead before the flames burn you. You won't feel a thing."

"No!" Tom shouted to his thoughts. There had to be a way out, but he couldn't think.

As Tom screamed, the dark mass suddenly fell away from Tom

and the Guardian Kapar was quick to slash across the demon, trapping him to the ground. The warrior reached down and grasped the thing around its snake like head.

"It looks as if you are no longer welcome here"

The demon screamed in pain as Kapar flung the demon into the air and followed its advance with his sword that slit the thing into. The demon disappeared into a cloud of red smoke that vanished with the wind.

"Okay Tom, now control yourself. There is a way out." Kapar spoke to Tom's spirit.

Kapar could see the growing mass that was beginning to merge from behind the distant ridge behind the fire. The enemy was attacking in force and would be near very soon.

Tom calmed himself somewhat.

"Think man," he said to himself, "there has to be a way out."

He looked behind him further up the ridge. The meadow was just too narrow. Maybe he could run down the lee side of the mountain. There had to be a burned out area somewhere to find a place of refuge.

Someone was calling on the radio. Others were talking about the new fire that was quickly gathering strength, preparing its red legions for a major assault on the mountain. Tom ran to the far edge of the meadow, his will to live taking control. The leading columns of gray smoke floated through the trees, scouts in front of a new offensive. Soon the embers would begin to fall with increased heat and then darker, black, acrid smoke that sucked the oxygen out of the air and replaced it with noxious gasses that would sear the lungs and cause an agonizing life unless death came quickly. Tom still had at least ten to fifteen minutes before the fire's front found his small enclave. There was still a chance. He couldn't outrun the fire, so the small meadow would have to do.

He had never deployed his fire shelter. His training had taught that to do so was a last gasp at life, deployed only after all other avenues of escape had failed. The shelter was made of fire resistant material similar to aluminum foil and resembled a small tent when deployed. As the wind increased, the meadow seemed even smaller than before.

Could he even deploy the thing in the wind? Would it truly protect him or would he burn alive inside? Fear grabbed hold of his spirit.

The first evil warrior appeared from behind the smoke and with a howl of lust, dove through the tree nearest Tom to drive his spear deep into the man's head with the metal of fear, but Kapar prevented the blow from going all the way through. A brilliant explosion of golden light shot outward from the Guardian's up raised sword as the warrior's spear point shattered on impact and the demon disappeared. That was close. Others were soon to follow.

Now that Tom was fighting for his own life, Kapar was free to fully protect his charge. Tom knew to call out to God for help in his time of need and the strength caused by his frantic prayer surged through Kapar as he prepared himself for the coming fight.

"Sarat!" Kapar called out.

"I am here my friend," the Gatekeeper stood next to the Guardian. Together they could defeat the enemy for a season, but if help didn't arrive soon all would be lost. The enemy was too many, but only the forward elements of their full detachment were nearby. The two angels could see the enemy swirling through the clouds in the far distance, streaks of red haze as individual scouts and skirmishers searched for their target.

Other Guardians that protected humans on the fire could not leave their charge, but could attack those that ventured close or threatened them directly. Tom, who was their target, had not yet been totally identified by the enemy and the scouts had to search across the entire area. Individual duals between warriors erupted in the heavens just above the tree line. Like a great air battle of air planes, the forces of light intermixed with those of darkness. Silent explosions of red flashed through the smoke as demons were either wounded or banished. Guardians took hits as well and several spiraled downward through the trees like stricken planes, trailing golden mist, however each in turn would quickly recover enough to stand guard again over their individual humans, even though wounded.

Only those Guardians whose charges allowed the onslaught to enter their spirit were unable to defeat the attack of individual scouts.

Their power was totally in the hands of the spirits of the men they guarded. They stood by and waited for their next chance to fight as Kapar had earlier.

The enemy was also engaging the warriors on the Beaver fire as strong winds erupted new fires along all of the active divisions. Frantic calls for reinforcements from several divisions were received at the Incident Command Post, but there were few to go around. All three helicopters were needed elsewhere on the fire where the lines held. The new fire was a priority to the Incident Commander, but not for the helicopters. Air tankers were being ordered up, but it would be a while before they appeared overhead. For the time being the new fire would have to wait. The helicopters could still do good work on the other divisions and were ordered across the fire toward the threatened sub division.

Jack received the order and called for Juliet to inform him that he could do nothing on the Mill Creek spot over. Tom heard the call.

"Copy that 7-Sierra Hotel."

"Are you in a good position?" the pilot asked.

Tom didn't know what to say. He was finally thinking clearly, but it was too late. He was on his own and would have to weather the fire the best that he could. The helicopter couldn't save him, but the air tankers possibly could.

"I think so, but if the air tankers come soon, they could make a few runs along the narrow meadow below the rock slide directly uphill from your position. That may give me a little breathing room."

Jack looked up the steep drainage to the ridge and for the first time, he spotted the bright, yellow, nomex shirt and hardhat of a fire fighter. Was that Juliet? That meadow was too small and there was no way the man could hump it through the brush to the rockslide in time.

"I see you Juliet. I'll put in the request, but I'm afraid the air tankers are over thirty minutes out. This thing will probably be on top of you before then. You best hunker down and deploy."

Other firefighters on the division heard the word deploy and suddenly all ears listened to the traffic on air to ground.

"Juliet this is Davis!"

Tom answered the Georgian. He was surprisingly calm.

"Are you going to be okay?"

"Yea John, I'm in a small meadow. I should be able to back up to the far side and find me a hole. There is a pile of rocks up here. I'll take shelter behind them and wait"

The crewmen crowded around the strike team leader searched far up the slope toward their division supervisor's location. They understood the assault he was facing and each found himself praying for Tom's protection. That is one thing about firefighters. No matter what their religious convictions were, in time of trouble and stress on the fire line, most knew enough to pray to God for assistance. It was sad that many did not truly know Him, but the saying was that if God listened to any ones prayers, He listened to firefighters. A firefighter once stated that if one of their own went down in the line of duty, he couldn't go to Hell, because he had already been there. That statement was terribly deceiving.

The smoke suddenly turned a deep charcoal gray with streaks of black and red and the firestorm erupted into an inferno of heat and flames, gobbling up the dead and dying timber on the slopes above it's outreached arms.

Tom saw the eruption below him, as did all of the firefighters on the ridge above Mill Creek. The ground crews at the helibase could see it as well as a giant plume of dark smoke billowed upward into the deep blue sky; the fire driven into a frenzy by the increased wind and it's on lust for destruction.

The fire crews on Division Juliet backed further into the black. They were totally safe, but still retreated further into the haven of blackened earth among the skeletons of a once vibrant forest. The wind blew strong across the scorched earth around them, filling the air with smoke and ash. Several snags fell and they retreated further to a blackened meadow void of any trees. The fire was not the only enemy that they faced.

Several took out cameras to record the show. The flaming front would erupt just below them along the fire line that they had been constructing throughout the day. Others, who had all the pictures they needed, just found a place to rest and wait out the approaching storm. All were apprehensive as the roaring beast emerged.

Davis ensured that all of his men were safe and then hiked the short distance back up to the fire line to peer down into the drainage below that was quickly filling up with dark, billowing smoke, the roar of the beast clearly audible even though the fire was still some distance from his position. This was his first trip out west as a strike team leader, his third trip total and up to this point he had never seen much action on the western fires. The Division, Tom MacKenzie, had been on many fires over the past ten years. Davis trusted that he was safe on the ridgeline above them. All they had to do was sit back, enjoy the show, wait for the fire to run its course, and then proceed off of the mountain.

Because of the increased fire activity, no further line was to be constructed. Davis set his radio to scan the other divisions and immediately heard the increased traffic as engines responded to the growing threat along the sub division. Several firefighters from the North Carolina crew had followed him to the ridge, their cameras ready. The helicopter circled the smoke column once more before turning upslope to clear the scene and respond to Echo Division as ordered by Air Attack.

The young firefighter next to him, a college student by the name of Stewart, pointed a blackened, gloved hand toward the helicopter. Something had gone terribly wrong. The helicopter suddenly shuttered and began to spin, disappearing behind the smoke.

"Oh God!" Jack screamed into the intercom.

The ship suddenly shuttered and Jack lost all control. Something had gone terribly wrong. The sudden turn of the ship caught the crew chief by surprise as he leaned partially out the open side door of the ship for a better view of the fire below him. But thankfully his harness caught him. For a moment he fell away from the aircraft and just as quickly snapped back into the ship. He fell against the seat, his head set pulling loose from the helmet and disappearing out the open door.

"Jack?" The crew chief called out and then realized that his headset was gone. The ship shuttered violently around him and began to spin.

Jack tried to maintain control, but something in the helicopter had totally shut down, but he still had some control. He directed the ship toward the only place that he could, the small meadow on the ridge below. He could see a firefighter below him, a moving speck of yellow that was growing larger all too quickly. His ship was going down fast. If he could just make the meadow, they had a chance.

"Mayday! Mayday! 7-Sierra Hotel going in, Mayday!" Jack radioed in. Everyone was startled by the calmness in his voice, but to Jack all was a blur. He glanced over his shoulder and below to where the crew chief was supposed to be, but David wasn't there. What had happened to him?

The ridgeline flew up to him in a blur of smoke and trees. He was going in too fast. He was going to die.

"Heather!" he shouted, his wife's beloved name.

From his position just behind and a little below the pilot's seat, David couldn't see the ridge coming up toward them as the helicopter descended, but he knew that the ship was going to hit hard, very hard. He also knew that his chances of survival were slim. Fear welled up within him and he began to shake terribly with the full realization that they were about to crash and there was absolutely nothing that he could do about it. His training told him to place his head down between his legs after fully buckling himself in his seat.

He thought of the old saying, "If you are about to crash, tuck your head between your legs and kiss your behind good bye." That seemed funny at the time, but not now, not as he was facing his own death

From where he stood in the meadow, Tom saw the helicopter suddenly turn abruptly and begin to plunge in his direction. "Oh God!" he thought, and keyed his radio just as the mayday call came forward. He switched to command and called the Operations Chief.

"The ship is coming down!" Tom told the Incident Commander of the fire who had answered his call to Operations.

"Do you have a visual?" the IC asked.

"Affirmative, I'm going to end up inside the thing if it gets closer!" Tom answered as he ran back from where it looked the helicopter would crash. He could see the pilot through the window.

"God help him," Tom murmured without thinking.

Others were watching and praying as well.

Both Sarat and Kapar felt the surge of power as the Spirit of God responded to the prayers of the believers along the fire line. But still the Guardians had to wait to be activated until the men on board the helicopter asked for their Savior. They watched from where they stood as a cloud of red smoke suddenly surrounded the helicopter, awaiting the deaths of the unbelievers.

It was then that the crew chief David on board the helicopter realized that he could do something.

He remembered the night years ago in a tent at a fire camp in Montana when a young woman, a firefighter herself, had told him about the love of Jesus who had died for the sins of the entire world. He had never been a religious man. In fact he had never even darkened the doors of the church except for his two weddings that had both ended up in divorce. He had lived his life since then alone for the most part, enjoying the pleasures of life as they came. On that particular night he had rejected the young woman's message. He had only been interested in the woman, not the message that she had shared with him. But he had never really forgotten it. Suddenly, now, when he knew that his time was up, the message came back to him with great clarity. He couldn't remember the girl, but he remembered the story that she told, that the man called Jesus had died on a cross, and had forgiven the thief that hung beside him on that same day.

The fear was great within him; swirling images of death and destruction, fires and smoke flooded his mind and he could hear voices within him saying that it was no use. The story was just a fairy tale. You have no hope. But he had nothing else to do.

"Jesus, please forgive me," He whispered.

That statement was all the man had to say.

When those words were spoken, the Guardians raised their weapons high and the explosive power of the Spirit came fully upon them. They watched as a brilliant white light suddenly exploded from the heavens above and encircled the stricken aircraft. The red cloud of the harassing spirits parted, cringing away from the light. A golden streak crossed through the smoke as another Guardian joined combat with the red spirits. In seconds they were all vanquished just before God himself entered the helicopter and the man inside. At that moment all of God's warriors shouted with joy across the entire mountain as another human came to know their Creator.

The helicopter clipped a tree that flipped it onto its side just before it impacted the side of the mountain below the meadow. It plowed its way across the opening, rotors still turning, tearing into the mountain, and breaking up into several pieces that flung across the ridge.

Tom dove for cover as twisted metal along with trees, dirt and rocks filled the air around him. He felt the searing pain as hot metal tore through his pants and sliced a gaping wound across his thigh. He had lost his hard hat when he had jumped behind the rocks and he covered his head with his arms as rocks pelted him. He heard dying sounds of the helicopter, the engines roaring, the rotors swirling above him, the metal twisting and breaking, but he dared not look for fear that he would see the wreckage plunging toward him. But suddenly with a final crash the aircraft stopped and it was suddenly very quiet. Tom expected an explosion and massive fire but there was nothing. The smoke swirling around him was from the inferno below the mountain.

He lay there a few seconds and then rose to his feet. He checked his leg and saw the gash across his outer thigh through the torn fire pants He pulled back the cloth to inspect the wound. The wound was not too serious, but would forever leave a scar and may even need stitches. Tom sat back down, glancing over at the stricken helicopter. He had to help those on board, but first he had to ensure that the wound was not worse than it appeared. There was no pain, just the warmth from the flow of blood and his heart raced with adrenalin.

He calmed himself and felt the first sensations of a dull ache. The wound was not too deep, but the object had sliced a section of about six inches across his thigh. The edges of the cut were black, the wound itself full of dirt. He had been burned. Smoking debris lay scattered around him.

The radio at his chest spoke, "Juliet this is Davis."

It was his strike team leader on the division's tactical channel.

"Go ahead," Tom answered and then pulled his fire pack from his back and opened it, searching for his first aide kit. He glanced back over at the helicopter. There was no fire, no smoke, but fuel and oil were everywhere and if just one spark or ember blew in from the approaching fire the aircraft would be engulfed in fire. He had to get the pilot and crew chief out of there before that happened.

"Did you see where the ship landed?" Davis asked.

"Yea, John. Its right here. I'm going to check the crew. Try to get them out."

Tom glanced down the ridge. The forest fire was spreading quickly. In just a few moments the smoke would cover the meadow and then the advancing embers that always came ahead of the final attack, like skirmishers of a mighty army, searching for weaknesses in the defenses of the enemy would blow in. He had to get the crew out before then, but where could they go? The meadow was already too small, now half of it was covered in the wreckage. The dried grass around it wet with fuel and hydraulic fluid.

Tom knew he didn't have the time to properly clean and dress the wound. He tossed the first aide kit back in the pack, but retrieved a clean bandana from the side pocket. The wound now hurt, as his senses fully understood that the skin had been torn, the flesh seared by the heated metal. He poured his canteen full of water over the wound to flush out the dirt and covered it with one bandana to stop the bleeding and then tied that one in place by another bandana. That would have to do, he thought, at least until he checked the helicopter for any survivors.

The spiritual enemy had finally located the primary target of their attack. Kapar and Sarat could see them clearly now, an entire troop of dark warriors, riding the smoke column in toward their position on the ridge. They would arrive ahead of the fire trying to attack Tom with fear and hopelessness and hopefully panic as well, as he attempted to make the rescue so that the fire itself would kill the target for them. The two warriors drew their great swords flashing gold through the smoke and stood just in front of their charge as he approached the helicopter.

A demon fluttered through the brush before them and landed just beyond the helicopter, his yellow eyes staring fiercely at the two warriors.

The demon pointed at the firefighter with a double bladed axe, "He wished to die. Let him be."

Kapar stepped forward, "You will have to defeat us before we yield."

The demon hissed, "There are only two of you. I have a full troop behind. You can hold out for just so long and then we will overcome you and he will be ours again. Depression and hopelessness have done their job well. He only broke the spell because of the crash, but soon he will feel that all is lost and it will no longer matter. Look around you warriors of the Most High God; the fires that burn in the natural will soon overtake him."

The demon paused, "We came expecting many more, but it appears that your Gatekeepers have failed you. You have received no help."

The dark warrior stepped around in front of the helicopter and eyed Sarat.

"Do you remember me, Sarat the Gatekeeper of the Rivergate?"

Sarat shook his head, "You are Nasi, the one charged to take the gate from us, but you failed. The Rivergate is firmly in the hands of the Gatekeepers now even after all those earthly years."

"Maybe, but it does the man Tom MacKenzie no good. There is no help coming, at least not in time to save him. You are on your own."

"Then that will have to be enough. It has always been so, even in the early days."

The two warriors, one a Guardian of men's souls, the second a Gatekeeper stood ready. There was just enough time for Tom to save the one man alive in the helicopter. They just had to hold out long enough for Tom to reach the portal behind them. Help would come, they knew. The Gatekeepers would not fail them. The Rivergate was firmly in their hands, the portal open and strong. But it had not always been so. Sarat had been there throughout the many earthly years guarding the portal, watching as it slowly opened over time, finally released when the portal opened in all its glory. Now it was time to see if the true Gatekeepers could wield its power.

CHAPTER EIGHT

NORTH CAROLINA MOUNTAINS
DAY TWO AFTER THE CROSS

A torrential rain had filled the river to the point of overflowing in the natural realm. The water was red with mud from mountain slides upstream. Trees and brush tumbled along the surface at times lodging along the banks, at other times breaking over new trees to join in the mad rush toward the distant ocean. The sun was bright, the sky blue as the last of the dark clouds blew away to the east.

An elk grazed among the lush grass in the meadows along the bottomland of rich, dark soil. A few birds fluttered among the thickets by the river's edge and un noticed by any of the creatures of the valley, Anah, one of the Gatekeepers of the Rivergate stood guard on the ridge overlooking the meadow.

He had been at his post for several days, even the day before when God himself had come to earth wrapped in the flesh of man and had been killed as all of the demons of the rebellion had howled with lust. A few had even attacked Anah's position, but he and his companion, Koah had vanquished them all, driving them back toward the distant ocean to the east. And then there had been a triumphal blast from the battlements of Heaven, announcing to all spiritual beings that God was alive again.

Now the war began on earth in the hearts of mankind as the Redeemed fought to again gain dominion on the earth, as was their birthright.

After the cross, Anah had earlier observed the first humans to find the meadows, a group of natives who roamed the mountains hunting and gathering. They were acutely aware of the spiritual realm and may have noticed his presence, but moved on as quickly as they came. A little later another group built small wooden lodges in the meadow and stayed, hunting the animals for meat and growing small gardens. They were a peaceful people, who did not know of the Cross, but did know of their Creator. They were totally unaware that the lands that they worked hid a portal to heaven itself.

A flash of red suddenly interrupted the quiet sky and Anah immediately drew his sword, searching for the attacker. Koah, who guarded the opposite side of the meadow among the human's camp drifted up through the trees among the light gray smoke of one of the cooking fires. Above the dark forest among the rolling hills to the east, a dark cloud swirled and then further off to the northeast near the great ocean, a brilliant white light shot skyward as a portal suddenly opened. The Redeemed had finally arrived from across the great ocean to the east. They were seeking a new world, a place where they could worship God in freedom. Soon they would find their way west and south. Hopefully soon they would open the Rivergate itself.

But of greater concern was the troop of evil warriors close in among the rolling hills down the same river basin that the two Gatekeepers watched over as well as the enemy that lurked somewhere nearby. Human Redeemed ones who knew of the Cross were approaching and the two knew that renewed battle might soon be joined. Anah flew quickly over the meadow to Koah's side, both watching intently as the dark forces rose high into the clouds themselves.

A trumpet blew and the sky parted, the very fabric of time and space broken as a detachment of Guardians entered the realm of men to reinforce the small group of Gatekeepers that could now be seen standing guard by a small village of stone and wooden houses that suddenly dotted the landscape along the shores of the great ocean. A portal was opening as devout believers began to pray in a new land of great possibilities.

The enemy suddenly charged, the forces driving down toward the growing town around the fluttering portal of light that reached heavenward and battle was joined. The two Gatekeepers drifted higher above the trees until they could see the fight more clearly, yearning to join their embattled comrades, but knowing that their true mission was to protect their own portal. For a few moments, the two armies fought earnestly among the heavens and then the enemy force was broken, their ranks decimated, the dark ones retreating back to the earth's surface to continue working their evil among men. The portal had been established, but the battle had weakened it somewhat. Now it was firmly in the hands of the believers, the true Gatekeepers. It was now totally up to them whether the portal would grow and expand or dim over time.

A single silver streak of light shot outward from the ranks of Guardians and Gatekeepers and moments later the light transformed into the Gatekeeper Sarat who landed among the alders by the river. Koah and Anah watched from within the portal as their commander stepped through the opening to where the two warriors now stood among the rocks that had been their defensive position since that first day after Eden.

Anah who was Koah's senior stepped forward to greet their superior, "It is good to see you again Captain."

Sarat, who stood a head taller than both of his warriors firmly clasped Anah's out stretched hand and hugged him and then turned to do the same with Koah, "And you to my friends."

"What news do you have for us? We watched, as several portals were opened. Is our turn soon?" Anah asked expectantly.

"Founded by humans who wish to worship God in freedom, the first portal that you saw was at Plymouth far to the north. The enemy fought us hard, as I'm sure you witnessed. Although a great nation has become established, one our Lord will use to help spread his message across the entire world, the enemy will counter attack violently. Be strong. Now there are only the three of us. Nasag will soon arrive and we will be four. Our only reinforcements will come from the Guardians and then only if the Redeemed will it to happen. Until then we must hold out at all cost to preserve the Rivergate until we can hand it over to the true believers."

CHAPTER NINE

BETHLEHEM SETTLEMENT, PENNSYVANIA COLONY, 1752

The letter originated in London, England. It was hand written by Lord Granville himself, owner of a great tract of land in the Carolinas to the south of the Pennsylvania Colony that stretched from the dark wetlands along the ocean to the distant blue mountains and beyond. The Carolinas were distant colonies separated from the small village of Bethlehem among the foothills of Pennsylvania by backward country, wilderness filled with dark forest, green swamps, and very few if any roads. A land only recently settled by the English, the small villages holding on tenaciously along the ocean and eastern rivers.

The Scotch-Irish were beginning to migrate down from the north in search of land. There was land aplenty in the Carolinas, land full of forest and woodland meadows, abundant streams and fertile bottomlands, open for the taking by those strong enough to face the great wilderness.

There were also natives in the Carolinas as well, but no different than in Pennsylvania. The Cherokee roamed the mountains along with the smaller Catawba tribe. The Tuscaroro, cousins to the northern Iroquois, once ruled over the eastern lands and had fought the English a half century before, losing their lands and forced to live on a small reservation along the coast near the Virginia Colony. They were soon to migrate north to join the Iroquois Nations. Other smaller tribes were scattered through the foothills, but small pox had already decimated their numbers. Only the Cherokee were powerful enough to present a problem to the settlers as they pushed westward into the foothills and mountains of the colony. At present the isolated confrontations between the settlers and the Cherokee had been friendly, but no one knew when that would change.

The letter had been written to the governing board in Europe of the Unitas Fratum or Unity of Brethren, a group better known as the Moravians, the name speaking of their ancestral homeland Moravia in Eastern Europe. With the letter was another one from the governing board to Bishop Spagenburg, leader of the Moravians in Bethlehem. Bethlehem was one of the Moravian's first settlements in the new world.

Their forefathers had founded the Protestant sect in 1457, following the teachings of John Hus. The Catholic Inquisition later burned Hus at the stake when he would not recount his firm belief that the word of God was above the Catholic Order and that all people had the right to understand its principles.

The young church was almost destroyed, but later revived in Saxony in 1730. Two of their fundamental beliefs were the importance of prayer and the support of missionaries abroad. When the New World was open for colonization, they started new missions in several countries including the settlement of Bethlehem.

They were a peaceful people who kept to themselves. They were hard workers and were able to thrive in the rugged lands of the New World. God was central to everything that they did and they were looked on strangely by their neighbors because of their order and discipline. The free spirited Scotch-Irish who lived around the Moravians clashed with their strong beliefs of order and discipline as well as the Moravians refusal to accept the Calvinistic teachings on predestination, the belief that a person's everlasting life was predestined at birth and people could do nothing about the decision, that was fundamental to the Scotch-Irish Protestants. The two groups were caught up in the same surge of religious freedom that flowed through the colonists as they spread across the new land in search of places to raise their families and worship their God free from government with little fear of the persecution as many of them had experienced in Europe.

The Moravians were anxious to branch out as well and so Brother Joseph, as the village called the Bishop, met with the council of elders soon after receiving the letters. Lord Granville was proposing to sell up to one hundred thousand acres of the land granted to him by the King of England. The governing board was greatly interested in the deal. All the Moravians had to do was find a tract that they wanted.

The town council met and a survey party was selected to accompany Brother Joseph to North Carolina to find the tract for a new settlement and outreach of the Moravian Church. The survey party included the farmer called Henry, Timothy Housefield, Joseph Miller, Herman Lash and John Merk, each with their own specialties including farming, mining, milling, land surveying and administration. Brother Joseph would lead the team and document their findings. There were several other men that would accompany the community leaders as well to assist in any way they could.

The men did not know the full significance of their actions. They were to found a new religious settlement in the wilds of North Carolina; but because of their obedience, they would also start a rolling series of events to cascade into the future that, if successive generations of The Redeemed would build upon, could pave the way for a future move of God, the opening of a powerful portal and the possible deliverance of two firefighters that were trapped on the side of a far distant mountain range.

But the enemy was prepared to stop the advance. They knew the significance of the Moravian survey party as well. It wouldn't be an easy trip south for the group of men. The enemy would make sure of that.

CHAPTER TEN

NORTH CAROLINA MOUNTAINS, 1752

Christopher Gist had lived in the valley for over two years, one of the first white men to build a permanent home there. His log home was situated on a low rise overlooking the wide flat bottoms that lay on both sides of the Reddies River that flowed into the larger Yadkin River from the north. From his front porch, he had a commanding view of the valley, both rivers and the low ridges to the south that had burned over several years before.

He was a careful man. He had to be in wild country so far from the settlements, building his home partially hidden among the great oaks and chestnut at the edge of Mulberry Fields, the name given to the meadowland along the river by the first explorers. They had seen the bright red berries of the mulberry shrubs that covered the wetter sections of the clearing from a distance and the name remained. Christopher farmed the land near his home, trapped from the abundant streams within the Reddies River watershed among the steep mountain coves and escarpments that rose behind his home toward the Eastern Continental Divide to the north and provided for his family as best he could.

The Cherokee Indians traveled through in small hunting parties from their settlements to the south and west, at times settling along the river near the home. He had befriended them, trading trinkets bought at the settlements for furs that he in turn floated down the Yadkin when he needed to trade for provisions of his own. He and his wife raised a family and moved west eventually, but in 1752, he was still situated on the high ground overlooking the meadows across the Reddies from the Rivergate protected by the Gatekeepers.

Christopher Grist and his family considered themselves Christians. There was no church or circuit preacher, therefore they read each day from the weathered, leather bound bible and prayed each night for the protection from the Almighty God and lived their lives the best that they knew how, surviving in a new world far away from civilization.

And in the spirit realm, a Guardian named Natan protected the Gist family. Natan also saw the battle of the distant portal and anticipated others of his kind moving into the valley as Redeemed ones migrated into the wilderness to build a new life. Across the river lay the Rivergate guarded by Gatekeepers. The Spirit of God was moving, talking to the spirits of mortals who prayed and who listened. Christopher Gist was one such mortal and Natan's assignment was to ensure that his charge was home on the appointed day when the Moravian survey team arrived.

Christopher Gist was a traveling man, but during this short time, he resided by the Yadkin. Soon he would travel with George Washington exploring the western lands. Indians would raid his home along the Reddies and destroy it although his family would be spared. Eventually he would travel through Tennessee and Kentucky, eventually lost to the pages of history. For now, however during this period of his life, he was settled exactly where Natan knew Christopher Gist needed to be.

CHAPTER ELEVEN

NORTH CAROLINA MOUNTAINS, 1752

The settlers called the river the Catawba, after the Indian tribe that inhabited the rolling hills and meadows along its course. Its watershed originated in hundreds of small mountain streams swelling up beneath thick mountain laurel and rhododendron, hemlock and chestnut among the steep mountain coves of the Blue Ridge, the western boundary of Lord Granville's land. The tributaries flowed out from the secluded ravines, high mountain peaks and fog covered slopes and into the low rolling hills where they converged to form the water course that now blocked the expeditions' western progress. Recent rains had swelled the river's banks and there were very few known fords in which to cross.

Night was fast approaching. The survey party was worn from days of constant travel, having left the small settlement called Salisbury over a week before. They had seen no one since. There were no trails except those used by the buffalo. The forest was dark, the understory shaded by thick foliage of the majestic chestnut and yellow-poplar, the smaller oak and maple.

Brother Joseph reined in his horse and dismounted near the edge of a small woodland meadow covered with flowers waving in the afternoon breeze. Across the meadow, the Catawba flowed silently. A buckskinned hunter trotted his horse across the meadow toward them. He reined in next to the waiting Moravians, his long rifle cradled in his left arm. He turned his head and spit out the last of his tobacco, juice running down his thick black beard. Brother Joseph turned away as the man dismounted. He disliked the hunter's uncivilized manner, but chose to overlook it. The party needed a guide who had been across the Catawba.

Salisbury was the farthest settlement to the west and few people knew the trails that led into the distant Blue Ridge. Even Lord Granville's agent who had met the Moravians in front of Tryon, the Governor's mansion in New Bern had not traveled so far west. The Hunter was said to know the way from Salisbury to the upper Yadkin, therefore the survey party had hired him the day before they left the small frontier settlement.

"Well Bishop," the Hunter called Joseph by his church title with disdain. He too disliked the ways of the churchmen, having no use for organized religion with their many rules and intolerance, "I've found your crossing. We'll camp here tonight and cross in the morning. Granville's grant is to the north."

"Have you been to the upper reaches of the Yadkin?" Brother Joseph asked.

"No, but there is a tributary of the Catawba just up stream from here that leads to the highest peaks of the Blue Mountains near the Hawks Bill and Grandfather. You can see the peaks from the Catawba fields nearby. The Yadkin is to the north and east of there."

The Hunter turned his horse toward the river, looking back over his shoulder, "Bishop, camp next to the river with the meadow between you and the forest, over there among the sycamore and keep a watch. This is now Cherokee land. I noticed sign of a passing hunting party that passed through not too many days ago."

"But I thought the Cherokee were peaceful?" Brother Joseph asked with some alarm.

The Hunter laughed, "Bishop, the red man is only peaceful in death."

The Hunter spurred his horse on with a swift kick, galloping across the meadow to the dark forest lost in the evening shadows. The Moravians paid him well for his services, but they did not pay him enough to listen to their nightly prayers and Bible reading. He disliked the Bible thumpers, but he needed their money and so he had taken the job of guiding them westward.

He would set up his own camp hidden among the pines within sight of their camp, but far enough away not to be bothered by them. But there was another reason why he decided to pitch his camp away from theirs. Ever since seeing the trail of the Cherokee the day before, he was worried, a growing fear deep within him rising to the surface. There had been talk back in the settlements about bands of Cherokee who were becoming alarmed at the western expansion of the settlers. Ever since they had pushed the Catawba from the mountains, the Cherokee were growing ever more restless. The Hunter knew that their main towns lay deep within the Blue Mountains and beyond, but lately small parties were roaming the foothills. They, too, were expanding their own territory and soon the two races would collide.

There had even been talk about war parties in isolated areas, roaming the foothills and he knew that one party on foot had crossed the ford nearby the day before. So he tethered his horse nearby among the darkness of the thick pines and sat back against a fallen log nearby, his rifle across his legs. The Moravians were out in the open. If the Cherokee were close and it was a war party, they would attack the Bible thumpers, he thought, and he would be safely hidden among the pines. He could sneak away in the night. They had paid him half his pay at the settlement, with a promise of more when they returned. He would be happy with half if something happened to them. He pulled a bit of dried beef from his pack and settled back to wait. He would sleep lightly.

Dark shadows floated among the trees above him, but he took no notice.

The Moravians secured their horses among the trees along the riverbank and then prepared a simple camp beneath the sycamores next to the meadow. They built a small fire just inside the tree line and began to prepare a light meal. They were tired, but happy to have finally reached the ford where they could cross the Catawba. Tomorrow they would strike out toward the northwest in search of the illusive headwaters of the Yadkin. Hopefully in a few days they would be in Granville's land and could begin their search for the place for their new settlements in the new world.

As was his custom, Brother Joseph settled down by the fire's light with his journals to record the day's events. As the meal was being prepared and the other men in the party prepared a camp for the night, He wrote a detailed account of what had transpired during the day.

"We made good time today, I think. Our guide seems to know the country well, which is a blessing to us. With out him, we would be totally lost. The country is remote and covered in timber with scattered woodland meadows. The forests are open, with all manner of trees of every variety. At times throughout the day, we could see the far off line of mountains. We made camp in a meadow on the Catawba near the ford that will take us across the river. Our guide says that this is now the country of the Cherokee. He seemed nervous today, more so than usual. He crossed the trail of a Cherokee party that may still be close and warned us to keep watch. I pray for the protection of Providence so that we will continue to be blessed with safe passage in this wild land. I know with renewed hope that Providence has led us thus far and will continue to do so, even though the travel is ever more arduous. We will persevere. Tonight, we will pray even more earnestly for protection."

Brother Joseph closed the leather bound pages and placed them in the protective oilskin and then in a leather satchel. The dinner was ready. The small fire flickered in the light breeze. The men would eat and then pray for protection.

Outside the glow from the fire, shadows darker than the night itself gathered close. Across the meadow a band of Cherokee crept ever closer. They could see the men gathered around the small fire. At the edge of the shimmering light, several horses were visible beneath the trees as well.

A shadow swirled among the horses, spooking them. Brother Joseph looked up quickly as did the men around him. One stood nervously and walked to the edge of the fire, looking out.

"Something's out there, in the darkness," He stated, looking back over his shoulder. Another stood up then, holding a rifle, standing in the light of the fire, unknowingly making himself a target for anyone hiding in the shadows of the forest.

Brother Joseph didn't move from his seat by the fire. He felt the presence of the enemy in the air around him, but he also felt the presence of his God. He began to pray.

"Heavenly Father, Bless us your humble servants. Protect us this night from the evil that surrounds us..."

The shadows shrank back suddenly, flying high over the meadow. A brilliant flash of light more brilliant than the sun exploded over the camp and golden swords clashed against red axes as a detachment of Guardians dived down through the trees and scattered the shadows that had encircled the camp. Several formed a defensive line just over the dark waters of the river, momentarily holding their adversaries back, but the power of the Guardian broadswords were too strong and one by one, the black warriors disappeared in vapors of red. The other shadows disappeared into the night.

The Hunter woke up suddenly with a start, panicked at first as the shadow over him screamed in the other realm and disappeared through the dark forest, chased by a streak of silver that disappeared over the horizon as well. He fumbled with his rifle and stood up too quickly, hitting his head on the low branches of the pine tree behind him. His horse stomped the ground nervously in the blackness behind him. He regained his composure and listened carefully, but heard nothing except the characteristic sounds of the night, crickets chirping out in the meadow; bullfrogs along the riverbank, an owl somewhere out in the darkness behind him. Across the meadow, the small fire flickered merrily. The scent of the fire floated on the soft breeze.

All appeared to be normal, but he shook deep inside as if he was cold, a chill climbing his spine. Something wasn't right. The Moravians were by the fire, their forms silhouetted against the faint glow. They were a strange breed, he thought, with all of their praying and Bible reading, their talk of starting a new settlement where the virtues of God could be followed. He had nothing against God, but he did have something against bible thumpers who thought they were better then everyone else and tried to force their laws on everyone around them.

Something had spooked him and his horse. Something was out there in the shadows, something not of this world. He knew the stories of witches and such and had felt evil in his time and that was the way he felt then. He didn't like that feeling and knew that it had something to do with the men over by the firelight. He decided then that he had had enough. They could find the Yadkin without him. He had led them to the fords of the Catawba and had pointed the way to the headwaters of the river they sought. He had never traveled the country further north and would be of no use to them anyway. He slowly reached for his horse in the darkness and led him out of the pines to the edge of the meadow.

The Cherokee had counted eight men by the camp, all of them sitting around the fire, easy prey. They could sneak through the tall grass and surprise them easily. But suddenly out of the shadows, a dozen riflemen arose from the grass and stood shoulder to shoulder just in front of the fire. Where had they come from? They had not been there before. The Cherokee faded back into the forest, regrouped among the oaks and decided that a dozen riflemen, standing guard, were too strong a party for them to attack. They retreated back to the buffalo trail that led to the Catawba fields up river.

The Guardians smiled as they watched the Cherokee melt back into the forest across the meadow.

"That ought to make them think twice before attacking again," the leader spoke as the twelve riflemen disappeared.

Three Guardians now stood by the fire. A fourth floated down from the trees and landed next to them, "Assap," he addressed the leader of the detachment, "the Hunter has left. Brother Joseph will have to lead without a guide."

Assap turned to look over the group of men who stood by the fire, facing out toward the meadow. Only their leader still sat, his head bowed, silently praying. He could feel the strength surging through him from the prayers of the men, especially Brother Joseph.

"Then he will just have to lead them the right way. We must watch carefully. In a few days they will reach the Yadkin. A detachment of Gatekeepers is hiding a portal somewhere along the river. It is different then the one that this group will establish, one that will rise up sometime in the future. I'm not sure where it is hidden, but they will expose themselves at the proper time. The enemy knows of its existence as well and I'm sure has forces standing by to attempt to gain control. When the Gatekeepers exit their portal. We will be there to assist."

Assap sheathed his sword and looked upward, "I need a Messenger."

The fabric of space itself split open and then closed just as quickly and the Messenger stood before the Guardians. He was small, lithe, armed with a short sword in the scabbard by his side. The Messenger bowed slightly and stepped up to Assap.

Assap placed a small parchment in the Messengers hands, "Take this to the Guardian Natan. Be careful. You may encounter resistance over the mountains to the north. Stay with Natan until we rendezvous with him."

The Messenger saluted and disappeared in a flash of silver, the only evidence of his existence a shimmering residue of mist that floated to the ground by the flickering fire.

The enemy warrior stood by the river, watching the log cabin beneath the trees on the hill overlooking the entire valley. He stood silently, hidden from view by the thick underbrush and his ability to blend in with his natural surroundings in both the physical and spiritual realm. Nasi stood silently. If he moved, the Guardian sitting on the roof of the cabin would be able to feel his presence. The Rivergate occupied the ground across the river, but he was unsure of its actual location. He knew there were Gatekeepers nearby, but they remained in the gate itself and therefore out of sight of all except other Gatekeepers. Sarat had been given charge over the gate, which meant that it was an important one to them. This land had always been under his control, even though the portal lay nearby. The Gatekeepers were powerless to do anything in his domain except protect their gate. He on the other hand had held sway over the entire region since the rebellion, controlling the few humans that entered his realm until just recently.

Now a Guardian occupied the high ground across from the Rivergate itself, which was an intolerable situation. Nasi knew that when the Guardians arrived near a gate, the enemy could be planning to activate it and that was something that could give the Gatekeepers great power. He too had watched the recent battle to the east. A gate had been opened and the land that had once been covered in the darkness of the rebellious forces now had an enclave of the Redeemed. They were slowly spreading across the land to the east like a plague.

Nasi had forces scattered across his domain, a full detachment hidden along the river, prepared to attack the portal if it ever opened. The others followed the scattered humans that entered the valley ensuring that they continued to remain ignorant of the cross. That had never been a problem, but all of that could change now that a Guardian was in the domain.

The Guardian Natan stood up and stretched, his charge asleep with the family in the house below him. He was alone, the only Guardian in the entire valley, but he knew that as long as his charge continued to pray, his strength was sufficient to protect the family. Across the river was a very important portal to heaven itself, one protected by several Gatekeepers. He had saluted Sarat earlier as he returned from the battle to the east, just before the Gatekeeper had entered the portal. It was a great comfort to know that they were there, even though hidden, as was their custom. Natan's charge was overseeing humans given to him by his Lord, a task that he relished, a task that he had been created for. The Gatekeeper's charge was the gate itself and he knew that they would have very little to do with Natan until the Redeemed activated the gate. That was okay with him. When the time came, they would be there by his side as he would theirs.

Natan scanned the surrounding countryside, seeing nothing that alarmed him, but deep within the recesses of his mind, he felt a presence that did. Somewhere, the enemy lurked, but he could not pinpoint their position. They had to know of the portal and definitely knew about his existence, but as of yet he had not been attacked. They, like him, were playing a waiting game.

The Messenger streaked across the landscape, only a wisp of sparkling silver shooting through the trees just above the ground, marking his progress. He flew through a steep ravine and over the top of a long stretch of mountains and climbed above the tree line before stopping, the silver mist transforming into his true form. Below lay the great valley of the Yadkin, the mountains rising suddenly to the west. He scanned the countryside carefully, looking not only for the Guardian, but also for any sign of the enemy. Assap had predicted trouble, but thus far the Messenger had encountered nothing.

He was in the middle of enemy territory, an area controlled by the enemy since the rebellion. He had not seen a single warrior to stop his progress, but like Natan, he felt their presence. The question was where were they and why had they not yet challenged his intrusion into their territory?

The river glistened in the moon's light as he slowly floated down into the valley. Across the river, he saw the Guardian and dashed quickly across the river, unknowingly over the Rivergate itself. The Gatekeepers saw the Messenger as well, but did not expose themselves. They felt the enemy presence and knew that they were vulnerable to attack if they opened the portal at the wrong time. The Messenger could only mean that the survey party was nearby. Sarat gave the order for his warriors to prepare for the coming battle. They were already prepared.

The Messenger stopped just shy of the cabin, a safe distance from the Guardian

"You are the Guardian called Natan." It was a statement.

"That would be me." Natan replied.

Nasi listened carefully. Because he had masked his presence by the cabin while Natan was away, he knew that he could not be located unless he moved. He was in a perfect position to overhear the message. The intelligence he could gather now would greatly assist him in countering whatever plan the enemy was trying to carry out.

"I am Malak. I have a message from the Guardian Assap," the Messenger stated and handed the parchment to Natan, who read the message slowly and then destroyed it by crushing it into dust with his gloved hands. He threw the dust up into the air to be carried off by the night breeze as the Messenger stood silently by his side.

Nasi was furious. He had stood silently for several days, waiting patiently to try to determine what the enemy plan was and they had countered him by delivering the message in a way that he could not hear. Enough!

He drew his long sword, the blade ringing loudly in the night and exploded from the dense underbrush with a fury, hurdling himself toward the two enemy warriors. Malak turned quickly, drawing his own short sword and parried the first blow, the force knocking him back through the log cabin and spinning out over the river. Natan stepped forward then, his golden sword brilliant against the dark sky, Nasi crashed full force into the Guardian, his red blade crossing the golden one, sparks spraying out over the trees. And then just as suddenly as he appeared, Nasi disappeared back into the darkness and was gone. The Guardian was not worth Nasi exposing his hidden troop who waited for the opening of the Gate. He would have to learn of the enemy's plans some other time.

Malak landed hard against the rocky cliffs south of the river, but recovered quickly. He jumped across the water with a single leap and met Natan on the roof of the cabin, his sword still drawn. For a moment the two watched earnestly across the country, but felt no remaining evil presence. They both sheathed their weapons and sat back down on the roof.

"What was that?" Malak asked.

"I'm not sure. I have felt its presence since entering the valley, but could never pinpoint its location. The enemy is here, but so far they have not exposed themselves to me until now." Natan answered.

"Then there will be another attack, I think," the Messenger proposed.

Natan looked over the river and agreed. When the Redeemed first claimed the portal, the enemy would most definitely expose themselves.

CHAPTER TWELVE

CATAWBA RIVER VALLEY, 1752

Heavy dew sparkled brightly on the tall grass in the early morning sunshine, a mist hanging over the valley along the river, shrouding the white barked sycamores in a ghostly pale. The men stirred around the small fire, having slept peacefully through the night. The heaviness around them from the night before had suddenly vanished and one by one, all had fallen asleep except for the watchmen who took shifts throughout the night.

The fire was stirred and fresh wood added. Soon the early morning mist began to dissipate and the sweet aroma of coffee brewing added a delightful fragrance to the fresh mountain air. Normally the Hunter would have already been to the camp with his own cup, but he was missing on this particular morning. Coffee was a rare commodity so far from the settlements, but the Moravians were fond of it, although their rations were growing slim. They would soon have to brew smaller portions each morning to stretch what they had for as long as possible.

Henry was the best cook in the group; therefore he usually did most of the cooking, although the fare was simple and each man was beginning to miss their own hearths, the cooking of their wives. The nights were growing longer as well, as the men remembered fondly the softness of the wife's skin, the fragrance of her hair, the way she walked around the room or how she combed out her hair just before going to bed. During the day, they were busy, their minds fully occupied by the grind of constant travel. It was at night just before going to sleep and in the morning with the beginning of a new day, that there was time to think of their families far away to the north. They each prayed daily for God's protection of their loved ones while they were gone.

They sat quietly by the fire for a few minutes; each with his own thoughts, waiting for the coffee before morning prayers. They had all volunteered for the trip, knowing that it was the will of God and that they were helping to secure a future for their people, but that did not make their loneliness any easier.

John Meek broke the stillness, "Where is the scout. He never misses Henry's coffee?"

They all looked around the clearing. That was strange?

"He made camp among the pines across the meadow just before dark," A tall, black-haired farmer by the name of Timothy Housefield stated.

He stood up, "I will check."

The simple breakfast was over and the men began to pack for the day's journey. The scout had said that they could follow the river northwest to the Blue Mountains, cross over the ridges to the north and find the western reaches of the Yadkin Valley, but the Hunter had never been so far west.

A few moments later, a shrill whistle echoed across the meadow from the pines still covered in the shadows of the morning. Henry was the first to see Timothy standing by the forest, waving his arms wildly above his head. The group ran to where their friend stood and stopped short of the tree line, gasping at what lay before them in the tall grass.

The Hunter lay face down in the grass., dead.

"Dear God help us! Who do you think did this?" Henry asked, looking over at Brother Joseph who stood white faced and trembling.

"He did say that he had spotted sign of Indians shadowing us."

The group looked around them across the meadow. If the Cherokee had been so close, why had they not attacked the Moravian camp?

Brother Joseph answered the unspoken question, "God has surely protected us this past night brothers. We need to give this man a Christian burial and then leave as quickly as we can."

They picked the body up and carried it back to the campsite, where they buried the man in the deep soil by the river among the sycamores, placing a wooden cross to mark the grave. The scout had been their eyes in a foreign land and now he was gone. They had put their trust in him to lead them into a wilderness known to only a few white men. Each wondered how they would continue, not knowing that forces were already at work to assist them. All they had to do was continue to place their trust in God. He would make a way. He always did.

When trouble comes, it is sometimes very difficult to fully place one's life totally in God's hands. Faith becomes buried under the depths of fear and unbelief. Each man in the survey party wrestled with these thoughts as the camp was broken down. The men were anxious, watching the forests around them as they worked. How could they continue? Where would they go?

The men gathered around Brother Joseph, only Lord Granville's man holding back as he studied the charts of the colony that he had brought along with him. They were of little use, he realized. Although the land east of the foothills was mapped, the western colony was shown to be unexplored, only a few rivers drawn extending to the mountains drawn randomly across the map.

"What are we to do?" Henry asked, "How can we continue now without our guide?"

"Brother Joseph, we have traveled through fertile land since leaving the settlements. Surely we can find the land that we seek back from where we have come," Timothy stated.

He had a point, Brother Joseph thought, but deep within him, his spirit told him that they had not yet found the place that they were to find. Something lay before them, not behind them.

John Merk, who ran a small mill back home, spoke of the heavily timbered slopes nearby, "We have timber for building homes here, plenty of water. A mill can be built on this very stream."

Granville's agent joined in the conversation when he heard the group contemplating locating their settlement by the Catawba, "Gentlemen, this area is not part of the offer. Lord Granville's grant that is available runs north of here from the coast to beyond the mountains."

"But we do not know the way!" Henry proclaimed.

"We can go back. Brother Joseph, we were offered the land vacated by the Tuscarora. The land there is flat, the ground fertile. Surely the area along the coast would make an acceptable location for a settlement. We will be closer to the ports. It will be easier to trade with others. There are no longer hostile Indians," Timothy stressed.

"But our future lies before us," Joseph encouraged, "Providence will guide us if we place our trust in Him. Before us lies a great land, an empty land, a land of great possibilities. We owe it to our families to seek out a new land that God Himself has ordained for us. There is much that we do not yet understand, but we must trust in Him to lead us."

"Brother Joseph is right," Herman Lash, the surveyor in the group, spoke for the first time. He rarely spoke, but when he did, he usually said something of great importance. He was older than everyone but Brother Joseph and well respected in his community. "Our future lies before us. The Yadkin Valley is to the north and west. We must go forward or we will not be in our Lord's perfect will. Timothy I too saw the black fertile soils of the land by the coast. You could actually grow a crop there. Not like that excuse for a corn field you grew last year."

The others laughed as Timothy smiled sheepishly. He was a young farmer, recently married and owner of one field that grew more rocks than corn.

Herman continued, "Yes the land is closer to the ports, but it is also closer to the English, closer to their government, to their soldiers," the memory of the Moravians past treatment by others was still strong in everyone's minds, "In this land we can raise our families according to our custom. We can build the City of God that we dream of. Gentlemen, no one said that this would be easy. But God did promise to be with us."

The groups stood silently. They all knew that what Herman said was truth, but each had to suppress the fear of the unknown within them and replace it with faith.

Brother Joseph broke the silence, "Thank you Herman for your words of wisdom. God has truly used your voice this day as He often does with you to encourage us. Gentlemen, I say that we continue on, but I do value your concerns. It is my duty as your shepherd and leader of this expedition to make the final decision as Providence leads me. We must trust God and continue or we will fail not only ourselves, but also our children and our Order. Let us pray for God's continued protection."

The survey party prayed then as the Guardians watched. The mortals had placed their trust in the Lord. It was now the Guardian's job to make sure that the Lord's will came to pass.

The group continued to follow the river into the mountains. They had been told that somewhere an overland trail crossed over the low ridges to the north and entered the Yadkin Valley, but after several days of travel, they still had not found the trail.

The summer was fast slipping by and soon fall would take over with crisp mornings, shorter days and the brilliant changing colors and behind the fall would be the winter. They were running out of time.

The river narrowed, breaking up into smaller tributaries, many of the stream banks choked with mountain laurel and rhododendron under massive chestnut and yellow-poplar, the forest dark and wet with few open meadows and very few trails. At times they had to walk ahead of their horses to cut a trail among the forest of deep shadows. Steep slopes rose upward from the stream, the ridges hidden from view by the thick canopy. In places great rock clefts extended down to the water itself, making the travel even more difficult. And then they reached a place where the stream widened and they were able to use the stream itself as the trail.

The Hunter had told them that if they missed the overland trail they could follow the stream to its source just below the crest of the mountains, climb to the top and then they would be able to see the valley to the northeast. When the stream widened, they could finally see the ridge, but it was still some distance off and appeared to be straight up. The valley gathered the shadows quickly as the sun disappeared behind the high peaks and exhausted from days of constant travel, Brother Joseph suggested that they go ahead and find a place to camp for the night.

A small meadow in a flat side drainage availed itself to them and they collapsed in the tall grass. They were lost, tired and homesick. They had somehow missed the trail that crossed the mountains. The seasons would begin to change quickly and they had yet to even enter the Yadkin Valley, much less search for land suitable for the new colony. All appeared to be hopeless.

A mantel of darkness covered the steep mountain slopes as the last pale glow faded in the west. In the realm of the Guardians, a black blanket of hopelessness gathered over the hearts of the Redeemed ones. A full troop of warriors launched a determined attack that forced the Guardian Assap and his detachment down the valley, momentarily leaving the group of men below them un protected. Brilliant arches of crimson flashed through the darkness, intersecting with equally brilliant flashes of gold as the apposing forces sparred among the chestnut grove.

The men tied their horses by the stream as Henry built a small fire and began preparing a stew. Timothy had shot a rabbit earlier and Henry added it to the pot. The group gathered around the fire quietly lost in their own thoughts. It had been several days since the death of the Hunter. He had told them the trail over the mountain to the headwaters of the Yadkin would cross the headwaters of the Catawba through a wide meadow just before a series of waterfalls. They had seen neither and must have traveled too far west. The river was now a small mountain stream. The maps were of no use. They had been adding to the map for the past three days, Lord Granville's agent carefully recording their travel along the river, marking side streams, mountain ranges and small woodland openings. But they had seen no trail to the north.

"What are we going to do Brother Joseph?" Timothy asked his spiritual leader over the warmth of the small fire.

Joseph could see the fear in the young man's eyes. They were all tired. Several of them were beginning to grow weak from the continuous journey. They had already lost several of their party over a month before in the swamps of the coastline to fever. The two men had stayed behind, unable to continue the journey. God seemed to have abandoned them, he thought to himself. The mountains over shadowing the group were too steep with no trail. Their food was running low, as was their time. The other men gazed through the smoke to him. He felt their burdens, their hopes, and their dreams. They had all volunteered with the dream of finding a new home for their people. What could he tell them now? Did he even believe that they would succeed in their mission?

Joseph gathered strength within his heart, his faith in God over coming the gathering shadows in his soul. You are their leader, his spirit told him. You must now be their strength as I am yours.

"We will eat our supper Timothy and then we will pray. We will sleep under the stars of heaven and tomorrow will be a new day. God will not forsake us, but will honor our obedience." Joseph stood and walked into the shadows. He too felt the fear.

CHAPTER THIRTEEN

NORTH CAROLINA MOUNTAINS 1752

Christopher Gist had traveled southwest for several days, taking his time, exploring new country along the extreme upper reaches of the Yadkin Valley. He had first thought about climbing to the peaks of Grandfather Mountain that on a clear day could be seen from the meadow below his home. A distinctive range of broken rock and dark spruce and fir covered slopes characteristic of mountains further north, Grandfather's profile from several angles resembled the face of a man with prominent bearded chin, nose and forehead. But he remembered that he wished also to locate other areas for his small fur business and so headed up the river instead, unknowingly listening to the suggestion from the Guardian Natan to his subconscious, who was following the orders in the message.

The woodsman rode silently along an ancient buffalo trail that meandered along the fertile river bottoms of the upper Yadkin, a constant broken ridgeline trailing along the south, another higher mountain range flowing down from the Continental Divide to his north. As he traveled, the valley narrowed, the trail leaving the open meadows behind and entering a great dark forest of chestnut and yellow-poplar, the understory open except along the streams and scattered lower slopes.

The trail slanted along the slope to the south toward the gap in the mountain on the divide. Further to the west, the highest shoulders of Grandfather lay hidden in a shroud of light afternoon clouds. Gist followed the trail to the ridge as the sun melted away behind the nearest ridgeline. From his vantage point along the narrow ridgeline at the edge of a small open knoll, a great mountain range extended to the far distant horizon, the deep valleys lost in the shadows, the farthest ridges highlighted in gold and lavender as the sun continued to retreat.

Hawksbill Mountain jutted distinctively above the lower ridges and further south Table Rock Mountain disappeared in the shadows. Gist had never been so far west, but had heard others speak of the western mountains that were the northern extremes of the Cherokee hunting ground. He had heard also, that the Cherokee were venturing out, spreading further north and east.

A soft breeze flowed upward out of the darkening valley immediately below him. The trail that he had been following dropped downward into the shadows. He dismounted at the edge of the opening, not wishing to plunge down into the unknown valley before him until the light of a new day. He would stop for the night, which his horse seemed to appreciate, having wandered to the lush grass across the worn trail.

The breeze shifted again and with the change a faint smell of smoke floated on the night air. Christopher stopped suddenly and turned, taking a deep breath, unsure at first that he had smelled smoke at all. Again with another turn of the breeze, the smell lingered and then just as quickly disappeared. His horse did not seem to notice. The mare contentedly nibbled at the grass.

Smoke meant two things, either a campfire or lightening strike. There had been no storms in the area; therefore somewhere in the valley below, someone had a small campfire. They had to be some distance off or the smell would have been more prominent or the fire was very, very small. In any event, he was wary. Strangers in a strange land could mean trouble, which was something that Christopher Gist was in no mood for.

Meanwhile Assap and his band of Guardians continued to fight among the forest, pushing desperately to again cover their charges from the onslaught of anxious worries that was overtaking them. Assap parried the blow from one warrior, just as a second axe sliced through the air, tearing a gaping wound across his left shoulder as he quickly turned to face his new adversary, a trail of silver smoke blowing across his face, red sparks cascading down through the thick foliage. The Guardians were out numbered, but held their ground. Hopefully the Messenger had gotten through and help was on the way, Assap thought as he retreated momentarily from the fight to adjust his shoulder and allow his wound to heal.

He felt no pain as humans did, but could feel his strength wane as the Redeemed ones lost their hope and faith in the Lord to help them in their time of need. If only they knew how his kind fought to assist them. If only they knew that his true power lay in their prayers and belief. But they did not understand and so he and his band were temporarily held back to fully assist them as they sat uncertain and lost.

"Pray!" Assap shouted, but the Moravians couldn't hear him, but the enemy did.

They answered his cry with mocking laughter.

On the ridge above, Natan and the Messenger Malak heard the cry and the answering laughter and knew that a battle had been joined somewhere below them. Malak shot heavenward, circling the dark valley so as to locate the source of the cry. A red streak intercepted him and for a moment he crossed swords with an enemy scout. The scout was strong, but Malak was faster and parried the attack, side stepping quickly and thrust below the scout's uplifted sword. The scout disappeared in a red vapor, his sword falling harmlessly to the ground where it disappeared.

Natan shouted to Gist as he stood listening carefully for any sound that may help him locate the source of the smoke, "Look down the trail!"

Gist turned and saw it then, a small red glow flickering in the darkness below him. He stepped further down the side of the hill and could then see several shadows vaguely in the light of the small fire. Concentrating on the light, he listened carefully and thought he could hear voices. There appeared to be several men around the campfire, but who were they?

Suddenly the distinctive sharp crack of metal on stone broke the stillness of the night and someone shouted. Was that the German language? Gist thought to himself. Who could be speaking German?

Natan spoke again to Gist's spirit, "Announce yourself. They need your help."

On a whim, Gist called out into the darkness, "Hello the fire."

At first no one answered, but he heard several people scurry among the trees and the fire was momentarily blocked from sight by one of them. His horse jerked her head up, peering down the hill below as well, her ears back, her head raised as she sniffed the air. She snorted disapprovingly and trotted over to where Gist stood.

Gist grabbed the reins. They had to be white men, he thought. No Indian ever spoke German.

Finally after a minute, someone below answered him, the voice carrying the heavy German accent, but the words were in English.

"Who is there?"

"Christopher Gist from over on the Yadkin." Gist called and immediately stepped to one side just in case someone down there fired a shot at the sound of his voice. You could never be too careful, "And who might you be?"

Again there was silence and then Gist could hear low whispers.

Another voice answered, this time with a distinctively English accent, "We are a survey party representing Lord Granville."

Gist laughed, "Well you are a far piece from the Granville grant. His property is from the coast up to the low foothills."

"You are mistaken sir," the Englishmen responded, " Lord Granville has a grant from the ocean to the highest mountains and even beyond."

The arrogance of the English, Gist thought. Those who lived on it, who worked it, improved it, and fought for it, owned land. How could Granville, who lived across the ocean claim land within this great wilderness?

Another voice broke in, this one with the German accent, possibly from an older man. Gist figured that he liked this man far more than the Englishmen.

"Sir, did you say that you live on the Yadkin River?"

The question had a deep yearning within its words and Gist understood somehow that this party was most likely lost.

"Yes sir. I have a small cabin overlooking the river near the Mulberry Fields."

Hope suddenly sprang forth into the spirits of the men and in the other realm; the Guardians were quickly able to beat the enemy back. The dark forces retreated just out of sight of the campfire and sulked, their yellow eyes peering from the shadows. Natan saluted his comrade from the ridge as Assap answered in kind. The Messenger had gotten through. They were one step closer to claiming the Rivergate. Hopefully the Gatekeepers would be ready, Assap thought and then dismissed the question. The Gatekeepers were always ready.

The river that the party of Moravians had followed began in a large bowl shaped valley, later to be called The Globe. The broken slopes of Grandfather lay to the west. The Blowing Rock jutted upward above the headwaters of the river and one ridgeline to the northeast laid the headwaters of the Yadkin River.

Christopher Gist made his camp next to the group of Moravian travelers and the next morning he led them back over the ancient trail that he had been following the day before. The upper Yadkin Valley was only a days journey, the Mulberry Fields two days. There the valley widened, opening in a great semicircle that emptied out into the lower foothills, the rich bottomland meadows covered in high grasses and flowers and dotted with buffalo, although their numbers were dwindling.

And across from Mulberry Fields, Sarat stood by the riverbank, watching as the party emerged from the forested trail and dismounted in the open meadow. He saluted the band of Guardians who traveled with the group. Behind him lay the portal, closed and protected by his own detachment of Gatekeepers.

Koah exited the portal and stood beside his superior, "Are they the true Gatekeepers Captain?"

"I don't believe so, but they are the ones that will first open the portal, this I am sure. If they are the ones to establish the gateway, I am not sure. Only the Lord himself knows this," Sarat turned to the younger Gatekeeper, "Prepare yourself for battle. The enemy lurks in the shadows and will no doubt attack as soon as the Redeemed ones open the portal. I will insure that the Guardians stand firm with us."

Koah turned and entered through the gap between time and space that was the portal to where the others waited. He too had felt the enemy presence all around him when he had been on the outside. Their numbers were many, but he was not worried. In the end they would be victorious, this he knew for sure.

The men camped by the Yadkin River across from the fields covered with the Mulberry shrubs below the small cabin where Christopher Gist lived under the watchful eyes of both Guardians and Gatekeepers.

Brother Joseph wrote in his journal late into the night after all the others were sound asleep. For the first time since leaving the settlements, the group felt totally safe. They planned to survey the surrounding lands. According to Lord Granville's agent, the valley opened further out into the rolling foothills and it was decided that although they would not establish their first settlement so far west of the settlements, they would survey a section of land in case they needed to expand westward sometime in the future. The men had made plans for the next few days with renewed strength and hope. Something about the place flooded their spirits with peace.

Brother Joseph placed the journal back into its protective cover and lay back, gazing up into the stars. A soft breeze blew across the valley, the scent of smoke from the small fire floating by. He breathed in deeply and thought suddenly of the patriarch Jacob on the night that he had seen the heavens open and the angels walking back and forth through the open door. Jacob had recognized that the place was holy ground, a place where heaven and earth touched.

Joseph sat up suddenly, looking around him at the sleeping men, the small fire, and the dark trees by the river. He felt the Lord stirring his soul, whispering to his spirit, prodding him into...something?

"What is it, Lord?" Brother Joseph whispered.

The Guardian Assap stood by his charge, Sarat beside him.

"They are not the ones to activate the gate." Sarat spoke.

"I know, but why did our Lord have me lead them to this very spot?" Assap asked, looking down at the man who was even then turning to kneel in prayer.

Sarat smiled and answered, "These are men of God, destined to help birth a great new nation. The Word says that wherever they place their feet, our Lord will give that place to them if they will but claim it. They have been brought here to claim the portal for the Redeemed even though they don't fully understand what they are about to do."

"Others will come then." Assap stepped back as the man began to pray, flooded with strength from the worship of the Creator.

He looked over at the Gatekeeper beside him who stood by the very portal itself that began to shimmer in the darkness as Brother Joseph prayed.

"Lord I claim this ground for Your service. Great and mighty works will be done here according to Your will. This is truly a holy place where the heavens meet the earth...."

"You know Captain that I will have to leave along with my detachment when they go." Assap stated.

"The enemy will attack soon, I think," Sarat smiled, "You can stay for the fun. It want take too long."

Assap drew his sword, "I wouldn't miss it."

The ring of heavenly metal echoed off the nearby hills as one by one the Gatekeepers emerged from the shimmering portal to stand by the Guardians on the outside, drawing their golden blades. The stench of sulfur then flooded the valley as red flashes dotted the surrounding mountains and a great roar thundered above. The battle was finally joined as the portal opened.

CHAPTER FOURTEEN

THE RIVERGATE
DAY TWO AFTER THE CROSS

In the realm of the Gatekeepers, time has no meaning, because in the spiritual realm of God's true will, time as humans know it does not exist. God lives outside of time itself, able to see the lives of mankind like one would view the pictures on a roll of film. At any given moment, God is able to see the past, present and future. Although the Gatekeeper and Guardians cannot do this, time to them is fleeting.

To God a thousand years is like a day and to His spiritual warriors this revelation most approaches the way time feels to them. And so as years goes by in the natural, in the spiritual only seconds slip away, although in truth time does not change at all, because in the spirit realm, the beings are immortal.

Sarat sheathed his sword, breathing heavily the acrid smell of sulfur, surveying the carnage around him. The enemy had been beaten back just before the open portal, but the faith and determination of the Moravians ensured that the Gatekeepers were able to protect the gate's integrity. Ghastly, blackened remains of demons lay sprawled through the forest, disappearing one by one as they fell into the abyss. The valley was covered in a thick red haze from the many demons who had been vanquished. The retreating army howled in defeat from beyond the mountain range, their yellow eyes glaring through the smoke. They had been defeated, but they were still defiant. Their wounded limped along the banks of the river, desperately trying to catch the others who had fled.

A horn blew from somewhere beyond the seething mass of yellow eyes and suddenly the enemy disappeared leaving the wounded to make their way over the mountain as best they could. One lone warrior remained standing across the river, floating just above the trees. It was Nasi, the evil prince of the valley who had claimed the land since the beginning of the rebellion. He stood defiantly before the gate, his broadsword upraised in one gloved hand, the horn in another. A swirling black cloud enveloped him as his body glowed, yellow beams of light shooting outward. His eyes glowed red with hatred and defiance. Sarat looked across the river to his adversary and shuttered briefly at what could have happened if the Redeemed had not claimed the gate in time. The enemy had power in this world, he thought, but only what the Redeemed allowed them to have.

"You may have won this battle Sarat, but you know as well as I that the portal is useless unless the humans are able to wield its power. I will work among men to ensure that they will never do that. I am still ruler over this valley. You are but a caretaker of what will ultimately be mine." Nasi challenged and then disappeared behind the cloud.

Sarat stood for a moment thinking of what the enemy had said. They would change their tactics, he thought now that the gate had opened. He hoped the humans could withstand the attacks or all would be lost. He glanced down at himself and then the others. He had been wounded by a poisoned arrow that left a nasty hole through his abdomen, the wound running with the blackened fluid that smelled of death. He would need the Lord's healing touch soon. Both Nasag and Anah had received severe wounds from the axe and sword, severe enough for them to momentarily retreat back into the portal itself. Nakar sat on a rock nearby, his sword across his knees, panting and gasping for air. He had suffered a heavy blow to the chest in the last attack, but appeared to be okay. The giant Koah appeared to not have been touched at all, his immense form shining brightly in front of the opening, his golden broadsword before him, the point in the ground, the shaft in both of his gloved hands before his breastplate that was covered in the red dust of vanquished demons like the blood of humankind.

The battle for the gate had been severe, but brief. The Guardian Assap and his band, as well as Natan, had fought for a moment at their side until they had left, replaced by countless others as time in the natural realm moved forward. Only the Messenger Malak had stayed the entire battle with them. He now stood by the river among the sycamores, covered in red dust, wounded and weakened and in need of a healing touch.

As the battle for the portal raged in the spirit realm, the humans began to populate the new country. Small villages sprang up along the river. Great farms covered the meadows. War raged across the mountains as the mountain people fought against themselves and the British Red Coats. Traitors hung under a huge oak tree near the gate itself. The Mulberry fields were cleared and the land worked by the Negro slaves of the large landholders. The Moravians lost title to their land surveyed, but they had established a strong settlement to the east and were destined to other works.

Smaller portals were activated across the land as believers established small meetinghouses, the first of these established very near the place of Brother Joseph's prayer. In the realm of the Guardians, the godly warriors continued their desperate battle as more settlers moved into the valley and new churches were formed. This brought reinforcements to the portal, but still the portal was not activated. It had only been opened through the prayers of the Redeemed who had first camped within its reach. Although God moved through his people over the generations, the regional portal that held the key to finally break the hold of the enemy over the region lay unchanged as the Gatekeepers fiercely guarded it.

War again ravaged the countryside as soldiers in blue fought their brothers in gray in great battlefields across the country and in house to house fighting throughout the land. The Civil War devastated the valley and left bitter barriers between families, cultures and races of man. The number of churches continued to grow, but the strength of the people began to wane as the pleasures and pride of life drew their attention from the portals that had opened around them. The enemy had infiltrated the very churches themselves and portals crashed down through the countryside as the Redeemed bought the lies of the enemy.

But the Rivergate and other smaller gates nearby remained pure. Others were damaged as the enemy infiltrated the ranks of men, but they could be repaired given time and a few were forever lost as the decay of sin continued to erode them.

Sarat ordered the Messenger Malak into the portal. After ensuring that all were safely inside the gate he too left the realm of the Guardians and entered the world of the Gatekeepers. His band stood around him. They had beaten back the enemy, but they all knew that the Redeemed would have to activate the gate soon or all could still be lost.

Sarat spoke as he surveyed the heavens around him, "The time is very near now. Rest for a moment and renew your strength. Our gate is strong. It has been claimed by the Redeemed and we have protected it for them. Soon the true Gatekeepers will activate the portal and our job here will be done."

The Guardians continued to fight sporadic battles to protect their charges, but Nasi had been beaten back. And for that he was thankful. He sat down to rest for a moment.

Malak suddenly stood at attention and looked far out in the distance, hearing a voice that no one else could hear. Sarat knew that a new order had been given the young Messenger.

"I must leave you now Captain." The Messenger stated with a bit of sadness.

Sarat stood before the smaller angel and saluted him, "You have fought very well Malak. We will miss you."

Malak saluted in turn, "Captain, look at the young girl there by the courthouse."

Sarat turned to look. Under the giant oak tree that had once been used to hang traitors of the new country stood a small girl wearing a simple homespun dress, her brown hair braided, her dark eyes bright.

"Watch her closely. She is the next human to be used to further open the portal," Malak explained.

Sarat nodded and firmly clasped the Messenger's hand, "If not before, then we will all see each other again at the great victory feast."

Malak disappeared in a silver mist, leaving the Gatekeepers watching the young girl beneath the giant tree.

Nasag stepped up beside Sarat, "She is no bigger than a minute, as the humans would say," he commented.

"Our Lord confounds the wise through small things, " Sarat answered and then smiled.

He pointed, "And see who is her Guardian, tis none other than the brave Natan himself."

Sarat stepped back from the gate and addressed his band, "Rest time is over gentlemen. We must now ensure that whatever plan our Lord has for this child is carried out. She holds the key now to the gate. When she widens it, Nasi is sure to attack again."

CHAPTER FIFTHTEEN

WILKESBORO, NC, 1948

The town was typical of small, southern, mountain communities that also served as the county seat. The old courthouse of white washed stone dominated the main street that was narrow and lined with businesses, homes, a few boarding houses, a couple of doctors offices and the cluster of small law offices. The town had not changed very much over the past few years. Older buildings lay in disrepair along the side streets as businesses moved.

A relatively new, three storied building almost as large as the courthouse next door was the largest private building in the town. Built of red brick, the building sported a wrap around balcony and lower porch. A large sign over the front door read, "Smitheys General Store and Emporium."

The first story housed a large department store filled with clothing, appliances, dry goods, hardware and an assortment of odds and ends that every household had need of from time to time. Along one side of the wall was situated a large bar from which snacks, candy, ice cream, sodas and light lunches could be had, including the now famous Smitheys Burger, a left over from the great depression and poorer times.

The Smithey family also had another store in the newer, sister town across the Yadkin River near the railroad depot. The town, appropriately called North Wilkesboro began with the building of the railroad that ended just across the river from the existing town.

Before the only bridge across the river was built, a ford was used to go from one side to the other. When the railroad depot was completed, the town grew up around it. At one time, the railroad had extended far up the river to the highest reaches of the Yadkin Valley, utilized by the lumber companies as they logged the timber within the remote upper watershed. But that had been before the great flood of 1940 that carried the railroad away as well as a large portion of both towns.

The two towns occupied the geographical center of one of the largest, most remote counties in North Carolina. Only the main roads through the towns were paved, the remaining graveled or even worse the further from town and the Yadkin River that one traveled. Large farms dominated the rich river bottoms, although the old plantations owned by the anti-bellum aristocracy had been broken up for the most part after the Civil War. Smaller hillside farms dotted the remote mountain valleys and coves, although many of these homes had been abandoned during the Depression after families left in search of work in the larger cities to the east. Entire villages of people had simple moved, leaving behind the skeletal remains of once prosperous farms.

Farming, logging, and to a lesser extend textiles and furniture were the main occupations of the majority of the natives. And of course, moonshining. Although illegal, many of the mountain families found that they could make more from their corn by converting it to liquor than they could by selling it for food and so there was a long standing tradition and understanding between the local authorities and the moonshiners themselves. A game of search and destroy as well as looking the other way played itself out throughout the more remote mountain coves as the natives continued to produce the shine and the local authorities half heartedly assisted the Feds with finding and destroying the stills.

Most people attended church each Sunday, as was the custom throughout the mountains. Only the most corrupt people did not claim to be a member of good standing in the local church. This also became a tradition, steeped in the culture of the people. Although there were many devoted believers, the true gospel had somehow been diluted by the very tradition itself and the influence of the church would slowly disintegrate over the next generation.

This time, however the church still held a lot of power over the community even though it was itself tainted by tradition. Although revivals were spreading across other parts of the country, beginning in the early 1900's in a small California mission church at Azuzu Street, tradition in the county had mingled with a religious spirit that held sway over many of the churches. The communities did not wish to change and yield to the move of God that was sweeping the nation.

Also like many mountain communities, the predominant white, Protestant natives distrusted new people moving in and barely tolerated other races within their midst. The local black community kept to themselves and strict boundaries of relationships were followed. The two races cooperated when needed, tolerated each other's existence, but primarily remained separated. This was especially true when it came to religion. Whites and blacks could possibly work together, their kids could play together, they could even live close to one another, but under no circumstances could the two races worship together.

There was a strong spirit that held sway over the people, a religious tradition that was afraid of any different move of God. And the small girl that stood by the tree between the courthouse and Smitheys Store held the key. All would have to be broken before the portal could be totally opened. New changes were blowing in from the throne room of God and like many times throughout history, God chose the small things to confound the wise.

"Eileen," the call came from the front porch of Smitheys Grocery. The small girl swirled around quickly. She had been picking the flowers that were planted in beds alongside the courthouse, "Yes Momma?"

"Papa says that we can eat before we go to your Uncle Tom's, Come on before he changes his mind."

"Alright!" Eileen dropped the flowers. She wasn't supposed to pick them anyway, and ran across the side street to where her mother held the Smithey's door open. They rarely came to town and she couldn't remember the last time that they had eaten out at a real restaurant.

Her mother patted the girl on her back as she ran in the door. Inside there were several older men looking through the hardware, and one other lady paying for fabric at the register. Eileen slowed her run to a stop when she noticed a teenage boy drinking a fountain soda at the counter.

She was just barely thirteen, almost marrying age to some, and fresh off the farm. Although small for her age, Eileen always attracted the attention of the young boys at school with her bright eyes and long brown hair. Now she straightened her dress and blushed as the boy, most likely her own age, smiled at her from behind his paper straw. Her younger sister, Mary, a dark haired smaller version of herself sat by their Papa, himself of short stature. Eileen sat next to her sister as her mother slipped into the seat next to her. Papa had already ordered hamburgers and sodas for everyone, plus a large order of French fries to be shared. It was a delicacy of vast proportions and the family waited expectantly as the cook flipped the burgers on the grill with one hand and opened the buns with the other.

The bell over the door jangled as two men walked in and quickly made their way up to the counter. It was approaching lunchtime and the place would soon fill up with townsfolk.

"Hey George, throw a couple of those on the grill for us." The first ordered and then situated his overly large frame on the small stool, looking over at the family who had just received their food.

"Hello friend, " the man spoke and then eyed Papa closely, "Are you by chance C.B. Jackson?"

Papa looked over to the man, immediately recognizing an old friend, "Why you know its me Henry. How the world you doing?"

"Good, good and yourself?" the big man answered.

"We make do," Papa answered, smiling.

Eileen glanced over at her mother as she ate the hamburger, noticing that she had suddenly stopped eating and sat quietly, looking down at her food.

"You okay Momma?" the girl asked, worried. Her mother was frail, her body eaten up with diabetes. As long as she took her medicine, she was okay, but the past year had been extremely difficult and medicine was very hard to come by.

Emma Jackson was a quiet woman, refined, once used to living above her current circumstances. The family was poor, very poor, living as sharecroppers on land that was not their own. It had not always been so, but just before the Depression they had lost everything. She was fifty-eight years old and had raised two families, giving birth to sixteen children in all, three of which had died before they were one year old. The older children had been born before the Depression back when the family had lived on a nice farm in the rolling foothills east of town. Those children had moved on, had started families of their own before the war. Her older son lived in Pennsylvania and had children older than her two youngest. Emma's second family included Eileen and the youngest Mary who had both been born after the Depression when they had lost everything. The older children had been raised in fairly prosperous circumstances. The two youngest were brought up in object poverty, moving from house to house, barely surviving on the land owned by others until just recently when the oldest son had moved them to a home he had purchased. At least now Papa farmed for himself.

C.B. Jackson had been born in 1885, orphaned son of a Confederate soldier who had died soon after his birth to a mother who died in child bearing. He was a quiet man who worked harder than most, even though he stood just barely over five foot three. He had a quiet since of humor and could play the fiddle better than anyone in the county. Like his wife, he maintained his pride and dignity even when all had been lost. Both went to church religiously, but like most mountain families, the mother seemed to be the dominant spiritual leader.

"I'm okay dear. I just took my medicine. I'll be fine." Emma answered her softly and continued to eat.

Henry took a bite from his own burger, the grease running down his beard. He wiped his face with his sleeve and took another bite, continuing to talk as he chewed.

"I heared you moved to the old Redding place."

"You heard right. The place needs work, but the ten acres along the river ought to produce a fine crop."

"That's great C.B. I wish you well." Henry took another bite, finishing the hamburger, "Hey George, I'll take another one of those and give me some of them fries as well."

C.B. Jackson smiled. No wonder the man was so large. He ate like his mule.

"Oh yea. You had to have seen the brush arbor on the Swann Creek Road coming to town. How bout them holy rollers with them women preachers and all that tongue talking." Henry said overly loud as a couple of other townsfolk entered the store. He loved to spread the local gossip.

Both Mary and Eileen looked over at the man upon hearing that statement. They had snuck over to the meeting just the afternoon before to see what was going on. Momma had said it was okay, but Papa didn't know about it.

"They seem to be fine folks Henry. I didn't pay them much mind." C.B. answered after finishing the last of his hamburger. Religion was a very personal thing to him and he always disapproved of making fun of those who worshipped differently.

"Well all I know that if you ain't Baptist, you ain't right," Henry continued, drawing a small crowd.

Many people had heard of the Holiness movement that was entering the mountains as they continued to hold services in temporary structures called brush arbors. There were even several small Church of God churches in neighboring communities that preached of the Holy Spirit and speaking in other tongues. It was new, it was different and to many it had to be misguided. Some of the congregations accepted the fact that the Bible spoke of such things, but they continued to teach that it was not for the church of this age. Other preached totally against the movement, saying that it was straight from the devil himself. One thing was for certain. If you wanted to draw a crowd, just start talking about either politics or religion. And Henry loved drawing a crowd.

C.B. Jackson paid for the food and stood up, ignoring his friend. He himself had stopped by the brush arbor on his way home from the fields before dinner a few days before and stood by the opening to the structure, watching as the small group of people were singing and worshipping God. One had a fiddle, another a guitar and several ladies banged away with their tambourines as some shouted and danced. They had seemed to be having a good time and the service sure wasn't boring. He was intrigued by the service, but being reserved as he was, he figured that he had better stay with what he was used to. But there was no cause to make fun of them, he thought to himself.

"Mother, you ready? Tom will be expecting us soon and we got almost an hour travel to Taylorsville.

C.B. turned to Henry, "See you later my friend."

"You too, C.B. Take care." The man went back to the group sitting down the bar from him, "I heared they handled snakes!"

"That's a fact. Margaret says they carry 'em in boxes and lets 'em loose as they sing and shout," another man said as the Jackson family left the store.

The Guardian Natan stood by the door on the front porch, laughing quietly to himself as Sarat suddenly appeared next to him.

"What is so funny?" he asked the Guardian.

"Nothing really. It is actually quit sad the way the enemy has deceived some of the Redeemed."

"I was told that the girl, Eileen, holds a key to open the Rivergate even more." Sarat continued.

"Yes, so it seems. I'm not sure what is in store for her and her family, but a few days ago she received a letter from one of her older sisters inviting her to a revival meeting. The Holy Spirit is moving among those who will listen. The letter has peaked little Eileen's interested in the gift. She has been studying the scriptures for herself and is ready to receive Him."

"Well then we must make sure that she does." Sarat shook Natan's hand and returned to the gate.

CHAPTER SIXTEEN

TAYLORSVILLE, NC, 1948

The two towns straddled both sides of the Yadkin River in the center of a horseshoe shaped valley that emptied out into the rolling foothills of western North Carolina. Steep mountains rose sharply to the north and west toward the eastern Continental Divide and the newly constructed Blue Ridge Parkway.

The southern county line followed the highest reaches of a long band of mountains called the Brushies. The Brushy Mountains were a remote section of high narrow ridges, crags and cliffs intermixed with rolling mountain summits, deep coves and hidden water falls. The range extended from the higher mountains to the west, driving a wedge between the Yadkin and Catawba River valleys.

The area was noted for its apple orchards, which spread out across the upland meadows. Deep mountain coves were choked with ancient yellow-poplar stands mixed with recently cutover areas, abandoned farms and the ever-present moonshine stills. There were very few passable roads through the mountain range that separated the Yadkin Valley from the Piedmont regions to the south. The main road across the Brushies left Wilkesboro near the courthouse and quickly climbed the first ridge along an extremely narrow, winding, gravel road that in the winter was almost impassible at times. The road continued through the wide upland meadows with their scattered orchards and farms before winding through a series of broken ridges along the southern shoulder of the range.

Here the road entered thick stands of hardwood forests covered with the bleached remains of giant American chestnut trees that had recently succumbed to the blight, forever changing the forest of North Carolina and ascended to an even higher summit overlooking a sheer rock cliff that offered an outstanding view of the rolling foothills far to the south toward the large city of Charlotte over eighty miles away. From the summit, the road wound down through deep ravines, passed several more farms and then finally ended at another road in the valley below. After passing several large farms, the road entered the small town of Taylorsville, county seat of Alexander County.

C.B. Jackson filled his tank with gas and with the two girls riding in the truck bed, he left the town and began the journey to Taylorsville. His second oldest boy lived in the small town, operating a small shoe shop on the main street. Recently married to a Wilkesboro girl named Francis Pardue upon returning from the war in Europe, Thomas Jackson had one young child of his own with one more on the way. The family lived in a small frame house near the shoe store.

Also living with the Thomas family was Eileen's older sister, Elizabeth, who was staying to help Francis with the new baby that was due any day. Elizabeth had moved to Taylorsville the month before. It was Elizabeth who had written the letter to her family, as well as to her younger sister, inviting Eileen to join her at a week long summer revival meeting sponsored by the Taylorsville Church of God. The church had been in revival services each Sunday for the last three weeks and God was moving. It was all new to most of those attending as the gift of tongues was being poured out on those who believed. Just like Azusa Street forty years before, the letter had said. Eileen didn't know where Azusa Street was, but she had heard the statement before at one of the Brush Arbor meetings. That didn't impress her too much but the scriptures that Elizabeth had told her to read did. They spoke of the baptisms in the Holy Ghost, speaking in other tongues, healing miracles and a deeper relationship with God. That was something that she was definitely interested in, especially the healing miracles. She had seen her mother sick too long. If she could tap into this power of God, she would do whatever it took and so she had pleaded with her parents to let her go. She didn't tell them everything that the letter said, especially to Papa because of what he might say.

They had agreed to let her go if Tom could bring her back, which a phone call from the small country store near their house to a store next to the Tom's shop had verified. So after the trip across the mountain, Eileen found herself standing on the front porch of her brother's new home. This was the fist time that she was to be away from home for more than one night. Papa, Momma and Mary stayed the evening and after breakfast, they headed back up the mountain road toward home.

That night was to be the first service of the Holiness revival meetings. This time they would be in a real church, not the quickly constructed shelter of rough timbers and tree limbs of the brush arbors back home.

The Taylorsville Church of God occupied a brick building on Main Street. The church had been in the town for over ten years and was somewhat accepted as a legitimate church by the community that often shied away from any church that claimed an affiliation with the Holiness movement that had begun to spread through the south before the depression.

The pastor was an older man who had moved to the town from Arkansas. Pastor J.W Galloway had been the leader of a Church of God in his home state, one of the first of the new Pentecostal denomination that was slowly spreading through the south. He had actually been to the Azuzu Street revivals and could give a first hand account of the miracles that he had seen there.

Although it was customary for the more traditional churches to have revivals in the spring and fall for people to repent and return to the church, this revival had not been scheduled and was in the middle of the summer, which was totally out of character for the mainline denominations that held sway over the mountain counties. God had moved in their regular Sunday services and Pastor Galloway had called for a weeklong series of nightly meetings so that revival could spread through the community.

The small church congregation had spread the word through town, called their relatives and mailed invitations to people across the region. Posters had been placed at the stores and on street corner signs as the community began to wonder what the Holiness people were up to this time. They had grown used to their Sunday night meetings with the music, shouting and long-winded preaching, but to have a revival in the middle of the summer? That was going a little too far, some of the townsfolk thought. Others paid it no mind, but a few were intrigued by their devotion.

And so, on the first night the little Holiness church was packed. All the seats were taken and more were brought out, even though it was hot. Simple cardboard fans were given out to everyone in the church as they came through the door by wide smiling young ladies as the musicians gathered on the platform. Farmers came in from the fields early, business people closed their shops and children filled the front rows, expectantly. Some came to gather information to make fun, others came because they liked the music, but all of them were there according to the will of God, especially young Eileen who arrived late because her older sister had to change clothes three times before she thought that she was pretty enough to be seen by the teenage boys that were sure to be there.

It had been a long time since Eileen had seen a church filled with people. The little mountain church that she attended back home with her family had seats for only thirty or forty people and usually there were only half that many people present on any give Sunday morning. There was a piano, guitars, fiddles, tambourines and even a small drum set on the stage. Her church only had a busted up old piano that barely played. She noticed that there were no spittoons next to the seats as was the case in her church and then remembered that Holiness people preached strong against tobacco use. That was a good thing she thought. She always hated to see old man Johnson spit in the spittoon at church. Most of the time he missed.

She shivered with the vision of the bearded man spitting and turned to her sister. Eileen was nervous, wringing her hands. Elizabeth smiled at her knowingly and pointed to one of the last seats available along the wall. Their brother, Tom and his family were seated up front,

Francis near the side door exit. If she grew any larger with that baby, Eileen though, she wouldn't make it through the aisle.

There were no more seats left in the church. People stood along the walls and out in the foyer. A tangible undercurrent of uncertainty, apprehension and expectancy flowed through the church as the pastor stepped up on the stage to stand behind the worn pulpit, the musicians growing quiet behind him. A mother scolded her child quietly. Someone coughed; a few whisperers silenced as the pastor begin to speak.

"Welcome to Taylorsville Church of God to all you visitors. May God bless you as I know that surely He will this night. Please stand as we go to our heavenly father in prayer."

Eileen stood up, but because she was shorter than those standing in front of her, she could not see the pulpit, therefore she sidestepped partially out into the aisle, bowing her head as the pastor prayed. She kept one eye opened, watching those around her. Back home, Papa would have scolded her if she had done that during the prayer time, but here she did not want to miss anything. She noticed several others were looking around the church as well.

The pastor finished the prayer and Eileen immediately begin to take her seat as a few others did as well until she noticed that the majority of the people remained standing. She stood back up as well. The musicians took center stage as the pastor stepped to the side of the platform near the door to the restroom. The church had one restroom that could only be entered by walking past the pulpit to a small hall that also went to the entrance to the baptistery, situated behind the platform under a large wooden cross attached to the back wall.

She definitely would not go to the bathroom, no matter how bad she needed to go, Eileen thought to herself.

The music started as the congregation was told to go to page 54 in the hymnal. Eileen found an old, worn hymnal in a small rack on the back of the pew in front of her and turned to the appropriate page. She knew the song and began to sing along, immediately caught up in the excitement of the music, people and the strong presence of God that she had never felt before. Something was going to happen tonight, she thought to herself. She just knew it!

"Please God, I do want more of you. Give me your Holy Spirit tonight." She prayed.

The music grew louder, the singing stronger as the congregation began to worship God with a freedom that many in the group had never experienced before. Surely the presence of God was strong. God was doing a new work and the spirits that held sway over the communities shuttered as they cowered in darkened corners.

There were several ministers that spoke on that first night of the revival, each telling a different account of how they had been filled with the baptism in the Holy Spirit and the miracles that they had seen. Eileen could not believe the wonderful things that were said. The more she listened, the more she knew that she wanted what they had. She did not fully understand, but she knew that there had to be more of God than what she now knew. Finally Pastor Galloway took the pulpit, asking everyone to stand.

"Acts 2:38 says to repent and be baptized in the name of Jesus that your sins may be forgiven and you shall receive the gift of the Holy Spirit. The promise is for you and for all who are far off."

He raised both hands and then pointed at the congregation, one hand pointed, it seemed, directly to Eileen's heart, " You are those that are far off. The promise is for you today, in this time and place. God has more for you than you can ever imagine."

He stepped from behind the pulpit as everyone listened intently, "The prophets of old said that in the last days, the Spirit of God would be on all flesh, young men will prophecy and the old will see visions. These are the last days. We are in perilous times. We have just come through a terrible war. Many of you saw its destruction first hand. And before that, we saw the tragedy of the first Great War. These are indeed the last days, because we see wars and rumors of wars. But God is ever faithful," he hit the pulpit with his fist as many in the congregation shouted resounding 'Amens', "I said that God is faithful and his Spirit is free to all of those who call Him Lord and Savior!"

Brother Galloway paused, eyeing the crowd as he took a handkerchief and wiped the sweat from his forehead and face. A soft night breeze flowed through the open doors to the church, but it was still hot in the little church. As the people stood, waiting expectantly, they continued to cool themselves with the small fans given to them before the service. A baby cried in the back of the church and the mother quickly took her son outside to stand on the front steps in the cooler outside air. There were several women already there with small children. A few children played quietly in the grass by the door under the ever watchful eyes of their mothers who remained close enough to the door to hear what was going on inside.

"Some of you came tonight because you are earnestly searching for more of God. You have sensed in your spirit that although you have been saved, God has a deeper relationship that He wishes to have with you."

Eileen leaned forward. He seemed to know what she had been thinking, what she had been praying for.

"Others came tonight to see if we were real, some to scoff, but now all of you have the opportunity to receive as much from God as you wish to have. He is here in this place tonight," the pastor draped the handkerchief on the pulpit and stood behind it, placing both hands on the worn, polished oak surface, "For those of you who wish to receive the Baptism in the Holy Ghost, tonight is your night. Come forward as the musicians play and we will pray for you."

Eileen felt the strong tug of God on her heart. She had been searching the scriptures for weeks herself trying to understand, knowing that there was more to God than what she was hearing preached from the pulpit of her church each service. The Holy Spirit was real, speaking in tongues was for the believer, and there was a deeper relationship with God than what she now had. She glanced over to her sister who was praying, her eyes closed, tears flowing down her cheeks, her hands upraised. People all over the church suddenly walked forward to kneel along the wooden alter before the pulpit. She knew that Jesus was calling her forward, and she took a step out into the aisle.

Her heart was pure, her spirit totally obedient. Eileen took one step and the heavens opened above her as the Guardians watched in the spirit realm, bowing before their Creator.

Eileen felt the Spirit of God flow through her body and then she fell back into the arms of her Savior as the Spirit of God filled her very soul, touching her spirit and bonding together as one and from her lips rose the glorious tongues of the angels in praise. She would never be the same.

A brilliant Messenger shot upward through the roof of the church and past the steeple, flying across the mountains toward the Rivergate. Just over Pores Knob with its broken cliffs and lonely fire tower, manned during the fire season by an older man who lived in the small cabin at its base, an enemy scout alerted other forces nearby and a full troop suddenly rallied to stop the lone Messenger. But the Messenger was too quick and darted downward, flying through the cabin itself, avoiding the enemy and arrived safely by the gate a few seconds later.

Sarat met the Messenger by the swift flowing Yadkin River, brandishing his golden sword. The small troop of enemy scouts ducked back toward the mountains, knowing that they were no match for a Gatekeeper.

"Captain, I bring good news from the Guardian Natan."

The Messenger handed a parchment to the Captain and stood silently before him. Nasag emerged from the portal as Sarat read the note and then crushed it in his hands.

"Thank you. Tell Natan that we will be ready to assist him." Sarat saluted the Messenger who answered in kind and disappeared.

"Captain, I don't understand," Nasag questioned, "The Spirit of God has been given to many, even here in this place. How does one young girl help with opening such a great portal as this one?"

Sarat looked over the valley and thought before answering. There were many small churches throughout the valley, several near the gate itself, many of them opening their own portals to heaven, but over time many of the portals had dimmed, and some had fallen in on themselves. Most believers did not realize that man's traditions had replaced true worship. Those traditions that trapped men in their religion had to be broken before the next move of God could sweep through the land, and the gate fully open. Suddenly Sarat knew the answer to the question.

"This little Eileen will be the first to challenge the Spirit of Religion that holds sway over this valley. We must be there to defend her."

He stepped back into the portal.

CHAPTER SEVENTEEN

WILKES COUNTY, NC, 1948

The little frame church stood on a low flat hill overlooking the deep valley of the eastern fork of the Roaring River under the shadows of Stone Mountain in northeastern Wilkes County. The building was typical of the small mountain churches that dotted the broken landscape, left overs from a not too distant past when people rarely traveled out from their secluded mountain coves. Even now, three years after the end of World War II, many of the mountain areas were secluded, but as more families acquired the automobile and the state continued to improve the mountain roads, people were able to travel farther distances, and go to town more often.

There had been a time when each mountain valley had its own church, own store and, in most cases its own post office. As more people moved to the larger cities for manufacturing jobs, many of the mountain communities had closed down, including the churches, leaving small ghost towns of dilapidated buildings. The little churches that remained, like this one, were places of worship for the few families that stayed behind to farm the land.

The church needed painting; a portion of the roof leaked and termites had infested a small section of the wall by the rear door of the building. A fading wooden sign out front told anyone who bothered to read it that the church had been established in 1882. Over the date were bold black letters that read, "Billings Chapel Baptist Church."

The small gravel road that passed the church before ending on the banks of the Roaring River two miles to the south wound northward through a low gap in the rolling hills to the small crossroads called Traphill. Once Traphill had been a thriving mountain community that boosted a small college before the Civil War. It had also been the home of the original Siamese twins late in the last century who had been farmers after their circus years.

The community was very remote, with only one road that traveled through the rolling hills under the shadows of the Blue Ridge escarpment. The road cut through some of the most difficult terrain in the mountains back to North Wilkesboro. The village was appropriately named to those who did not wish to be there. Late in the last century there had been a thriving logging community, but as the great forests were cutover, even these logging camps disappeared. Several miles to the north along Basin Creek under the high cliffs near Brineger's Cabin on the crest of the Continental Divide, a large community of over seventy homes, a church, several stores and a post office thrived. Now only the skeletons remained, many of the families leaving, the remaining homes destroyed in one night during the great flood of 1916. A forest fire had ravaged the mountains during the Depression, burning most of the empty homes as well as a few occupied ones. Over the years since then, the mountain had slowly taken over the village, growing over the foundations, scattered chimneys and small cemeteries, leaving very little evidence of what had been before. Much like what was happening in the spiritual realm.

The mountain people were a self-reliant breed, untrusting of outsiders or of anything new that threatened their traditions. The small church reflected this sentiment, even more so than other churches closer to town. They were generally good folks. Many of them went to church, but even that had become a social tradition to most of them. There were still devoted prayer warriors and people that wished for a renewed spiritual revival, but their numbers were few. The people lived day to day, surviving in a difficult time, a changing time that would in one generation re arrange their entire lives as an influx of outsiders would begin to move into the mountain coves, building retirement homes, golf courses, mountain retreats. New roads would open up and people would begin to flock to the remote mountains to escape the growing cities in the east. But now, they were still isolated, many knowing very little about what was happening in the outside world.

A narrow dirt road turned off of Billings Road by the church and followed the edge of a broken stand of beetle killed Virginia pine to a small frame house overlooking fertile bottomland fields next to a small tributary of the Roaring River. The fields were covered with corn. Nearer the house was a large vegetable garden, fenced in to keep out the free ranging cattle that utilized the surrounding pasture. The house had two stories with a porch that extended down the front and one side of the structure. A kitchen extended out from the back of the house. Several outbuildings made from graying chestnut boards as well as a large, slightly leaning barn surrounded the farmhouse. A well house was situated immediately behind the back door that entered the kitchen from a small back porch. Brilliant colors from flowers planted in beds edging the house contrasted greatly with its fading white paint of the house itself.

C.B. Jackson worked the fields each day until dusk, tending, plowing, and pulling weeds, driving out the occasional cow that found holes in the fence. On this day, he was still working even as the sweet smell of freshly baked bread and apple pie floated on the soft breeze from the open kitchen window. The day had been extremely hot, but with the onset of a cool afternoon breeze, the heat became bearable. Approaching clouds promised a much-needed evening shower, which Papa was trying to beat. The back screen door screeched and then closed with a loud bang as Mother brought in a jar of last year's green beans from the cellar to add to the evening meal.

And meanwhile two young teenage girls sat under the shade of a cluster of sycamores along the stream behind a low hill behind the barn. Eileen and her younger sister Mary read from a worn Bible. For the past year, the two girls had met each day that they could to pray for their mother's healing. As time went on Eileen especially began to earnestly seek a closer relationship with God, searching the scriptures for a deeper understanding. The preachers that she listened to each

Sunday and Wednesday night seemed to only have a portion of the truth. And now since her experience at the Church of God revival meeting, she understood what it was she had been searching for. Now her younger sister was searching as well and Eileen began to share with her what had happened the week before.

"Mary, I can't explain it as much as I try. All I know is that I was filled with God's presence so much that I seemed to be floating. He was all around me, all within me. I could hear the music. I could hear the people around me, but I seemed to be in a different place. I remember going forward at the altar call and then suddenly I was speaking a language that I couldn't understand."

"Speaking in tongues?"

"Yes, I guess I was. But Mary, I know now that it's really not that important that I speak in tongues. What's most important is that God has filled me with His Spirit and I feel different, stronger somehow, closer to God."

"That's what I want Eileen. Can you show me how?" the younger sister asked expectantly.

"I can't show you Mary, but I know that we can pray for you to also receive the baptism."

The two small children held hands in the pasture as they had been doing for several months and began to pray and seek God for His Spirit to come upon them. Natan stood back respectively ever watchful for any sign of the enemy, but they were nowhere to be seen. The prayers of two children had driven them away, Natan thought as he basked in the strength of their prayers that smelled like sweet incense to his spiritual senses.

Suddenly the sky exploded around the girls and Natan bowed in reverence as the Holy Spirit descended in the spiritual realm and settled over the girl Mary, who began to cry and speak in a language, that even Natan's ears could not comprehend. It was just like when the Spirit had descended on King David those many earth years before, he thought, but this time the presence of God stayed. The victory at the cross had made that miracle possible.

The next day was Wednesday, the day when most churches opened for a mid week service and Billings Chapel was no different. Eileen and Mary changed quickly into their simple, homespun dresses reserved for church meetings and special occasions and kissed Mother goodbye. Papa was still out working in the fields. Mother was sick again and didn't feel like going to the service. The church was within sight of the house. The girls could see a few cars already parked in the gravel lot next to the road. Another pickup turned down the lane and backed into the spot closest to the front door and a large man in bib overalls and worn hat stepped out from the driver's side and spit the last of his tobacco onto the gravel as the girls walked by. His wife, a small, quiet woman who always wore the prettiest dresses to church smiled widely.

"Hello Eileen, and you too Mary. Where are your parents?" she asked as her husband entered the church.

"Papa's still working, and Mother is sickly tonight Mrs. Hutchinson," Eileen answered.

She liked Mrs. Hutchinson who always had a kind word, but distrusted her husband who had a way of looking at her and her sister that always made her feel uncomfortable. She had stumbled on his moonshine still one morning while taking a new route to school and he had been drunk. He had grabbed her, throwing her to the ground and fell across her, the smell of alcohol on him so strong that she gagged. She tried to struggle, but he was too strong. He pulled at her clothing and she screamed as she tore at his face with her fingernails. Somehow one hand found a rock and with all of the strength that she had in her, she slammed the rock across his face, tearing away flesh. He jumped back off of her and stumbled back against a tree, and she grabbed Mary's hand and ran. She had never told anyone about that terrible experience.

"I'm sorry to hear that. Make sure you tell her that we missed her at church," she smiled again and followed her husband in the door, the two girls following behind.

Inside, the church was small, two sections of old wooden pews with a single aisle between, a simple altar and pulpit. A dozen older couples as well as a few children were already sitting in their respective seats when the two girls entered the room. The pastor of the small church had not arrived and one of the elders stood behind the pulpit. He looked at his watch and decided that it was time to start the evening service. Eileen and Mary slipped into the last pew on the right side of the church.

Yellow eyes peered down on the small group from the rafters above. Several Guardians stood by their charges as well. There were good people in the congregation that truly loved God, but the church had no open portal to heaven. Evil had infiltrated the ranks. Therefore, although still able to protect their charges, the Guardians were powerless to drive the enemy totally away. Even in the midst of the enemy, God could work through the Redeemed ones who sat in the pews.

One of the first religious spirits of the enemy that held sway over the region was going to be attacked. The attack would come from two unsuspecting girls who had just experienced just a part of what God desired for all in the valley to one day experience.

The deacon led the small congregation in a simple prayer, well meaning but void of power, a prayer that offered very little strength to the scattered Guardians overlooking the small church. The enemy snickered from the shadows, the Guardians watching, only slightly interested in what was going on around them. They had become accustomed to the church services, the hidden sins, open hypocrisy and lack of spiritual authority exercised by this particular congregation.

But suddenly something stirred in the spiritual realm, something small, insignificant. The enemy felt it and so did the Guardians, especially Natan. He looked back to where the two girls sat, past the spirits of lust and alcohol that held Mr. Hutchinson captive, past Mrs. Hutchinson's Guardian who fought valiantly each day to keep his charge sane in her world of hidden torment at the hands of her husband. The Spirit of God sparked ever so slightly within the older sister, joining with her own spirit. Then as the spark grew into an open flame within her heart, the girl began to tremble ever so slightly as if her flesh was cold, but it was not.

Natan took a step closer, the yellow eyes in the shadows disappeared as the harassing demons retreated back.

The deacon's prayer over, he began his announcements. A deacon meeting was scheduled for the next week. A workday was set for two weeks away where hopefully the church could be painted, but they had to decide on what color first. A child shifted uncomfortably in the front row and someone coughed, very loudly, and then excused himself politely as the deacon waited before continuing the announcements. He was about to run out of things to say and looked nervously out the side window of the church to the parking place of the pastor. They usually sang from the hymnal just after the announcements, but the pastor's wife was the only person who could play the old piano that sat in the corner across from the pulpit.

"Pastor is running late tonight, so we'll have a testimony service until he arrives," the deacon announced, and then waited for someone to stand up and give a testimony.

Sarat entered the church suddenly through the roof and hovered just over the two girls and greeted Natan, who saluted the Captain.

"I thought this would be interesting to see. I felt that it was time for Nasi to be directly challenged."

"We have not seen him for some time Sarat. If he knew that she was chosen, surely he would watch to see for himself, " Natan commented.

The other Guardians stood ready, fully expecting an attack from somewhere but nothing materialized, though they could now feel the Spirit stirring within the young girl. Suddenly, she stood up, and all turned to watch, including the enemy who gathered in the shadows, wondering what was going to happen.

Eileen stood nervously, but she knew that she needed to share her new experience with the church. Surely they would be happy with what had happened to her. She stammered nervously before the Deacon spoke.

"Go ahead child. It's okay. Just tell us what God has done for you."

The teenage girl began, tears running down her face as her younger sister sat beside her, looking up into her eyes, "I don't quite know how to say this. But a few weeks ago, I went to a revival meeting in Taylorsville. Lately I have been praying for God to reveal Himself to me in a stronger way. I have been praying for God to heal my Ma."

"Now you know that if it is God's will, He could heal your Ma…" the deacon interjected, suddenly uncomfortable with what the girl was saying.

Eileen continued as the Deacon fell silent.

"Like I said, I have prayed for something more, a deeper understanding from God. My sister told me about the Holy Spirit. How she received the baptism and I knew that that was for me. That was what I was searching for."

The small congregation stirred, a few people mumbling to themselves. The Deacon paced nervously behind the pulpit, but for some reason he could not think of anything to say. If only the Pastor was here, he thought. He would know what to do.

The Guardians stood silently watching, smiles spreading across their faces as the young girl cleared her throat to continue her story. The Spirit was strong within her now and soon she may not be able to contain the power within her mortal body. If Nasi had known that a great crack was in the process of being created in his control over the valley, he would have sent his entire army to attack them. Only the harassing demons now fluttered nervously over the church, falling back as the Spirit grew stronger within the girl.

"So I went to the revival and God," she began to cry no longer able to contain her composure, "God filled me with the Holy Spirit and I began to speak in an unknown language. What the scriptures say in the Bible are true. The gift of the Holy Spirit is for all generations, not just those in the Bible. I have been lied to all of these years. The…"

"Young lady, you need to set down. We will have no more talk such as that!" Mr. Hutchinson ordered and began to stand up.

Natan drew his sword and knocked the enemy warrior that approached his charge back through the door where he fell in a heap among a pile of chicken manure that had recently been dumped next to the pasture behind the church.

"Fitting place for him," Sarat remarked as he drew his own sword, signaling the others to do the same. Nasi may yet try to stop this, even though he could not. The Spirit was in full charge of both of the girls now, and no army Nasi deployed could withstand them.

Eileen ignored the man as Mary stood next to her, trembling herself. The two girls did not understand what was going on, but they knew what they had experienced was Truth and knew that they were to proclaim that truth loud and clear. Little did they know what they were starting in the small country church would begin a process that would ultimately lead to the opening of a great portal that would usher in a new move of God through the land.

"The gift of the Spirit is for me, healing is for me, dominion is for me. I don't understand what has happened to me, but I know that it is true and I will never be the same."

The girls began to tremble then as they began to cry and then from their mouths, they began to utter a most beautiful language that even the Guardians could not understand. They were worshipping God in a way that had never been done before in the valley inside church walls. The enemy warriors immediately shrieked in pain and covered their ears as they crouched in the far corners of the church. The harassing demons were immediately gone, flying far over the mountains. The Guardians radiated with renewed strength as the language of God himself flowed from the young girls' lips. The two were not loud, in fact Mary spoke in just a whisper, but the language shot through the spiritual realm to the very throne of God. And the dark master of the valley cringed at the hearing of them.

Mr. Hutchinson stood up angrily and reached to take Eileen's arm with thoughts of throwing her from the church, but his wife stood between her husband and the girls.

"No Thaddeus leave them alone. They're just children!" Mrs. Hutchinson pleaded, knowing that a beating waited for her when they returned home. But she was encouraged by an inner strength that told her she would soon be free from that abuse.

Thaddeus Hutchinson glared at his wife, his trembling hand poised to hit her and then he remembered where he was and turned to the Deacon, " Do something Bob! These girls are crazy."

He grabbed his wife's arm and pulled her out the door just as the pastor and his wife pulled up in their pickup truck. The girls continued speaking in an unknown language, oblivious to what was going on around them. Others filed past them and out the door, visibly shaken by what they were seeing, some outwardly frightened, praying for God's protection from the work of the devil. The Deacon was the last to leave the girls just as the pastor and his wife walked toward the front door of the church hurriedly.

"Brother Hutchinson? What's wrong?" the pastor asked as the Hutchinsons pushed past him to their vehicle.

"I'm sorry that we're late Brother Bob. We had a flat tire on the way to church," the Pastor looked at the others standing nervously around him, "Why are you leaving? What has happened?"

"It's those Jackson girls, Pastor. They're inside the church shaken and a shimmering all over the place, talking about the Holy Ghost and jabbering on. I didn't... we didn't know what to do?" the Deacon answered.

The heavenly host gathered around the girls couldn't help but laugh at the humans' reaction to what the girls were doing, even though it was saddening that the enemy had so blinded the Redeemed ones. That was going to change.

The portal at the River suddenly shifted through space, opening further with a myriad rainbow of colors catching the Gatekeepers who guarded it somewhat by surprise. Both armies who fought for control of the valley had taken the little girl for granted, but no more.

"It is not over Natan. Nasi was caught off guard this time, but prepare yourself. He will no doubt try to destroy her testimony soon," Sarat commented to those around him.

CHAPTER EIGHTEEN

WESTERN WYOMING
PRESENT DAY

The thick gray smoke blew in over the stricken helicopter with its crew of two where it lay on its side. Tom cautiously approached the front of the machine, and then glanced over his shoulder. The fire was gaining strength. He would have to move quickly. He could see the pilot slumped sideways, held in still by the safety belt, the glass shattered in front of him. He was unconscious or possibly dead. The only way to gain entry into the ship was from the open side door that luckily was on the side of the helicopter facing the sky. Tom pulled himself up and peered into the dark interior of the aircraft. The body of the crew chief lay toward the back of the ship, his vacant eyes staring out the door.

Tom climbed into the craft and checked the man's pulse. He was dead, his blue eyes staring into eternity. Tom would not leave a fallen firefighter on the field of battle to be torn apart by the red claws of the coming dragon. He gingerly pulled the dead man back to the opening and placed him so that he could pull him out of the aircraft from the door. He then made his way to the front where the pilot lay, still strapped into his seat. The man groaned in pain and turned his head to look upward toward the sky that was filling with smoke. Soon the embers would come and then the fuel would catch fire.

Tom gained access to the front, "Easy now. Let me help you out."

The pilot struggled with the harness across his chest. His face was covered with oil and he could not see because the oil covered his eyes as well. Tom pulled the headset and helmet from the pilot and disconnected the harness.

"David? Where's David?" the pilot asked, struggling for breath.

"He didn't make it."

The pilot slumped forward, wiping his eyes.

"Can you move?"

"I think so," the pilot turned to climb out of the seat and then cringed in pain, reaching for his side.

"Easy now," Tom climbed around in front of the pilot, " Let me help you out. You may have a few broken ribs."

The pilot was an older man with graying hair and sky blue eyes. He was also tall, making it more difficult for Tom to pull him from the seat and back into the rear of the ship. The man was also strong and even though he had a cut across his forehead, most likely a concussion and possibly broken ribs, he was able to stand.

"I won't leave David behind," the pilot stated when he saw the crew chief's body propped upright below the open door.

"I wasn't planning on it. But first let me get you out and then I'll get David."

The pilot agreed and Tom climbed back out of the door. Bracing himself, he reached back and grabbed the pilot by the arms pulling him out from the door. Tom then climbed back into the helicopter, but he could not carry the body back out. The pilot leaned back in the opening, reaching hands downward, the pain evident on his face.

"Lift him up and I'll pull."

Tom followed the order and together they were able to retrieve the body from the ship and were soon on the grass by the under belly of the craft.

"We don't have much time. The fire will be upon us soon and we need to get some place safe." Tom ordered, still unsure about where that place was at the moment.

"Are you Juliet?" the pilot asked.

"Yes, names Tom McKenzie."

The pilot shook his head, "Jack Darnell. Thanks for pulling us out."

"Can you walk?"

"Yea, but where can we go?"

"There's a place behind the rocks where I think we'll be okay. It's going to get hot but with the shelter I believe we'll get through."

For the first time Tom realized that Jack didn't have a shelter with him. It was back on the ship.

All of the personnel on Division Juliet saw the helicopter fall behind the smoke, as did the personnel at the helibase at the bottom of the mountain. There was a moment of hushed alarm as the ground crew watched in horror. Everyone heard the frantic cry for assistance before the radio went dead. Heather heard the "mayday" call as well and ran from the trailer across the road from the air operations tent.

A strong wind bent the trees along the river, flapping the tent flaps and causing the wind sock situated on top of a metal pole at the edge of the helibase to stand straight out. Great, blackened plumes of smoke covered the mountainside, drawing strength from the wind. She had seen this many times before when past fires had suddenly come alive to prey upon the unsuspecting fuel.

Off to the north, she sighted the medium helicopter making a water drop near the threatened homes. That meant her worst nightmare had suddenly come true. She stood by the road as several trucks pulled into the field beside her, trailing clouds of dust that quickly enveloped her. She turned her head to shield her face from the onslaught and closed her eyes. She recognized the Air Ops Chief, who walked past her and entered the communications tent. She followed as far as the open door. Inside there was a frenzy of activity.

"Where did he go down?" Air Ops asked. She didn't know the man's name.

"Somewhere high up on Juliet," a young woman with unruly brown hair answered. Her name was Gloria, but Heather wasn't sure

Oh God! What if? Heather could not complete the question.

No! Jack was smart. He would make it out. He had to!

A large topographic map covered the table suddenly as papers were shoved to the side and on to the floor. Another assistant quickly gathered the loose documents and placed them on a chair. Outside the helibase crew watched the fire climb upward across the mountain, each with their own thoughts, their own fears. Several had flown on the ship the days before. The sudden realization that they could have been on the helicopter when it went down brought a flood of fear as well as relief. They had not been on the ship, but two men that they worked with had been.

Inside the tent, the phone rang. One of the crew answered as Air Ops called once more on the radio for the stricken ship.

There was no answer.

The crewman hung up the phone and turned to Air Ops, "That was Safety. He'll be here in a few minutes along with the Incident Commander."

For a moment everyone stood silently. Air Ops was responsible for all of the aircraft assigned to the fire, including the remaining helicopter, scout plane and inbound air tankers that were soon to arrive. He had a fire to fight from the air in coordination with the ground troops, but he also had a search and rescue to do. What was the policy on this? Thankfully he had never been on an incident where a ship had gone down. He worked for Operations and would need to keep him informed, but surely the IC would take over.

"Air Ops, this is Ops." The radio broke the silence.

Air Ops carried his portable in his back pocket. He quickly answered.

"Safety and the IC are in route to your position. They will assume control of the incident. I need you to handle the incoming air traffic. This wind event has caused several blow ups and dispatch has sent us two tankers."

"Copy that Ops. As soon as they arrive I'll turn search and rescue over. I am going to divert the medium for a quick recon to locate the site."

"Okay, Let me know, Ops clear."

"Air Ops clear."

The gods were smiling on him, Air Ops thought to himself. He turned to order the medium helicopter back to Juliet, but noticed that the Helibase Manager was already on the radio with the pilot. He could see the helicopter in the distance bank around behind the low ridge and disappear behind the smoke.

Air Ops turned back to the map. He settled himself. First they needed to locate the site. Next..... he had to think. Too much had happened too quickly and his mind was being overloaded. It didn't help that he had worked 16 hour shifts and longer for the past ten or was it twelve days? He rubbed his eyes and focused on the map.

Division Juliet was approximately three miles long, starting at the bottom of the mountain and following a narrow ridge to where it intersected with another higher ridgeline above the timberline. Okay, there were personnel assigned to the division. Maybe they were close and could help? He checked the COM plan for the Juliet frequency and turned the dial on his radio to channel 8.

"Juliet, this is Air Ops"

No answer.

He repeated the call.

"Air Ops, this is Strike Team Leader, Davis on Juliet."

"Davis! Are you anywhere near the crash site?"

"Negative. The crews have pulled back to a safety zone to wait the fire out. We are blocked from reaching the site until this thing makes it's run. But Tom is nearby. I talked with him a few moments ago. He is within site of the helicopter and is attempting to get the people out."

Every one listened intently to the radio. They could hear the roar of the monster in the background as well as shouts from the crew. The fire was very close, too close from the sounds.

Air Ops looked through the IAP that showed all of the personnel assigned to the various divisions. Tom would be the Division Supervisor.

"Davis can you get back in contact with Juliet?"

"Let me try"

Davis called several times, but no answer, which could be a bad thing or maybe Tom was too busy to answer. The fire had to be very close by this time.

"No answer," the strike team leader stated.

"Okay, Keep trying. Hopefully he can assist until more help arrives.

You are the closest resources that we have to the site at this time. As soon as you can, try to make your way to the site."

"Copy that,"

Again, the ground crew could hear the fire's hot breath in the background. Hopefully the crews were in the black.

Across the fire, another radio was scanning the traffic. The blue four wheel drive Jeep Cherokee, a rental from Jackson Hole, marked it's progression down the winding road through the purple sage back to base camp with the ever present yellow dust. Inside the team's Information Officer and a young reporter from Jackson were on their way back to the camp after visiting several of the divisions earlier in the day.

The reporter, a young upstart from the Jackson Times by the name of Jason Stanley had been sent out to do another story on the Beaver fire. It was a slow news day and although the fire had been covered several times already, he was back again to get an update. He didn't mind it too much. This was his first fire and he had a lot to learn. The Info Officer, an older firefighter from New Mexico that everyone called Joe, was a big help, even if he was Zuni. Jason smiled to himself, remembering the night before at the Silver Dollar Saloon in downtown Jackson Hole. He had referred to Joe as Injun Joe to everyone's amusement as he recounted his last visit to the fire with much embellishment. The cute girl next to him had laughed at his story and he had bought her another beer, hoping to get lucky. But nothing had happened. All he got for his money was a kiss on the cheek and a sweet goodbye. Later she had gone off with one of the firefighters who were spending their leave in Jackson. His smile suddenly vanished then. He didn't particularly like firefighters after all. And then he heard the "Mayday" call.

"What's going on Joe?"

Joe slowed the car and pulled off of the road to let the truck behind him pass safely. He switched the channel to Air Attack and quickly learned that there had been a crash. He looked over at the reporter beside him and turned the scanner off and changed the channel to the command frequency. Joe had been in the business long enough to know that reporters could be a real pain in the butt at times, especially when something exciting was going on, especially young ones who were trying to get a feather in their cap. The worst thing that could happen in the case of a death or injury, especially in the case of aircraft was for reporters to release information on the victims before the proper time. He also knew that there would be a tremendous amount of traffic and although firefighters were trained not to reveal names over the radio, in their rescue attempts, the names could go out. As information officer, it was his job to assimilate accurate and timely information concerning the fire to the news media, but at the same time ensure that no news got out before the IC allowed it to. So he turned the radio down, relieved that the young reporter didn't seem to notice.

"There appears to have been an accident of some kind, possibly one of the aircraft," Joe answered as he pulled back out on the road and continued toward the camp. He had to get rid of the reporter and get in touch with the IC. As soon as the media found out, they would overrun the place and he would have to ensure that they didn't get in the way.

"Could you take me back to the site?" Jason asked excitedly. He understood enough of the chatter to know that an aircraft of some type had gone down.

"We're almost back to camp. I need to check in and get more information." Joe continued driving. He needed to ditch the kid and make a few phone calls. Soon the place would be buzzing with reporters from all over. He had to make sure that he was prepared to receive them. Just ahead behind the low rise, the American flag fluttered in the breeze, only the very top extending over the sage. The camp was hidden in the valley behind the ridge.

Fire camp spread across the prairie, a city of tents that had grown as the fire had grown, covering perhaps 40 acres. There was a great bustle of activity as new replacement crews were waiting to check in, the crewmembers loitering nearby their respective school buses as the crew leaders signed all of the appropriate paperwork at the various administration tents.

The supply and logistics areas were receiving additional gear ordered the previous day from the central fire cache as Job Corp crews quickly unloaded the trucks. The command tents were active as well, especially now that the helicopter had crashed. The only area that lay desolate was the area filled with the multi colored tents of the crews spread over the side hill across the camp from the cluster of large canvas tents marking the food and supply units. All of the crews were on the fire line except for the ones that sat by their buses along the dusty entrance road to the camp. Each crew had located their tents in circles, some marking their territories by their state flags that they hung proudly in the center. Other crews shared a common large tent with smaller tents for their gear or for areas to hang out later at night away from the sleeping areas.

Like battalions in the military the individual crews had their own respective personalities. The North Carolina crew 45 was camped next to Pennsylvania 11, both state flags attached to an aspen pole that had been brought in from the line on the first day, the two flags flying side by side in the afternoon wind. Virginia 23 clustered their tents next to their sister crew number 24, their flag fluttering in the wind from a line that secured their large crew tent. Mixed with the Type 2 crews were Type 1 crews as well, including the Carson City and Silver Lake Hotshots. Unlike the type 2 crews that were brought together from various state forest service agencies, the hotshots trained and worked together all year and were federal US Forest Service employees.

Joe climbed the small hill and carefully navigated the turn into the front entrance to the camp, passing the buses. A water tender slowly drive by, spraying water over the dusty trail that circled the first row of command tents and ended behind the food unit for dust abatement. He pulled the jeep next to a row of an assortment of government and rental vehicles, all of them covered with the yellow dust. Joe shut off the engine and pressed the emergency brake, and quickly exited the car, leaving his portable radio in the seat.

Jason had noticed that the information officer had turned the radio down. He opened his door as well, but hesitated. As he watched, Joe walked quickly to the command center. Then he reached over and turned the radio up, and changed the channel to air attack. He was young, but he had been trained well. The second helicopter had to be searching for the crash site and would relay information as he saw it, which Jason would carefully take down.

This would be big news. He smiled to himself. And he was the only reporter on the scene.

The radio crackled briefly and then he heard a female voice. Was the pilot a female? He listened intently.

"Air Ops, this is Foxtrot Seven-Nine." The voice spoke among the characteristic background engine noise of the medium helicopter. The pilot was a female.

"Go ahead, this is Air Ops."

"Okay, I have a visual. The ship is on its side in a small meadow on the ridgeline about two-thirds up the mountain. The fire is making a strong run straight toward the ship."

The woman, Teresa, was a young pilot from Arizona. She lowered her ship for a closer inspection. Already the gray smoke from the fire below was beginning to blow over the meadow. She circled the meadow twice before she noticed the first yellow shirt. That had to be ground crew, she thought. The pilots wore green nomex flight suits. The person was running away from a pile of rocks back to the helicopter. Okay, there was hope, she thought. She had known both Jack and Heather for several years. If the individual was running to the ship, then there was a chance that the crew may be alive. But they would not be for long if they didn't find cover.

When she passed over the rocks, she saw the metallic silver of a deployed shelter and behind the rocks themselves the green shape of a man, lying on his back, his face looking skyward.

The pilot switched her radio to the onboard frequency to talk to her crew chief, "Can you see that John, the shelter? Is there a body there among the rocks?"

The crew chief acknowledged that there was a body among the rocks. Both pilot and crew chief knew then that there was one casualty, one deployed in the shelter and a third entering the helicopter.

But for what purpose? An answer came a few seconds later. The man climbed back out of the helicopter, unfolding a shelter as he ran. He had retrieved one of the shelters from the ship.

The pilot switched back to air attack and called for Air Ops.

"There are three men in the meadow. Two are deploying. A third appears to be dead, but I can't be sure. I know that only two are deploying. The third is lying among the rocks. They still have a few minutes before the fire front reaches them. I may be able to make a couple of safety drops with retardant along the meadow to cool them down a bit..."

Suddenly the helicopter exploded in a ball of flame as embers from the approaching fire found their way into the ship, finding a broken fuel line. The pilot instantly jerked the ship up and away.

Teresa screamed into the microphone, "The ship just exploded! The whole meadow is on fire!"

Tom managed to find the shelter located next to the pilot's seat and quickly retrieved it. He climbed quickly back out of the open door after noticing blowing embers entering through the broken window. He had to hurry! Once more fear gripped its arms tightly around his heart, but he was able to hold it in check. If he lost it now, he would surely die.

In another realm, the Guardian Kapar quickly jumped across the helicopter and Sarat flew through the machine to intercept another group of demonic tormentors who slashed toward Tom's spirit with broadswords of crimson. Their attack was stronger now, more determined and the two warriors barely survived their onslaught, but was able to force them back just as Tom jumped from the ship. Nasi, the demon's Captain, laughed and then blew a strong breath of smoke and red embers across the ship itself.

"You can't hold out for too much longer." Nasi taunted just as the fire found the fuel lines and the helicopter exploded in a fiery ball that covered the entire meadow.

The explosion knocked Tom to the ground, pelting him with fiery darts of fire and debris. For a moment he laid there, his ears ringing from the impact, disoriented and temporarily blinded by the black smoke that billowed over him. Luckily the shelter had fallen over his face, shielding him from the fire. Realizing that the ground around him was on fire, he quickly jumped up and ran toward the rocks where the pilot's shelter shone brightly. Overhead a helicopter passed by. His consciousness registered the fact that someone was above him. Hopefully help would soon come. He ran as fast as his wounded leg would allow, holding the shelter over him. There was a small area by the rocks where he could deploy if there was enough room.

Teresa regained her composure and brought her ship around again for a closer look. She knew that she would have to locate the shelters exact position so that she could return with retardant. For a moment she could not see the person who had just emerged from the helicopter. Then she saw him jump up from within the flames themselves and run to the rocks, where he quickly fell next to the deployed shelter and disappeared under his own metallic tent.

Baked potatoes, she thought to herself and then quickly dismissed the thought. She turned the ship toward the water source as the crew chief prepared to insert retardant in to the bucket. Teresa realized in her excitement that Air Ops had called her several times.

"I am going for water." She answered Air Ops question.

"What shape are they in?" he asked.

"Pretty bad, but they have deployed," Teresa answered and then spoke to her self before disengaging the microphone, "They're dead!" She didn't mean for anyone to hear the statement, but several did, including Jason Stanley, who heard what he had wanted to hear. He had a story all right, one confirmed by the people on the scene.

He didn't need the information officer. He had a cell phone and would alert the paper before any one else even had a chance to know that the crash had occurred. He had scooped them all! Jason turned the radio down and closed the door to the jeep. He walked over to the bulletin board where the division assignments list had been posted. Running his finger down the list until he located Juliet division, he wrote the name down. Tom MacKenzie from North Carolina. He already knew who was on board the stricken ship from the interview he had done earlier in the day. All he needed now was a private place in which to call his boss. News like this would go straight to the top.

CHAPTER NINETEEN

WILKES COUNTY, NC
PRESENT DAY

Nicole Mackenzie stared at the hand written letter from Tom. Surely he would not act on it? But had things actually gotten so bad that he would? The thought frightened her, a growing, sickening fear building within her stomach, moving upward through her chest. Old demons raised their ugly heads, demons that had once held sway over her own spirit as she had traveled the same road that her husband seemed to have traveled. He had always been there for her, even when she had tried to take her own life in time when her spirit and soul were held bondage to the depression and fear. Tom was the strong one. He would never do that, but then again?

"You must pray for him, Nicole. Everyone must pray for him," an audible voice spoke to her spirit.

Nicole jumped and quickly looked behind her, but there was no one there. The children were in the other room playing. Water was running in the bathtub. She took the letter back into her shaking hands and read it once more.

Dearest Nicole,

How much can a man take in this life and still keep his sanity? Life has a way of piling failure upon past failure; calamity upon disappointment, until man finds himself buried beneath the rubble of his life, unable to breath, his heart faint. The human body is very resilient, but over time the stresses of life itself will break even the strongest under its weight of heaviness and despair. What are we to do? I cry out to a God that doesn't seem to hear me. I have nothing left within me. I am only an empty shell; my hope drained away into the catacombs of failure that is my life. I press forward to do the right thing, to discipline myself to follow what God tells me to do through his word, but to no avail. The brokenness grows, the rubble increases, and the heaviness. Everything that I do not only affects me, but my family also. You depend on me to care for you, to be your spiritual leader, to protect you. And even in this have I failed. It is an honorable thing to give your life for those that you love. The Bible says that this is the greatest love of all, to give your life for a loved one, to sacrifice yourself for your family. I battle with the thought almost daily. Would my family be better off without me? If I gave my life in such a way that all of your needs would be met, would this not be the right thing to do. I would gladly lay down my life to protect you from harm. If I died while protecting you and the children from harm, I would be remembered as a hero, a man who died protecting his family. That is the ultimate responsibility of a husband and father after all, to lay his life down for his family. This is the most honorable way to leave this world. Would this not be the same? I could sacrifice my life in such a way to insure that you, my beloved wife would have everything that you needed. My children would have all that they needed. I would not make any more wrong decisions that continue to destroy you and the children. Would not this be honorable as well? And so, my wife, I choose to do such a thing. I have tried to make you happy and have failed. I have tried to overcome all that has fallen upon us and can no longer hold back the tide. You deserve so much better. Please accept my gift to you in the love that it is intended. I have worked everything out

so that you and the kids will be well taken care of for the rest
of your lives. We have grown so far apart, even though I still
love you and I know that you love me as well, but I can no
longer look into your beautiful blue eyes without feeling such
great guilt. It tears at my soul. My failures are too many. I
promised you that I would take care of you, that I would be
your knight in shining amour. I have tried, but I have failed.
So now I give my whole self. I do this because I love you.

Tom

Nicole began to cry. How could he do this? Didn't he know that he would destroy them all if he were gone? How could she live knowing what he had done? Anger built up within her at the thought of what her husband was thinking. And then deep within her spirit she felt the tug of the Holy Spirit. She needed to pray, needed to get to church and quickly so that others could pray as well.

Remember when you, too had the same thoughts of death Nicole, her spirit told her. They were lies, but lies that held a strong power over you. You would have succeeded in ending your life if it had not been for Tom by your side, his prayers for you, his love. He never gave up on you. You must not give up on him.

She wiped the tears from her eyes and stood up, stuffing the letter into her pocket. A strong urgency to do something, do anything rose within her, but what could she do?

Pray! Nicole pray!

Yes! She needed to pray for her husband; she wanted to get to church quickly, speak to her Pastor, let him read the letter with his wisdom, and pray. She knew that her church family would pray as well.

Nicole picked up the phone to call her dearest friend, her former pastor's wife, Shelley Carter. Even after Tom had resigned from the youth ministry and he and Nicole had begun attending another church, the two women had remained strong friends. The Carters too had moved on, locating to another city where Shelley's husband had taken another church. They regularly talked by phone, email and an occasional letter.

Nicole was disappointed when she heard the bright voice of her friend on her answering machine, "You have reached the Carters. Please leave a message and we will get back with you as soon as we can. God bless and have a wonderful day."

Nicole waited for the beep, "Shelley, Tom is in trouble. Please, when you get this call me. Pray for him Shelley. I'm afraid."

She hung up the phone, "Kids hurry up and get dressed. We have to get to church!"

The Guardian Raham pulled her weapon from her scabbard and blanketed the entire house with the strong radiance of God's power, chasing harassing demons from the home. On this night, even little Megan would be no trouble getting ready to go to church.

Raham glanced toward another warrior who had been sent from the throne to assist her, "Laham. When the family leaves for the Gate, you strike hard at the enemy. Take as many of them as you can. I will shield the car. As Nicole prays more will join us."

The warrior drew his own broadsword and placed it before him, the point touching the hardwood floors of the living room, the pearl handle clasped tightly before him with gloved hands. He smiled, "Yes Lady Raham, your way will be easy. My blade will see to that."

Raham had no doubt about that. She had seen this giant before in battle. His kind was a special breed of angels, created to worship God and to destroy His enemies. They were not Guardians who ministered directly to the Redeemed ones or Gatekeepers who fought constantly to protect the portals to heaven. They were warriors only, ordered to assist the others in battle. They gained their strength as all did, by the prayers of the Redeemed and worship of God, but because they stayed by the throne in worship at all times until called forth to battle, they were especially lethal to the enemy.

With the kids dressed and in the car, Nicole felt for Tom's letter in her pocket and closed the front door behind her. Even though it was late in the afternoon the heat was still oppressive. There was no breeze, no relief, only the bright cloudless sky and an overly large ball of white-yellow sun that bore down mercilessly on the land below. She knew deep down inside that she needed to tell her pastor, let him read the note and pray. Deep within her spirit she felt that her husband of fifteen years, the man that she knew would be hers from the time that she was thirteen, was in some type of trouble. She had to reach someone, to tell them, to be comforted, to somehow get Tom help.

The summer air did not stir as Nicole started the van and pulled out of the driveway onto the dusty gravel road, but all around her the air was full of disturbance. Raham had shielded the van as the family entered and closed the doors. Now she floated above the van, expecting the enemy to come. Her weapon was drawn and her body radiating a fierce brilliance. Suddenly a full detachment of enemy warriors crashed out from the trees and attacked her, but before it could reach Raham and the van she protected, the giant Laham sliced through them with his golden blade, most of the demons disappearing in puffs of red smoke.

Only a few made it past his blade as the van turned out into the highway and headed for town. Raham beat them back and noticed another enemy detachment hovering ahead at the city gates. She looked skyward. The Spirit of God was working, answering prayers and she knew what she needed to do. The Messenger of God called Malak appeared before her. He was fast, and stealthy and could get a message through when no others could.

"Find the woman called Shelly Carter. Impress upon her the need to pray not only for Tom, but for Nicole as well. Especially Nicole. If the Gatekeepers can be fully activated by her request, the portal will open fully and Tom can be saved."

Malak saluted and disappeared. In his great speed, even Raham could not see him as he streaked northward, but another could. An enemy scout hovered in the shadows of a deep forest by the road as the van drove by. He watched as Malak received his orders from Raham and immediately flew after the Messenger. Time and time again Malak had been instrumental in helping to achieve victory for the Gatekeepers of the Rivergate and the demonic scout had been ordered by Nasi himself to intercept the Messenger in this battle.

He, too was fast and quickly caught up with Malak over the hills of northern Virginia.

Just over the Potomac River, the scout dove down through a thin layer of clouds, his sword drawn. Up ahead a vast aerial battle between the forces of light and darkness waged in the heavens. Brilliant flashes of silver, gold and red exploded against the backdrop of the light blue sky. Wounded Guardians spiraled downward, trailing silver smoke as reinforcements climbed higher to fill the gaps in the line. A black cloud of enemy warriors rose suddenly from the ocean and attacked in a great wave that pushed the Guardians' line back. Malak pulled up suddenly to allow the enemy forces past. He did not wish to get caught in another battlefield and, as he did, the enemy scout swept past him. His sword hit Malak high on the shoulder, tearing a great gash through his upper arm, spinning him violently around. Malak drew his own sword and parried another blow just as the enemy ranks crashed against the Guardian battle line with a lustful cry for blood. The air around him quickly filled with the red dust of the vanquished. Below a great portal opened as a gate was activated by the Redeemed and suddenly a troop of Gatekeepers cut through the dark lines, driving the enemy back.

Malak turned to find his assailant, but he was too slow. He felt the sword slice across his back, the blackened poison of evil infecting his body.

"Not so fast now are you?" the scout mocked as Malak moved toward the new threat.

The Messenger was able to parry the third blow, but he was already losing strength from the poison that stunk of sulfur and decay and dripped down his chest and across his tunic. He began to float downward toward the river until strong hands grabbed him from behind and spun him around. A black hand clasped his neck as another knocked his sword from his weakening arm that was growing numb.

"You have troubled Master Nasi for too many years Malak, but now you have failed," the scout mocked him.

"You can't destroy me. You know that," Malak responded defiantly, his breaths coming in gasps.

"Yes, but I can hold you here until Nasi has gained victory," sneered his enemy.

"Nasi has tried to destroy the Rivergate since the rebellion. He failed to keep it from being activated and he has failed in keeping the portal closed. The Redeemed ones are now in full control of the gate. They are expanding it with each passing day. How can he win a victory now?" Malak countered.

He knew he was losing strength. The scout squeezed tighter. Malak looked past the scout to the battle waging above them. Gatekeepers were everywhere but they did not seem to notice his predicament. Then he saw one turn toward him. Hopefully that one would come to his aide.

"Master Nasi holds a grudge. He will succeed in destroying the Gatekeepers themselves, starting with the firefighter who stands on the edge of the abyss himself. Then the woman Nicole who still fights the darkness of her past life. There are others throughout the assembly that you call Gatekeepers of the Rivergate. He will destroy them one at a time until it will no longer matter if the portal is open and active. Without the Redeemed, you have no power."

The scout smiled, his yellow eyes glowing in the darkness, his breath hot against Malak's face. Malak could no longer breath. The scout pushed Malak down further toward the river. Suddenly, to Malak's surprise, the demon scout disappeared in a cloud of sulfur and Malak fell away. He hit the pavement hard. He had to smile as a bus drove through him as he lay on his back looking up to the heavens above. The battle was won. The enemy had retreated, the victorious army was gathering the wounded and retreating back to their portal as a strong wall of warriors guarded their way.

"Thought you could use a little assistance," a voice spoke from behind him, "You dropped this."

Malak sat up and then rose to his feet and turned around. Before him stood a great warrior, standing over eight feet tall and wearing the tunic of a Gatekeeper, five gold bands across his chest, signifying the rank of General. Malak immediately bowed, never having been in the presence of one with such rank before. The giant stepped forward and gave him back his sword and he raised his head to accept the weapon.

"You have been wounded." The giant spoke.

"Yes but I'll heal quickly. I must continue. I have a message to deliver and I have already wasted too much time."

The general looked over the Messenger's wounds. They were black with poison.

"You won't get far with those, Messenger, but I may be able to assist you if you tell me where you have come from and who you seek."

Malak backed up suddenly his sword before him. He would never reveal that information to anyone no matter his rank or kind. That was the one rule of the Messengers that could never be broken.

"I can not tell you that sir. If you were truly a Great One, as you appear to be, you would know that. I thank you for destroying the scout, but I must be on my way."

The giant smiled and saluted the Messenger, "You have spoken true brave Malak of the Rivergate." He touched the wounds and they immediately healed, "Tell Sarat when you see him next that I look forward to seeing him again if not soon then at the great victory supper."

"You know who I am my lord?" Malak asked.

"Yes I know. I was sent straight from the throne of God to assist you. Now go on your way. Deliver your message brave one. And remember to tell Sarat that Michael sends his greetings."

The giant vanished, leaving Malak standing in the middle of a highway at the edge of the river across from the great capital of the new nation. Before in his existence he had only seen Michael from far off. Now this great General had been sent straight from the throne to assist a lowly Messenger. Malak shook his head in amazement. Malak shot upward with a renewed zeal and seconds later he drifted down through the trees over a small house in a small town of western New York.

Below a car pulled into the driveway and a woman, carrying a bag of groceries, walked up to her door. Placing the bag of groceries on the chair next to the door, she unlocked the door and entered the house. She threw her keys on the kitchen bar, and placed the bag of groceries next to the sink. Quickly, she began to put them away. She was frustrated and late. Her husband was at the church next door preparing for the Wednesday night service and she was supposed to have already joined them. The house was empty, her two children still at home already at the church. Just before her husband had left for church after having worked all day at the mill, he had asked her to pick up a few items for the dinner the church had planned after the service. She left those items in the bag and turned to leave the kitchen. The blinking light of the answering machine caught her attention. No time to listen now, she thought. It was most likely one of the church members anyway with another complaint. There seemed to be more of those with each passing day.

Malak entered the house and saluted the Guardian. He explained what must be done, then immediately disappeared to return to the Rivergate. The Guardian looked at his charge. She had been ever more despondent lately, stressed because of the growing problems that the family had endured. The church was not doing well, her husband was gone all the time and she did not wish to be here in the first place. He sighed and placed a hand on Shelly's shoulder.

"Shelly, check the answering machine," the Guardian whispered.

Shelly looked at the light again and then at the clock. She had to go. Church would start in fifteen minutes.

The Guardian spoke again, and the Holy Spirit began to talk with her spirit. She pressed the button and knew immediately why the Spirit wished her to listen. She began to pray then, forgetting about her own problems. She prayed for her friend Nicole and then for Tom. A warrior immediately left the throne room. Help was on the way.

CHAPTER TWENTY

WESTERN WYOMING
PRESENT DAY

J ason Stanley found a secluded place by his personal vehicle from where to call back to Jackson. Nervous with excitement, the young reporter paced back and forth by his truck, waiting for the receptionist to answer.

"Come on, come on..."

"Jackson Times."

"Julie, this is Jason, Is Bruce still in," Jason looked at his watch. Four thirty. Plenty of time to get front coverage on tomorrow's paper, plus if the news went on the wire, it could be picked up nationally. It was six thirty back east. Yes! Plenty of time for it to make the evening news back east.

"Yea, I'll transfer you." Julie answered and with a beep, music came through the line as Jason waited.

"This is Bruce."

"Bruce, Jason. I've got big news! There's been a major incident on the Beaver Fire. A helicopter crash!" Jason in his excitement was talking too loud and too fast.

"Slow down boy," Bruce ordered, "Are you sure?"

"Yes, absolutely! I was with the PIO and heard the call come in on the radio. They are already trying to put a lid on it, but I tuned in to the air traffic and got confirmation from a circling helicopter. Three are dead, two pilots and a firefighter from back east."

The line was quiet for a few seconds, something that Jason could not stand.

"Did you hear me Bruce? This is big news and I am the only reporter out here."

"Yea Jason, but before we can run this, we need to get verification on casualties. You need pictures if possible. Gather more info and get back here as quick as you can, but not before you get verification and pictures. I'll change the format for tomorrow's paper and make room on the front page."

The front page of the Jackson Times was not good enough for Jason. This was his big chance. A gold nugget had dropped in his lap and all his boss worried about was printing it on his small town paper.

"But Bruce, this can go national. When word leaks out and you know it will, the news stations will be all over the place. I've got the info now! We need to put this out on the wire and scoop them all."

"Patience, Jason. You need verification first. You said it yourself. You are the only media out there. Just do your job and get as much information as you can. Then we'll send it up the line," Bruce looked at his watch. He had an appointment in five minutes that could not be missed. What bad timing he thought. He had sent the young reporter out to a fire that was low on everyone's radar screen on a slow news week and something big had happened.

"Jason I've got to go to a meeting. You get the verification and call me. We'll decide then what to do. Call me in an hour."

"Okay, I'll call back, but we got to hurry with this one!" Jason couldn't believe what he was hearing. Big news like this and the boss wanted to sit on it.

"Patience, Jason. You'll get your story. I've got to go."

The line went dead. Jason stared at the phone angrily before throwing it in the seat. He climbed in his truck and shut the door. Verification! Bruce wanted verification. He had the information straight from the pilot on the scene. He had the names and had heard what had happened from those present at the scene of the accident. It couldn't get any better than that. He looked across the dusty parking area to the ICP tent filled with people as they tried to get a handle on what was going on. Joe stood by the tent door, talking on the phone.

"I knew it. The old injun is calling other media. He had to be, that was his job!"

Jason slammed his fist down on the steering wheel. The TV cameras would be all over the place very soon, most likely interviewing the Indian and stealing his story. Jason fumed. The greatest story in his young career and that stupid Indian was taking it away from him. He never really liked the man. In fact, he didn't care for any of his kind. Well he was not about to set around and allow Joe to beat him to the story. He started the engine and backed quickly out from the parking area, taking the far exit out of the camp. The helicopters were working from the helibase. He could go there and interview those directly involved. The pilot had a wife who traveled with him, he thought. He could interview her as well. And he could at least get pictures of the choppers and the growing fire.

The narrow road wound past the entrance to a secluded ranch through purple sage. Several miles away along the flanks of the high timberland, the cloud of smoke billowed high into the otherwise clear blue sky. He spotted the black dot that was a helicopter circling a ridge high up near a tumble of white rocks before the road dipped down into a small valley. He would call Bruce from the helibase with verification. If his boss didn't let the story out, he would do it himself.

The fire shelter was manufactured of aluminum bonded to fiberglass cloth that will reflect 95% of radiant heat, but was not designed to withstand direct contact with fire for any great period of time. Required PPE, personal protective equipment, for wildland firefighters on federal fires, it was designed for deployment only when all other alternatives for escape had been exhausted.

When deployed properly, the shelter looks like a bright silver, one-man pup tent. The shelter is carried in a plastic container, contained in a nomex cover that is usually attached to web gear or below a wildland fire pack that can be easily retrieved by the firefighter, even while running. Once the tightly folded shelter is released from the airtight wrapping, the firefighter can open it by shaking it loose like a plastic garbage bag, before draping it over the back, stepping over the straps underneath and falling quickly to the ground. Once underneath the tent, the firefighter ensures that the inside flaps are secure under the arms and legs for a tight seal to the ground and the tent is pushed upward to expand to its full height. The more air space within the shelter, the more breathable air and cushion from the heat there is.

All state and federal firefighters are trained in its use, but few place much trust in its ability to save someone, although it has saved over 300 firefighters since its development. But many others were burned alive within its cover when deployed in impossible situations. Everyone knew that if you fought fire wisely and safely you should never be in one of those circumstances. It was an insurance policy for use only if something went terribly wrong.

The shelter was designed to be utilized in a deployment zone, which is an opening of sufficient size to ensure that no direct contact with flames occurs. Most firefighters who have deployed within these zones survived the experience, although many received burns from the radiant heat. The people that have been killed while in their shelters had, for the most part, deployed in areas where the fire front itself had passed directly over and against the shelter.

The meadow was very small, even smaller now that it contained a burning helicopter, but it was the only place to go. Hopefully, there was enough space in the low grass where intense flames would not pass through. Tom tucked the flaps under his knees and feet and pushed the top of the tent upward as he had trained. He then dug away the ground in front of his face as much as he could to give more space for cooler air to settle. The cleanest air would be at ground level. If he could dig a depression in the ground, he could place his head lower against the cool dirt and breath fresher air. Or so he had been taught.

Inside the shelter, it was surprisingly dark, only bits of light shining through scattered small pinholes in the shelter itself. A strong breeze tugged at the edges of the shelter from the outside, like an unseen hand trying to pull the flaps up as Tom more strongly secured the small opening with his knee. Panic was building deep inside of him as the walls of the structure felt as if they were closing in on him. He had to get out of here! What had he done? He began to breath quickly, focusing on his breaths to take his mind off of the tightening fear that spread through his heart. The fire roared just across the meadow now. Soon it would swallow him with its angry heat.

And you wanted this to happen, Tom. A still small voice spoke to his soul. Why fight it. Stand up and take a deep breath as the fire passes and it will all be over. That, after all, is what you were prepared to do.

Tom fought through the thoughts. He had been a fool. Once again he had made a stupid decision. This time it could be fatal. What had he been thinking? What pain to those that he loved would his decision make? How could he ever rise up from the crumbling life that he had built around himself? Despondency grew within his soul, but deep within him was the God given desire to live, to somehow survive, and to rebuild his shattered life. He had to somehow survive.

Outside the protective walls of the shelter, the fire grew closer, red walls of pure energy, a living, breathing organism of heat, noxious gas and destruction rolling up the steep slopes like a wave. The wind increased, dark clouds of black smoke filling the meadow and totally covering the crash site from view from above. Red embers flew ahead of the main front, igniting patches of dry grass across the meadow, torching individual trees near the rocky outcrop, pelting the silver tents in an attempt to gain entrance to destroy the humans inside. The shelters held as they were designed to do, but the heat inside was already climbing to uncomfortable levels.

The spiritual war grew in intensity as well as the combined forces under Nasi attacked Sarat and Kapar who stood between the dark ones and the two firefighters. But Sarat could feel his strength growing. Soon reinforcements would arrive, but the fire would consume the humans first. The heat would be too great when the main fire swept over the meadow. The meadow's opening was too small.

Across the country in a small ranch style brick house, an elderly lady was eating an early dinner as she always did on Wednesdays before getting ready for church. She was a widow and mother of three, including a firefighter who was now somewhere in the West helping to battle the fires that were sweeping across the countryside. As she ate, she suddenly felt the strong presence of the Holy Spirit and knew that he was in danger. Something was terribly wrong. Immediately she dropped on her knees as she had once done many years ago in a pasture behind her house on a little backcountry farm under the shadows of Stone Mountain and had been doing all of her life since. She began to pray with all of the strength that was in her for her son's protection. By her side, a shining figure enveloped her with wings of love. The Guardian Natan caressed her cheek, feeling the moist tears as he had her entire life.

"That's it Eileen, pray," Natan spoke to her spirit. It would be her final prayer this side of the portal to heaven.

"For you will command His angels concerning you," Eileen quoted from Psalms 91, "to guard you in all of your ways…"

Eileen suddenly looked up and for the first time, saw the Guardian who had been with her all of those years. She was not afraid. Natan smiled at her and reached for her hand, now youthful and full of new life, not the shriveled, arthritic hand that it had once been.

"I always had a sense you were here. Especially these last few years since Thomas passed on," she said to Natan, "But why do you show yourself to me now?"

"Your time here is over my dear. The poem that has been your life has come to an end," Natan answered.

"But my son. He is in trouble. I must continue to pray for him," Eileen stood up as she spoke, noticing her hands.

"You do not need to worry Eileen," Natan spoke, "Your prayers have been answered. Now is your time to see the fruit of your labor."

Natan pointed to a brilliant light that shone through the back door to the house. At first it was small, piecing through the window like the early morning sun, but then it grew until the light completing covered the entire door.

"Come with me Eileen," Natan led her toward the light.

The white light opened in the middle and expanded as she walked toward it, the inside revealing a field covered in flowers with a snow capped mountain range in the background. Across from the field there was a sandy shoreline. She could hear the crashing waves of the ocean. There were people there.

She squinted her eyes from the glare and gasped! Was that a fishing pier extending its way out into the sea? She stepped through the portal as Natan let go of her hand. It was a pier. A man stood on the pier, his back to her. He held a fishing rod in one hand, casting the rod over his head. She had seen him do that many times before. He set the rod down against the railing and turned to face her, smiling and waving his hand. She held her hand to her heart, tears of joy rolling down her face. She noticed first him and then others. Her husband! Her parents! Her Savior! A true Gatekeeper had come home.

Across the country within the burning meadow, the situation appeared to be a lost cause and then suddenly a warrior appeared from the dark smoke in a flash of silver. He was a Throne Warrior, a pure fighter straight from the throne room of God. He brandished a huge claymore, red with the dust of fallen demons. The giant emerged from the smoke and stood before Sarat. The attacking warriors retreated momentarily as the giant cut a swath through their forward ranks with one mighty swing of his weapon. The enemy needed to access the new threat. A new power had arrived on the battlefield to assist Sarat and Kapar, upsetting the balance of force. More powerful warriors would have to join the attack. Nasi directed his forces to reform as he ordered a stronger detachment to attack as well, answering the greater force of the Throne Warrior with more force of his own.

The Throne Warrior saluted first Sarat and then Kapar, "I have come from our Lord at the request of a mighty Gatekeeper, a woman named Eileen. I am Barak."

Sarat smiled. He remembered the small girl standing by the oak tree that day many earth years ago. She had battled much, won much and now her great strength as a Gatekeeper was preparing the way for a great victory.

"We must hold this position until the Rivergate forces are assembled Barak. You have come just in time."

The enemy was preparing for a new attack.

CHAPTER TWENTY ONE

WESTERN WYOMING
PRESENT DAY

When fires explode up slope the way the Beaver Fire had done, they create their own winds, often much stronger than those created by the weather patterns. As the heat rises with the billowing clouds, enormous amounts of energy is released, sucking the air upward from all directions and creating drastic down drafts with swirling winds. These are strong enough, at times, to pull trees out from the ground. The same currents can cause fire shelters to fail if they are not secured well enough.

Tom continued to fight the growing panic rising within him. The approaching monster of smoke and red flame roared outside his shelter. Already the wind ripped at his fire shelter, and flying debris pelted the outside. Small amounts of smoke drifted in from several locations where the shelter had blown up from the ground. A thin patch of dried grass caught fire next to the shelter and ignited a spot at the inside edge within the shelter by his leg. He frantically beat at the flame with his gloved hand.

"God help me!" he prayed aloud and heard a violent crash just outside the shelter, a resounding snap.

He stopped and listened. The sound was familiar. What was it? And then he knew. The wind was blowing over the dead snags alongside the meadow, the same ones that he had flagged earlier in the day so that the chainsaw crews would fell them.

Tom peaked out from the side of the shelter away from the oncoming fire. Through the gray smoke and flying red embers, he saw the second shelter, a ghostly silver glistening, shaking in the wind. There were several large snags beyond the pile of rocks, their tops already burning. The closest of the trees crumbled suddenly from the top, showering the rocks with burning embers. They were twin snags, very near. If one fell, Tom knew that he and Jack would be crushed, but where were they to go?

"Jack!" Tom screamed over the wind and roaring fire.

"Okay Teresa, you got it. You are clear," the crew chief remarked over the ship's channel. Foxtrot Seven-Nine had just filled its bucket with several hundred gallons of cold, mountain water from Beaver Creek.

"Copy that," Teresa replied and switched to air attack, "Juliet this is Foxtrot Seven-Nine."

No answer.

"Juliet, Foxtrot Seven-Nine," she repeated.

Again no answer. The pilot called Air Ops who did answer.

"Okay, I'm going in for a drop over the deployment site. I think I can help."

Teresa circled over the crashed helicopter, partially hidden by the dense smoke. It was still burning violently, adding energy to the approaching firestorm. Just a little lower and she could drop the retardant across the lower side of both shelters. She eased the helicopter downward, slowly, carefully. The violent winds shook the ship, but she maintained control.

Again Tom shouted, "Jack! You okay?"

Faintly from the other shelter he heard a muffled reply, but could not understand what the man had said. The two shelters were immediately beside each other. In fact they touched along their entire length. Tom then heard the unmistakable engine noises of a medium helicopter just above them. The snags! If the helicopter came too close, the rotor wash could break up the snags and cause them to fall.

He reached for his radio to warn the pilot, but he had lost his radio somewhere. The harness was empty except for the spare battery, incident map and a pen.

"Left just a few more feet, Teresa, and the drop will be right next to them," the helicopter crew chief spoke over the intercom, guiding his pilot for the very important drop. This was their only chance before the blinding smoke and heat would chase them away.

All eyes that could see the helicopter from the mountain below the fire watched and listened, many praying for a miracle.

The crew chief suddenly saw the twin snags as the smoke suddenly lifted from below the chopper. The trees were only a few feet below the bucket itself. Had that been a silver flash? He thought and screamed over the intercom, "Teresa, up! Abort! Abort!"

Teresa responded to the crew chief's command immediately pulling back hard as she released the water, but it was too late. The retardant dropped through the smoke, missing the trees, but the rotor wash did not.

Tom saw the helicopter suddenly through a break in the smoke. A red veil washed downward, spraying the ground in a line nearby as the retardant dropped and then the closest snag suddenly snapped high up in the tree, a large chuck of dead wood falling directly down toward Jack's shelter.

He reached quickly under the shelter and grabbed the first thing he felt, which was Jack's arm and pulled him violently up as he rolled away from the on coming tree toward the rocks. The limbs crashed down around them and then suddenly to Tom all was strangely bright and then there was darkness.

The helicopter rose higher above the smoke that now covered the entire meadow including the deployment site. Teresa steadied herself, holding the stick with both hands between her knees. That had been entirely too close, she thought, "Can you see anything?" she asked her crew chief.

"No. They are on their own now."

Teresa, still shaking, called in to Air Ops for further instructions.

Kapar, wounded from the last attack fell through the portal with his charge, followed by Sarat. Only the giant Barak remained just outside the portal as a rear guard to divert the enemies' attention from what had happened to the humans. The Gatekeeper Nasag stood by the portal as well, watching the gathering forces just outside the door.

"Why do they attack with such strong forces Sarat?" he asked.

"Nasi was defeated at the Rivergate. He knows that this is the first test for the true Gatekeepers. He knows that if he does not defeat them now, he will never have another chance." He looked down at the two humans who swirled in the blinding lights toward the other end of the fallen portal, "Tom helped to open the gate. He too is a Gatekeeper, but because of his past failures, he doesn't believe that. He must once again meet the God of Abraham, Isaac and especially Jacob. Make sure they arrive safely and be prepared to help them exit when the moment comes. I will stay with Kapar and help with his wounds. Soon the forces of the Rivergate will come and we can destroy the enemy that is after Tom's soul once and for all."

Nasag disappeared and the portal suddenly shut, leaving Barak, Kapar and Sarat once more on the rocks just outside the portal.

Swirling lights of the rainbow, violent winds, periods of white light and complete darkness. Unearthly screams, shadows floating, the sun exploding over the distance horizon only to disappear again and again and again... Complete blackness. Soft whispers. Rustling garments. Cool wetness followed by intense heat. The smell of roasted meat. The deep ache of a broken bone mending. The far distant roar of a waterfall.

Tom lay on his back under the shade of a small grove of pines on some type of mat. Through the haze that was his sight, he saw the bearded face of a balding older man lean over him and then there was darkness once again. He could hear whispers, but could not understand the language. What had happened to him? Someone else lay next to him, but through the growing darkness, he could not tell who it was.

CHAPTER TWENTY TWO

WESTERN WYOMING
PRESENT DAY

Teresa circled behind the smoke, shaken at what she had almost done. In her attempt to get as close to the deployment site as possible, she had almost added her ship to the carnage below. The entire meadow was now engulfed in dense smoke and flames, but at least the retardant drop near the shelters appeared to give the firefighters below a small cushion of protection. Hopefully that would be enough.

"Foxtrot Seven-Nine this is Air Ops."

"Go ahead," Teresa answered after gaining back her composure as she backed the helicopter up and away from the growing smoke column. The wind was beating her up pretty badly and she knew that she had to leave.

"Teresa can you give me an update," Air Ops requested.

"I made the drop. Hopefully it will help, but I have to leave. The wind is too strong. The main fire has reached the meadow and is crossing it now, but it appears to be losing strength. Numerous spot fires are all across the ridge over the fire line."

Teresa looked carefully through gaps in the smoke over the piles of rocks for signs of the deployed shelters. Usually the silver glistened in the sun and could easily be seen even through smoke, but for some reason, she had lost total sight of the two shelters. She could see the fallen snags, but not the shelters. Where could they have gone? She tried to circle closer for one last look, but the wind was too strong and erratic and she was forced to leave. They had to still be there among the rocks, she thought. They had nowhere else to go.

"We have to go back Teresa," the crew chief interrupted her over the ship's radio.

She nodded and turned the helicopter back toward the helibase.

Meanwhile, down the ridge at the safety zone, the crews watched as the fire roared up from the thick timber below. There were places along the line where the towering inferno had blown out along the ridge line, throwing embers across to the lee side of the mountain and starting new fires that began to burn back up to the top or continue onward with the wind. All of the ground troops in all divisions were ordered to their safety zones to wait out the monster and allow it to run its course. Hopefully the fire's attack would be a short one and run out of steam as the afternoon progressed. If the weatherman had been correct the wind event that was causing the problems would blow through western Wyoming and be gone by nightfall. Everyone had been briefed on the coming front, but no one had expected the wind to be as strong as it now was.

Strike Team Leader Davis stood off to himself watching Teresa's helicopter circle above the smoke. There were firefighters up there, possible wounded, even dead and he was at the moment unable to go to their assistance. He watched along with all of the men as the helicopter dropped the retardant. It appeared to be a miniscule amount in relation to the wall of flame that was quickly progressing toward the deployment site. What was needed were tanker drops, but all available resources were used up and the tanker requested was still almost thirty minutes out.

One of the crewmen from the North Carolina crew approached, holding his hardhat in his hands. Davis looked away from the helicopter as the young man placed his hat back on his head.

"Davis, Tom is a friend of mine," the man said. Davis knew that he was the crew boss but for the moment he could not remember his name.

The crew boss continued, "We can't just stand here and do nothing. There are three firefighters up there that may need our help."

"I've been thinking the same thing," Davis answered and then remembered the name, "Tony there may be a way that we can go in behind the head of the fire, through the burned area. I was up there yesterday and the terrain below the meadow is not that bad. It would still be a hard go. There would be a lot of heat yet, but if a man took his time and was cautious, he could go in behind the fire as long as he stayed in good black."

"I'll go and I know that my entire crew would if need be."

Davis gazed back up through the smoke as the helicopter made one last turn. He heard the pilot tell Air Ops that she was leaving the scene because of the increased turbulence. He suddenly had an idea.

"Hold on a minute, Tony," Davis switched the radio frequency to the air to ground channel and called the chopper.

"Can you give us a recon from our position up the ridge behind the front to see if we can make it to the crash site?" he asked after the pilot had acknowledged his call.

Teresa circled behind the billowing smoke cloud and over the smoking lunar landscape where the fire had just crossed. There was still a lot of heat as individual stumps and fallen logs burned as well as scattered torching snags. She knew that because of the lingering heat, anyone walking through the black risked melting boots and eventual exposure. The heat would have to cool down somewhat before it would be safe to cross the recently burned area.

She reported what she was seeing, "There's still a lot of heat, but it is good black all the way from where you are standing to below the site. But you will have to wait some time," she suddenly glimpsed a trail below her, "Hold on. There is an old road running parallel to the ridge top, possible an old logging road. There is a lot of smoke along the entire trail, but you should be able to follow the road to where it forks. At the point of the fork, you need to hike directly up slope to the crash site. Its about three hundred yards below the meadow at the forks."

"Thanks Foxtrot Seven-Nine. We'll see if we can do that." Davis answered.

"Copy that Davis. Be careful and good luck. As soon as this wind dies down a little I'll be back. Sorry I can't stay with you. Foxtrot seven-nine clear."

"No problem, we completely understand. We'll see you when you get back," Davis commented, and turned to the group of men and women that now surrounded him.

He had never met any of them before this tour of duty, but for the past week he had worked with them all each day and had began to appreciate each of the crews strengths and weaknesses. They came from all walks of life and from different parts of the country with different dreams and goals for their lives, but now they all had a common purpose. They were a unit, a group of professionals that were thrown together to battle a common enemy, an enemy that now held several of their compatriot's hostages. And Davis realized that he was their leader and they waited for him to make the final decision.

"Okay you heard the pilot. There is a way that we can get close to the meadow. It's good black but there's still a lot of heat and smoke. I need a couple of volunteers to go with me."

A dozen hands immediately went up including Tony's.

"Okay," Davis smiled, "Tony pick a couple from your crew and make sure that they have thick boot soles. It may get a little hot."

Tony picked two from his crew as Davis turned to the Falling Boss who had raised his hand, as did his entire chainsaw crew of four.

"Petroskey, you're strike team qualified, so I'll need you to stay with the crews. Just hang here unless you hear from me. Otherwise you're to stay here until end of shift or when it's completely safe to hike back off the mountain. I'll keep in touch to let you know if we need anything. Give me two of your men in case we need to do any saw work."

Petroskey motioned for his most experienced sawyer team, Jake Ayers, a tall, lanky cowboy looking man who reminded Davis of one of the Sackets from a Louis Lamoure Western and his shorter companion Andrew Johnson, both sporting handle bar mustaches and thick, wavy black hair.

"Ayers and Johnson, you up for it?" Petoskey asked, knowing the answer. Of course they were up for it. Sawyers always were.

"You bet boss," Sacket replied. He immediately left to gather his saw and associated tools, his younger partner in tow.

They were cousins from the same small mountain town in western Oregon who logged when there was timber to be cut and fought fire when the government called. They were both professionals who could do things with a chainsaw that most firefighters only dreamed about.

Davis meanwhile informed Operations about his plans who reluctantly agreed, reminding Davis that he didn't want the group to play hero. If they felt in danger at any time they were to return to their safety zone, a statement that caused the crew to grin. If they operated that way they would have stayed back at fire camp with the camp slugs. Firefighting was a dangerous business and there were certain unbreakable rules that you always followed when doing it, but you could never totally remove all of the danger. It was part of the job.

Davis gathered the squad around him, pulling his map out from his radio harness.

"Okay according to the chopper pilot there is a road just below us that travels under the slope to below the meadow where it forks. That should be pretty easy to find. We'll be in good black so the biggest danger is falling snags in this wind. Keep your heads up and look out for reach other. Remember our LCES. " Davis referred to the safety plan. The LCES stood for Lookouts, Communications, Escape Routes and Safety Zones. Davis looked over to Petoskey, "Could you place a lookout somewhere higher up on the hill to watch the lee side of the mountain for any potential problems from that area?"

"Sure thing."

"Thanks. Okay, when we arrive at the forks we'll be able to determine if the heat has cooled sufficiently for us to travel overland to the meadow. Watch for burning snags and stump holes. There will still be a lot of heat in places and if you fall, you could be in trouble. Petroskey, I'll call you when we reach the forks and when we reach the meadow."

Davis looked at each one of his men, "Be prepared for the worst, but we'll believe for the best. Have we forgotten anything?"

"Yeah," Petoskey answered, "Do you have an EMT with you?"

Davis swore to himself. He had forgotten the obvious. They needed someone with medical training because there were sure to be injuries. The last word from Tom was that he was approaching the helicopter to search for survivors. No EMT was on the division.

"Yea, I'm one," Tony raised his hand, "I'm carrying my kit."

"Okay, thanks Tony. If there are no questions, then lets get going."

The group made one last inspection of their gear and headed down the fire line in single file, Davis in the lead and Tony bringing up the rear. They dropped immediately from sight when they turned off the fire line and into the old black toward the trail below them. The slope was steep, their footing worsened by the thick layer of fine ash that in places had the consistency of flour. Their progress could be seen by the individual ash columns that rose up with each step before blowing off into the wind.

Nasi watched as Kapar and Sarat disappeared in a brilliant flash of light and then re-appeared a second later. He gathered his forces close. It was no matter now. He had saw the twin snags crash down and across the silver tents just before the thick black smoke covered the humans in front of the deadlier red mass of heat. All he had to do was wait. The frailty of the human body would soon give way to the onslaught of power and force that had befallen Tom and he would perish. Just as he had wished. The enemy could stand guard all they wanted. They guarded a corpse. Nasi smiled and then ordered his troops to form a perimeter around the meadow just in case humans were trying to rescue their fallen comrades. In a few minutes the first Gatekeeper would fall and then others would soon do so as well. The Rivergate may have opened, he thought, but what good would it do the enemy if the Redeemed had no faith in its power. He had destroyed others before; this one would be no different.

CHAPTER TWENTY THREE

WILKESBORO, NC
PRESENT DAY

Nicole realized that she was driving too fast, well over the speed limit. She could see the town of Wilkesboro nestled into the valley alongside the Yadkin River from the low ridge that the highway crossed before descending down to Main Street where she would turn off at the overpass exit just over the river bridge. She slowed down, looking in her rear view mirror. That was all she needed, for a state trooper to stop her, she thought. Thankfully the smaller kids were watching a movie on the van's video player. Her older son sat next to her, not fully understanding why his mother seemed to be upset, but he could tell that she was worried.

Main Street in downtown Wilkesboro occupied the same location that it had always had, but the town had grown up around it. After leaving the highway, the two-lane road passed one of the largest employers in the county, the Tyson chicken plant and a few smaller manufacturing plants before entering the older part of town. Several large churches graced the tree lined street as well as the overly large federal building, Board of Education building and police and fire station. Rows of neat little houses mixed with small shops and restaurants. The older courthouse stood like it had for almost a hundred years to the left, but it was empty now. Next to it the Smithy's Department Store was now a health food store and restaurant, housing small offices on the second floor. The hanging tree behind the courthouse had long since died from old age and the ravages of several storms. A small black oak had been planted in its place next to a plaque telling the tale of the original tree.

The location of the first, original meetinghouse was said to be somewhere near the old courthouse, but no one knew for sure. The mulberry fields still lay across the river from the high bluffs as they had always been. Although a few buildings had encroached into the bottomlands, most of the area near the river was still in open fields and cornfields with sections within the boundaries of a new town park that extended alongside the Yadkin River.

The ridge once occupied by the cabin of Christopher Gist had been covered by the plantation home of General Gordon through the past century, that home finally destroyed before construction of the hospital in North Wilkesboro that now commanded the upland overlooking the wide flat bottomland. Thick wooded tracts of hardwoods occupied the steep sections along the river on the south side down to the highway bridge, where recent manufacturing plants had been built near the spot where the Moravians had first camped those many years before. On a low rise next to the bridge a series of buildings covered the tree dotted landscape along the banks of the Yadkin, including an old school and that had been there for over half a century. Now, North Wilkesboro Assembly, a new progressive, multicultural church that had sprung up several years before owned those buildings. The church had quickly grown to be the largest church in the region because of a fresh, new vision where the religious and racial walls that had dominated the valley for hundreds of years had at last been broken.

Nicole stopped at the intersection of Main Street and West Street at the red light. The road crew was working late, paving the road. A female crew worker in a neon orange vest held up a stop sign, taking precedent over the newly changed green light. They appeared to be having trouble with some type of equipment and it would be a few minutes before the traffic could continue. She was still several blocks from the church, but could see the large white church sign across the top of the red brick building. Several cars were already parked in the front parking lot.

Nicole began to shake inwardly as fear tried to grip her mind with its deceptive lies. Her younger children were blissfully ignorant of the turmoil within her, but upon glancing at her oldest boy, just turned a teenager, she knew that he understood something was going on. He had always known even back when the demons had haunted her own spirit, even though he was but a small boy. She pushed the lingering guilt away and stared back at the sign. She desperately needed to get to the church to be among the believers, feel the power and love that radiated from within. She wanted their pastor to pray for Tom and herself.

The road was still blocked and by the look of things it would be a few more minutes before they would let her pass. Suddenly, Nicole saw the church building as it used to be. It was again the school and the front steps were full of teenagers, both black and white, filtering through the front doors as the sound of cheering and electric guitars filled the air. Tom stood by the front door. He was greeting the different youth groups as they entered the building, shaking hands with youth pastors and senior pastors from small churches across the county who had brought their kids. Large groups from the established, older more traditional denominations joined ranks with the kids from back country holiness churches. Black kids sat next to white, rich kids next to poor. The gym was filled with youth from all denominational backgrounds and races, from different parts of the region. The churches that they represented had very rarely worshiped together because of the religious walls that separated, but the kids themselves had. In a series of youth meetings, culminating with the latest outreach, the youth had bound together under one common banner like no time before. The Spirit of God was moving and kids from all denominational backgrounds were experiencing the Holy Spirit in a fresh and new way. Walls of racial injustice were being broken, denominational lines crossed. Tom and Nicole were so excited to be a part of what God was doing.

Then suddenly, the movement began to fall apart. The youth from main line denominations were suddenly barred from attending the meetings because the elders of their respective churches disliked the youths' new found exposure to the Pentecostal experience of the Holy

Spirit and the numbers began to shrink. The youth in the community were ready for change, but many of their parents were not. And then suddenly that bright new youth ministry was finished.

That had been when the trouble had started with Tom, Nicole thought. They were in terrible financial trouble she knew, but they were actually beginning to work their way out. At times it appeared to be an impossible situation, but if they would continue to operate according to the principles of God and be faithful in their obedience to God, they would eventually work themselves out. But the despondence in her husband had continued to grow, more so then she had ever dreamed until reading Tom's letter. Now she knew what was really working against him. She had faced the same demons in her own life. She recognized them for who they were. Now they controlled her husband.

"Mom," her older son brought her back to the present reality, "she wants you to turn here."

"What?"

"The woman. She's motioning for you to take a detour. I don't think they are able to get the truck working. The whole road is blocked."

Nicole wiped the tears from her eyes and turned down a side street, the church building lost to view behind the rows of older homes that surrounded the courthouse.

"Mom, you okay?" her son asked.

"Yeah, just my allergies," Nicole answered with a half-truth and then realized, just as quickly, that it was a half lie. Her son knew.

"Nathan, your dad's in trouble," she finally stated as they stopped at a second red light.

"What's wrong? Does it have something to do with the papers you are holding?"

Nicole realized that while they had waited at the roadblock, she must have unconsciously taken the letter from her pocket. How was she going to answer that? She didn't want him to see the letter, didn't want him to know the desperation and hopelessness that his father had revealed.

"Nathan, he'll be okay. We just need to get to church and ask Pastor Dave to pray for him."

She began to get frustrated. What was taking the light so long? God please let me get to church, she prayed silently.

The Guardian Raham floated over the car, wounded from the last attack. Next to her stood the giant warrior, Laham, also wounded. Another attack like the last one could overwhelm them. She felt the prayers of her charge, but Nicole's fear made them ineffective. She glanced up over the nearby buildings to the brick church beyond to plan her next move. As soon as Nicole entered the church and asked the Redeemed ones to pray, then forces could be gathered to assist in the battle for Tom's life.

The Rivergate stood fully open now, a portal that connected earth with heaven. It was from where the angels of God ascended and descended to do the Lord's bidding just as the patriarch Jacob had first seen and recorded centuries before.

After years of being fully protected by Sarat and his small band of Gatekeepers, the keys to opening the portal fully had finally come together. First a new move of the Spirit had begun those many years before in the small church through the girl, Eileen, and then the walls of racism had first been challenged among the youth just a few years before. Unknowingly, Tom himself had been among the first to begin to break that wall down. Now, God's people were operating fully within an open portal, the Redeemed ones themselves being the true Gatekeepers who held the power over the region.

What had begun through the simple prayer of a devout man of God those many years before as he camped in the meadow by the Yadkin had finally come to fruition. Now that the portal was firmly in the hands of the true Gatekeepers, the potential of the portal to expand the kingdom of God was only limited by the Gatekeepers themselves. In the heavenly arena, many Guard units stood ready to do the Lord's bidding on the behalf of the Redeemed to drive away the enemy and fully reclaim the land. They waited only to be activated by the Gatekeepers through prayer, worship and faith.

The portal was no longer just an opening in space as it appeared in its infancy. It now had expanded itself across the valley, anywhere where believers operated within its fullness. In the midst of these the center stairway ascended upward into the heavens. Surrounding the stairway were massive walls of translucent rock, battlements with colored banners blowing in the winds of heaven and watchtowers that faced in all four cardinal directions. Mighty Gatekeepers stood within each of the towers as Guards patrolled the lower battlement walls. Brilliant lights of the rainbow cascaded over the walls, like rain falling from the heavens.

All around the Rivergate were smaller portals scattered across the countryside. None were as large as the one by the river. The church within the protective battlements of heaven was destined to be a great regional base of power, but only the Redeemed ones or true Gatekeepers determined just how effective the portal would be in influencing the country around it.

A warrior leaned over the front gate tower and pointed below to the enemy forces massing for an attack on the two warriors guarding Nicole's van.

He motioned for the Captain of the Guard, "The one Sarat spoke of before he left has arrived. The enemy appears to be laying an ambush for them."

The Captain joined his subordinate and leaned slightly over the battlement. He saw the Guardian Raham and another warrior by her side, one that he did not recognize.

"A Gatekeeper somewhere has been praying. Look, that is one of the Throne Warriors. But more is needed for the Lord's will to be done."

"The Messenger Malak was sent north just moments ago. He must have succeeded," the guard commented and pointed again to the dark shadows hovering below the battlements just outside the colored lights that radiated around the portal. "The enemy is strong against this one, Captain. We must help. They are so close. Surely once inside the Rivergate, the woman's prayers will be sufficient to bring her husband's salvation."

The Captain tilted his head as if listening, deep in thought for a moment before responding. "The woman has the power to call the forces of heaven, but she has yet to fully believe in what our Lord has done for her through his redemptive act. Like most of the Redeemed, she does not truly understand the authority that lives within her."

The Captain turned to the warrior beside him. Someone was praying for the woman and he was stirred into action, "She is trying to reach the portal so she can tell her story. The combined prayers of the Gatekeepers will be sufficient, but the time is short." The Captain hesitated, "In fact, her own prayers would be sufficient."

The cloud of dark warriors continued to gather just around the corner from where the car stood still, waiting for the light to turn green.

The voice spoke from deep within the recesses of Nicole's mind, a troubling echo from her past, "Nicole, all is lost. He is not like you who did not have the strength to carry on with what was ordered. He will succeed. You have done this to him. All of those years of sickness, the late nights he waited by the hospital bed, the cuts he took to protect you from your own hand, the abuse, the loneliness when you turned away from him, the confusion brought on by your sickness. You think that you have driven me out. But I am still here, waiting for the chance to once again take control. With Tom gone, who will stand with you? He is already dead, Nicole. You killed him!"

The light turned green, but for a moment Nicole did not move as she fought to control her thoughts.

You have no control over me anymore! Nicole's spirit shouted the words within her.

The Captain called to the warriors guarding the battlements, "First Guards stand to arms! Second Guards secure the walls!"

Immediately a full troop of warriors stood before the walls, their golden swords before them, their bodies shining brilliantly among the cascading multicolored lights of the rainbow. The Second Guard took their place on the battlements.

Raham placed her hand on Nicole's shoulder and caressed her mind to comfort her from the lies of the enemy that lurked around her.

Tom is not dead! There is still hope!

"That's it Nicole. You can do it!" Raham encouraged her charge silently, even as she turned to the warrior, Laham beside her. "Prepare for another attack!" she called, glanced through the row of houses. She thought she saw the banner of the First Guards flying outside of the portal walls. Hopefully help was on the way.

CHAPTER TWENTY FOUR

WESTERN WYOMING
PRESENT DAY

Hold on Tom, Help is on the way. Davis thought to himself just as a particularly violent gust of wind blew his hard hat from his head followed by an unexpected fire tornado that had crested a narrow side ridge below the group as they trudged through the tormented landscape. The whirlwind pelted the rescue party with ash and debris as well as live embers as it swirled past them, a funnel cloud of gray ash that rose over a hundred feet into the air. Davis instinctively closed his eyes and pulled the bandana tighter over his nose, turning away from the force of the wind as the funnel clawed through the deep ash and swept up the hill before suddenly bouncing upward and disappearing in the lingering smoke column.

All around them lay the ghostly remains of a once proud forest of evergreens, now just a sea of smoking, blackened snags, many broken and lying across the ground. Others were still burning in the very top or at ground level and below. Smaller whirlwinds raced across the deadened land, small funnel clouds that could pull deadened snags from their roots and blow burning embers across the fire lines. The wind blew strong across the mountain, casting a gray veil that limited visibility and forced the firefighters to pull their goggles over their eyes and tighten the bandanas over their face.

The greatest risks were from falling snags, but luckily most of the trees had burned through at the base and had already fallen. However, up ahead, Davis noticed a heavy concentration of smoking trees that were still standing. Even though the wind howled forlornly, it was otherwise uncharacteristically quiet. No scratching animal sounds, no calling birds. It was the sound of death, Davis thought. A crash echoed across the face of the mountain and a huge ponderosa pine tumbled from the cliffs above, breaking up several of the smaller aspen below it before finally settling down in the final throes of death on the logging road ahead of the party.

"Did you see that?" one of the crew asked.

"Yeah, heads up guys," Davis replied.

He looked over at Ayers who had set his saw down to take a drink from his canteen. There were several large snags across the road ahead that blocked their path. The debris along the road ahead was still burning, the ground heavy with smoke and still very hot. Live fire was still spreading through previously unburned fuel. The main firestorm was above them along the ridgeline and across the other side of the mountain, but they were entering a hot zone with a tremendous amount of heat still consuming the last holdouts of the dying forest. Green islands of unburned vegetation lay scattered above the road.

"The pilot said that everything was black. She missed the areas above," Davis commented, "What do you think, Ayers. We go around or stay on the road"

Ayers looked up, testing the wind that was calming somewhat now that the firestorm had passed over the lee side of the ridgeline.

"We can clear the road. This ground's steep and there is still too much heat. Hopefully the fork in the road is close, but I wouldn't go near the islands. They could heat up pretty fast."

"You're right. If you think you can safely clear the path, we'll continue on the road."

"We can do it boss, just keep a close eye out," Ayers said and turned to his partner. "Let's go Andy."

The sawyer returned the canteen to its pouch and placed the saw over his shoulder. Both men then walked past the other crewmen. Up ahead, a dozen, large pines had fallen across the road, several of them still actively burning at both the base and top. Older jackstraw remains of dead trees were piled along the road and were still burning, the flames reaching upward over twenty feet into the air.

The wind calmed because they had approached a sheltered section of the mountain protected from the overhead winds by a ragged cleft of red rock that loomed dangerously above them. All was strangely quiet except for the crackling of the fires around them. From their vantage point, the crew could see far down the slope to the green meadows along Beaver Creek that lay below the black and gray, smoking world of death.

The first saw cranked up with the characteristic buzz of the Still chainsaw and then the second as both sawyers began cutting a path through the fallen timber. Davis watched as they worked for any signs that new snags would fall. It would take a while to safely cut the path. He motioned for the other crewmembers to find a place to wait and looked at his watch. They had been gone for close to ten minutes. By the look at the progress the two sawyers were making, they could continue in another ten to fifteen. No telling how long it would take them to get to the meadow. He drank from his canteen as he gazed upward through the smoke toward the ridgeline where the fire had just crossed. Somewhere along the ridge there were the fallen firefighters.

The radio was quiet, so quiet in fact that he checked to see if his own radio was working and the volume was up, both of which were true. He switched over to the command channel, which was also quiet. That was usually the case, he thought. In the heat of battle, as the fire was exploding all across the lines, and crews were being pulled back to safety zones in some areas and fighting valiantly to hold the line in others, the radio chatter often became confusing at times. But as time progressed and resources settled down to their new assignments or retreated from the line, the radio often became silent for a time. He heard Foxtrot Seven-Nine call in to the helibase as the pilot approached for landing over the air to ground before he switched back to the division tactical frequency. Someone had just called for Juliet again, but there was still no answer.

CHAPTER TWENTY FIVE

THE PORTAL

"**M**om, tell us again about what happened at the old church," a youthful Tom Mackenzie asked as he pointed out the car window at an old, weather beaten church building, long abandoned and now used for storage. The boy was only seven. Youngest of three children, he was short for his age with wide brown eyes and a round face that matched his full belly. His sisters were thin, but short, both taking after their mother's side of the family.

Tom's father, E.T. Mackenzie looked out the window as he turned down the gravel road and commented to his wife, "Honey that church hasn't changed since we were married. Looks like somebody's storing hay under the porch. Look there," he pointed as he pulled over into the parking lot, now grown up with weeds. An old tractor, long since abandoned for scrap sat next to where the church sign had once stood. A faded white board leaned against the tree by the tractor, several black letters still visible.

"B-I-L-L," Tom read aloud the few letters that he could see on the old sign, "What was the name of the church?"

"To tell you the truth, sweetie, I can't remember. I think, Billings Chapel, but I may be wrong."

Eileen Mackenzie clasped the hand of her husband of sixteen years, "There's very little good that I remember about this place. They named the community rightly when they called it Traphill. I was trapped here for two years."

"You were trapped?" Tom's older sister, Emily, asked surprised.

"Well not exactly, but when we lived here, Ma was so sick. There were times when I thought she would die. All of my brothers and sisters were gone, married and living far away. It was just Mary and me. I felt trapped because I had no friends, we never left the mountain and some of our neighbors were not very nice. Sometime, when you are older I'll tell you about that."

"But what about the church?" Tom asked again. "Tell us about the time when you spoke in tongues and scared everybody off. "Tom began to laugh. "That's funny."

"Well Mary and I received the Holy Spirit in that very cow pasture. I was only fourteen."

"Did you know Daddy then, Mom?" Emily asked.

"No that was two years before we moved to High Point where I met your Daddy. Anyway, the next day was church. So Mary and I got ready like we always did and walked to church. It was a Wednesday night and the pastor was late so the deacon started the service. The deacon asked for people to give their testimony and I was so excited about what had happened to me that I stood up and began to tell them. I didn't know that they didn't believe in the baptism in the Holy Spirit or speaking in tongues. It was such a great experience for me that I thought everyone there would thrilled."

"But they wasn't." Tom stated

"That's right son, they were not thrilled. In fact they were mad, afraid. I really don't know. All I remember is that I began to speak in tongues and before I realized it they all left the building and cut out the lights. When the pastor came up, somebody told him that us Jackson girls were inside shaken' and a shimmering. I remember the deacon telling him that."

"What happened next?" Emily asked.

"Well, I looked at Mary and she at me and at first we were a little embarrassed, but then we began to laugh. We knew that what had happened to us was Truth. Well, anyway, the next Sunday we come back to church and during the singing, we started speaking in tongues again. This time, the pastor took us outside the church," she pointed to where the sign leaned against the tree, "Right there by that old tree, he took us there and tried to explain that what we were doing was wrong. That it was not the Holy Spirit, but only our childish emotions. He said that there was no need for anyone to speak in tongues and we should never do it again."

"What did you do?"

"It had to be God, because I was taught never to back talk your elder, especially a pastor. But something rose up within me and I told him that he was wrong. That he lived a lie, that what had happened to me was real and was what God wanted for all believers. I told him that because he had forsaken the move of God, that his ministry would fall and so would the church. I told him that for a full generation, the church would cease to exist."

"Mom, you told him that?" Emily exclaimed.

"Yeah, I guess I did. Like I said, I knew that that had to be God. Mary looked at me in total surprise and I could not believe what I had said."

"Did you get in trouble?"

"No, the pastor just turned around and walked back inside and we went home. The next week, old man Hutchinson found the pastor....." Eileen hesitated, trying to think of the right words. "He found the pastor with another woman that was not his wife."

"Ooooh, that's a no no," Tom exclaimed.

"That's right Tom, The pastor was found to be in adultery. He resigned the church and moved away in disgrace. And ever since then the church has been empty."

"You put a curse on the church?'

Eileen laughed, "No, honey. I just spoke what God said. The people put a curse on themselves for not accepting the move of God that was coming to the valley."

"Wow, that's cool."

"There's your old house, honey," E.T. pointed to a farmhouse down the road in the middle of the field. The barn had long since been torn down and someone had replaced the tin roof and added another room and side porch. E.T pulled the car off the road again at the entrance to the driveway as Eileen strained her eyes to see. She had not been back to the place for at least ten years and much had changed.

An elderly woman sat on the front porch swing in the warm spring sunshine. She noticed the car stopping briefly at the driveway entrance before turning around and proceeding back down the road by the old church. She stood up and entered the kitchen door. Her husband would be home soon and she was cooking a roast for dinner. The woman in the front of the car had looked familiar, she thought as she closed the door behind her. She straightened the picture on the wall of her and her husband, children and grand children. For some reason her thought turned to the girl, Eileen, who had been a neighbor's child those many years before.

Had it been Eileen in the car? She thought of her first husband, Thaddeus Hutchinson, of how awful he had been and of that terrible day when Eileen and her sister had walked by the house on their way from school. She knew that he had attacked the girls like he had done others before and after. He would hurt no one again, she thought. That had been a long, long time ago.

The dust from the passing car blew over the nearest grave that stood in the old cemetery by the road behind the abandoned church. Thaddeus Hutchinson had died in a fire in 1949, freeing a wife that had lived too long in abuse. She was a Miller now, with two children and five grand children and her life had been a good one since the day he had fallen in a drunken rage in the fire set by his own hand. Mrs. Margaret Miller smiled again as another car pulled up the driveway. Her husband was home.

The Gatekeeper Sarat stood by the old church, saluting the Guardian Natan as well as several others including Kapar, a new Guardian in the valley.

"It seems but minutes ago when young Eileen sent the pompous Nasi flying over the hills," Sarat commented and then greeted the dark haired Kapar. "You are Tom's Guardian? I am Sarat, Captain of the Rivergate."

Kapar studied the Gatekeeper and then saluted him. "What interest do you have in young Tom?" Kapar asked.

"He holds the next key to activate the Rivergate. Guard him well Kapar, for in time he will return to the valley and begin opening the last door to the portal. There is but another who will open it fully."

Tom Mackenzie woke up suddenly, his head bursting with the lights of a thousand suns. The smell of roasting meat lingered on the breeze as well as the pungent aroma of pines. He lay still, confused, waiting for the pain to subside and as it did, clearing his vision. He lay on his back on a bed of straw? He looked around him. He was in the deep forest under a shelter of some type.

The dream had been so real. It had been years since he had thought of that day back when he was just a boy when he had first seen the place where his mother had lived. It didn't seem to be a dream at all. He felt as if he had actually been there. He could still smell the flowers, the dusty road, the sweet smell of his mother's perfume, and the pungent odor of the chicken houses. But it had been a dream or was he dreaming now?

What had happened to him? Where was he? For a second, a wave of panic rose within him as he suddenly thought that he might be dead. No that couldn't be.

He touched his chest, looked at his hands, one of which was bandaged, and then down at his bare feet. Where had his boots gone? The wound across his thigh appeared to have been cleaned and freshly bandaged.

All around him were the trunks of large pine trees, ponderosa pine, he remembered. The sun sparkled through the heavy canopy, dotting the ground with golden rays. A small fire crackled cheerfully near another shelter where someone slept. He heard the person's heavy breathing. Tom lay back down and stared up at the pine roof. What had happened to him?

At first he couldn't remember what had happened. He glanced to the side of his lean-to and saw the yellow fire shirt. He looked down at his chest again. He wore his Forest Service tee shirt and still had on his green fire pants, although they seemed to have been cleaned. But how?

He sat up in the bed and placed his bare feet on the pine straw matted floor, working his toes down through the pine needles and into the rich, cool dirt below, a habit from his childhood. The fire shelter lay next to his shirt, crumbled up in a ball, torn and blackened from soot. Well, the fire had been real, that was for sure. But what of this place? He remembered reaching for the pilot just as the snag had fallen across him, remembered pulling the other shelter back over the rocks and then he had blacked out.

This had to be a hunter's camp, but how did he get here? There were no camps that he knew of, and if there had been some on the mountain, the hunters would surely have left long ago with the onset of the fire.

"Well, well, you have finally awakened." A voice spoke from behind the sidewall of the shelter.

Tom turned quickly to face a short, balding, older man wearing a heavy wool robe, tied about his waist with a black leather belt. He vaguely remembered seeing him once before. Tom stood up.

"How long have I been asleep?"

"Oh, I'm not sure. Time doesn't seem to matter here, but I do know that you took a nasty hit, burned your hand you did. Nasty gash across the leg as well young man. It was good that I found you when I did. And your friend there, he has been unconscious the whole time. Bad bump on the head, that one."

The man stooped over the fire, where a pot was situated by the coals, simmering some kind of meat and what appeared to be potatoes. Tom realized that he was famished.

"What is this place?" Tom asked.

"Yes, yes, I have asked that many times. It drove me near mad at first, but then I began to get used to it. I haven't seen a soul for days, but then again, time has left this place."

Oh great, Tom thought, I have been rescued from the fire by a nut. But the food did smell good.

"My friend. You said that he has not awakened. We need to get help. I lost my radio in the fire. Do you have a way to call for help?"

The man looked puzzled, "Who would we call. There is no one. Just us. At first it was me, but now we are three."

He placed the wooden spoon on the ground next to the fire, "Supper is ready. You need to eat."

He stood up and smiled, "Oh my. What manners. My name is Markus O'Reilly at your service, recent cook for Coronado himself."

Tom shook the man's hand, "Tom Mackenzie"

"Oh a Scottish lad. You are indeed a long way from home. Pray tell me how a Protestant finds himself in Spanish lands? Oh, no matter. It makes no difference in this place."

Tom eyed the strange little man for a moment before the gnawing in his stomach took over and he reached for the bowl of stew being handed to him. He did not sit down, however, but walked over to the second shelter of tree limbs and glanced inside. The pilot lay sleeping, his head bandaged. There were several scars across his face, but otherwise he looked to be okay. There were three shelters built among a grove of Ponderosa pine, with the small fire situated between them.

"Sit lad, your friend will be fine. Not only was I the cook, but surgeon as well. I have pulled a many of the savage's arrows from Coronado's men."

Tom sat down on the log by the fire in somewhat of a stupor, confused, a dull ache deep within his head. He took a bite of the stew hesitantly at first. The stew was very hot, but delicious. He took another bite, realizing that the meat was venison or maybe elk. It was very good indeed. But where was he?

Markus was busily eating his own stew and seemed to have dismissed Tom entirely, lost in his own world in another time and place. All around them were lush pine forest that extended back from a rocky outcrop of red sandstone behind them toward what appeared to be an open meadow several hundred yards away and below them. Strange outcrops of black rock jutted out from beyond the last trees among green grass and multicolored flowers. A soft breeze stirred, blowing the light gray smoke from the fire across in front of Tom.

The fire! Tom placed his bowl down and stood up, Markus continued to be oblivious to his presence as he continued to eat. Where had the fire gone? He could see a bright blue sky above him through the canopy and there was no smoke column, no lingering haze, and no clouds of the constant yellow dust.

"Markus where are we? What has happened to us? A few moments ago I was working on a fire?"

"Monumental questions lad, very good questions in fact, but questions that I am afraid that I cannot answer." Markus had finished his bowl of stew and was dishing out more, "I have found this past week that if I dwelled on those very questions, I would go quite mad you see, so I try not to think of them anymore. You wish for more stew lad? Coronado himself said that I prepared venison better then any of his cooks before."

Tom placed the bowl on the log, suddenly alarmed. Who was this old man?

"What I need is to contact the Beaver Complex fire camp. You got a radio around here somewhere. I need to get Jack to a hospital."

Markus looked at him puzzled, "Lad I'm afraid I don't know what you are talking about. Believe me when I say this, there is no one to contact. There are no hospitals in this place, only mountains and trees, meadows and forest and the God forsaken Malpais out there beyond the trees."

"Malpais?" Tom looked back through the trees to the meadow and the jagged black rock beyond. The Badlands here in Wyoming? He knew of no lava flows in this part of the state. There were places in New Mexico, Colorado, areas in the Dakotas, but not here, not anywhere around the Beaver Fire!

"Markus, you must tell me. Where are we? How did I get here? A few moments ago I was on Juliet Division on the Beaver Fire in western Wyoming. The fire had escaped and was rushing toward me. There was a helicopter crash and we deployed in our shelters. I remember trees coming down, the thick smoke, heat from the fire and then, suddenly I was here in this place."

"Truly, Mackenzie, I do not know. You have been here for three days I think, but then time is different here somehow. I have been here for I think a week, seven days and nights. I returned from killing the deer and you and your friend were laying by the rocks at the edge of the lava beds. Those strange tents were over you and at first I was frightened, but then I saw that you were indeed human. I pulled you to my camp and tended your wounds. Now you are awake. That is all I know. I can't answer anything else. There has been no fire, no smoke, no... how you say it, no helicopter crash, whatever that is. It was just me, now it is us three."

Markus set down by the fire again, staring into the flames deep in thought for a moment as Tom tried to come to grips with what was happening to him. There had to be a logical explanation for this, but what? The fire was spreading quickly toward him and then the tree had fallen? He must be dreaming, but how to wake himself up? Then again, maybe the old man somehow took him and Jack from the fire line. Unconscious, he would not have known how far they could have traveled by vehicle to this place, but for what purpose? Get real Mackenzie, he thought. How could the man have pulled both of them to safety? There was nowhere to go, no way to leave the mountain but by back down the trail. He looked across the fire to the man. He looked to be in his sixties, maybe even older. There was no way that he could have hiked up the trail and carried both Jack and himself off of that mountain. But what other explanation could there be?

You are crazy Tom. You finally dropped off the deep end and look where you have landed. In the middle of a forest with a crazy man who thinks that he is Coronado's personal servant. Tom shook his head to clear his thoughts. He had to find a way to contact someone for help. Wherever he was, there was a way out. He just had to find it.

Markus began to mumble something under his breath and then he spoke louder as Tom looked deep into the old man's troubled eyes.

"I was his cook you know and a good one. We had been traveling across the desert for weeks with no sign of the savages. There had been a few skirmishes. But nothing serious and then the Captain told us to stay at camp with the wounded and he and the rest would travel onward. They promised that they would return in a few days time. It was a day such as this one here. We were camped by the Malpais beneath high cliffs and an archway of rock. There was a spring with fresh water and shade back against the cliff just below the archway that looked from a distance to be a gateway to heaven itself."

Tom was immediately drawn into the old man's story.

"I was young and naïve, a true believer that wished to share the gospel of our Lord with the native people. But the soldiers were harsh. They rode under the banner of the cross, but they did not follow our Lords commands. They were cruel and treated the natives with increased cruelty all in the name of God. They would laugh at me because of my prayers, but like I said, I was a good cook and could treat their wounds, so I guess they tolerated me. We camped there by the spring for a day and a night, tending to our wounded. There were seven of us. We were to stay hidden and not show ourselves to any one who happened by. Unknown to us, a dwelling place was on top of the very cliff that we were camped by. The second day three of the natives walked up on our camp, three young women in fact. The soldiers took them as I pleaded for them not to. They raped them again and again until their savage appetite was quenched and then left them by the spring to die. I knew then that I had been calling the wrong people savages for it was the soldiers who were the true savages. We broke camp and fled then, but the lava beds blocked our travels for several miles. A party from the village intercepted us as we tried to hide in the lava itself. I watched as one by one the soldiers were killed. I ran, praying that God would protect me, and suddenly I was here in this place. I have been here since."

"That was only seven days ago?" I asked, overwhelmed by his story. Either we were both crazy or something very strange had happened here. I began to remember books I had read of people vanishing and then returning, rifts in time and space, but it all seemed to be just science fiction stories to me.

"I have been in this place for seven days, but then time is different here. I am no longer a young man. I have aged. Like I said before if I continued to think on such things, I would go mad."

He was telling a story that would have happened almost five hundred years before during the time when the Spanish first traveled through the American west in search of treasure. How could that be?

"Tom, I did not wish to die and prayed for God to deliver me and he did. You on the other hand wished to die, yet God seemed to deliver you as well."

Tom stared in disbelief at the statement. How had he known his most secret thoughts? How could Markus have known what he had been planning this very morning?

"What do you mean, I wished to die? I don't want to die. I have a wife and three beautiful children."

"Oh, but you did wish to die. You have thought that you are a failure, that you have failed your wife, your family, your God. By dying you think somehow to overcome your supposed failures. But you are wrong Tom Mackenzie. You only fail when you give up." The man continued talking through a sudden mist that enveloped him.

Tom closed his eyes and opened them again. Markus was still there telling his story, but Tom could no longer hear his words. A voice from somewhere deep within the forest, beyond the cliff walls was talking to him, a voice that echoed strangely through the trees. His world was spinning around him, the trees a blur. The rocks swayed and a bright white light exploded over him as he fell backward from the log.

"Juliet, this is Davis. Juliet can you read me."

Tom looked for his radio to answer but it was not in his pouch. The heat was beginning to grow more intense.

The office was small, the oak desk in front of him too large for the office itself. Tom sat in a leather chair in front of the desk. Along the wall beside him were a small couch and a filing cabinet. The couch was covered with stacks of papers, magazines and books, as was the desk. Tom was dressed in jeans and a black sweater, a fiery heart emblazoned on a small logo over the left breast pocket that was the youth ministry's symbol. It had been one of the worst days in his life. He had just resigned as youth minister. The strain was too great. The financial burdens too much to overcome, his wife's continuing sickness a yoke that he felt he could no longer bare. He had failed the church, his wife, his children and God, and now it was over. He left the church a defeated man that day, not fully understanding that the youth ministry he had led for five years had broken the second wall that held sway over the community and had unlocked the second key to the Rivergate itself.

The Gatekeepers in the Spiritual realm had won a great victory, but to Tom he had been a failure. The black tentacles of depression clamped down across him that day and grew stronger over the next few years as the Rivergate opened all around him. A depression that ultimately led him to this very spot, somewhere in the lost worlds of collapsed portals, portals that originally were created for man to have free access to God himself.

"The portal still exists, Tom," voices whispered through the blinding lights as shadows swirled around him.

"What do you mean portal?' Tom answered.

"All of mankind can still open the portal in their own heart and enter into the most Holy of Holies to commune with their God. Jesus made sure of that on the cross."

"But what would God want with me anymore after I have failed Him and all the ones that I truly love?" Tom asked of the shadows.

"If you only knew how important you truly are to Your Savior, you would not ask such a question. A man only fails when he gives up. If you have the Spirit of God within you, you can never fail. You may fall, but you must always get back up."

"But I wished to die. I planned for it. My God I even wrote Nicole a letter stating what I was going to do. What have I done? How I have hurt her once again," Tom responded.

CHAPTER TWENTY SIX

WESTERN WYOMING
PRESENT DAY

The windsock fluttered violently on the silver pole across from the landing zone. Teresa had to come in from a different angle than before. She noticed that the other ships were already on the ground. A tanker drove by the dirt road alongside the field, laying down a trail of water for dust abatement. Out ahead of the truck, yellow dust swirled over the road surface and across the meadow toward the creek, but luckily the wind blew the dust away from the helibase. Before her on the ground a crewman motioned her toward the landing zone, guiding her with hand signals.

The strong wind frustrated her approach as she slowly lowered the aircraft toward the safety of the grass meadow, thinking of the bright silver tents through the swirling smoke. Where had they gone? One moment the two shelters shone brightly from under the smoke and then with one puff of black smoke they were suddenly gone, vanished or so it seemed. Her mind raced with the images of fire, smoke, the dark green image of one pilot among the rocks, the sudden appearance of the man running across the field, the explosion, both shelters deployed among the rocks. Then the snags rising suddenly up from the ground from beneath the smoke itself.

She shuttered inwardly at the closeness that she had come, how the bucket had almost foiled itself around the burning snag. She had pulled up suddenly, dropping the retardant near the shelters. There had been a quick shift of the smoke and the field had been momentarily clear. Where had the shelters gone? She thought she had seen one of the snags fall as the retardant crashed over it. And then there had been a brilliant flash of light. Had the rocks themselves moved, shaken by the giant snag? Had the rocks crashed around the two firefighters?

Finally the helicopter touched the ground. As soon as the wind reduced to acceptable levels, she would go back up and take another look. The two shelters could not have just vanished, she thought. They had to still be there somewhere among the rocks. Hopefully the two could survive. Teresa unbuckled her harness as the rotors slowed, the ship vibrating under their reducing strength. She saw the communications tent, now full of people, yellow shirted men and women darting in and out as several more government vehicles pulled up behind the tanker. She had never in all of her career been on a scene where an aircraft had crashed and had no ideal what was going on within the tent. The fire had gone south in a hurry, she thought and the crash had just added insult to injury. She would have hated to be in the IC's shoes.

Her crew chief had already exited the chopper and she sat for a moment, watching him walk past the front of her ship, holding his cap on his head as he walked under the rotor blades. It was characteristic of most people to bend over when walking under the rotors even though there was no way that a person could walk into the blades, but her crew chief was one of the few people that did not. Of course he was only five foot five. Teresa on the other hand was a tall five foot eleven and always stooped over a bit, even though she knew that the rotors were several feet over her head.

She dreaded the questions that they were waiting to ask her. She began to second-guess herself. Had she done everything that she could to help those men on the mountain? Or had she killed them when the snags had fallen? She shivered inwardly at the thought. She had never believed in God, never had a use for him. How could an entity that was referred to as a father be loving and caring. The only father that she had ever known had found his pleasure in liquor and whatever woman he could find to bring home at night. And when he could not find one, he broke into the locked door to her own bedroom. She had very little use for men, distrusted them in fact if they were kind to her. She respected the men that she worked with, was friends with most of them, could kid around and drink with the best of them. But if they ever tried to approach her romantically, she immediately shut them out. There were times when she would respond to them, but only for the physical pleasures that they could share together and only on her terms. To say the least, she had never had a steady relationship with any man.

Most women, especially married women of the firefighters she worked with, saw her as a threat. She knew she was thought of as a very beautiful woman, a curse that she had learned to live with since her teenage years when her father began to notice her flowering womanhood. Therefore she had very few women friends as well. The one woman that she did have a friendship with, however, just happened to be the wife of the pilot that may even now be lying dead on the mountain. Teresa saw Heather standing by the tent, swirling yellow dust blowing, casting a veil over her. Heather had always been kind to her, had shared with Teresa her faith in Jesus and how her life had changed when she had accepted Him into her heart. She wasn't pushy at all. She just shared her life and Teresa drew strength from having her as a friend. And now she stood by the tent, watching as Teresa climbed out of the helicopter. What was she going to tell her?

Hello Heather, I think I just killed your husband by my stupidity.

Teresa gathered what little strength she had and followed the crew chief toward the tent. She would tell her the truth. She didn't know what had suddenly happened to the two shelters, but hopefully the retardant and the small deployment site was enough to keep them safe until the fire blew past them. As soon as the wind died down, she knew that she would go back to find out for herself.

Teresa looked straight ahead toward the open door of the tent. She feared facing Heather, feared what she might say, guilt building up within her. But at the last minute, she looked up and into Heather's blue eyes of concern. Remarkably calm, Teresa thought as the woman took a step toward her.

Teresa stopped, again not knowing what to say.

"Did you find them Teresa? Are they alive?" the woman asked.

Heather had heard Teresa's remark over the radio as many others had, but she had refused to believe that her husband was indeed killed. God would protect him. He always had. It was not his time, not now.

"I saw shelters Heather. They deployed in a small meadow, but that is all..." she was telling only a partial truth. Heather was one person that she could not lie to.

"Heather, one appears to be dead, but there were two people that deployed shelters in the field. I'm sorry, but I could not tell who. I tried to drop retardant to create a better safety zone, but the wind was too strong and I had to land. I'm sorry."

Heather could see the pain in her friends eyes, could feel her shake as she held her hand. Inwardly, her heart rejoiced. Two shelters meant two men that could survive. Her husband was alive. She knew deep within her that her husband was one of the two that had deployed.

"It'll be okay Teresa, Jack is okay. He'll be fine. Thank you," Heather looked deep into Teresa's dark green eyes, "Thank you. I know you did what you could. It'll be just fine."

How could she be so sure, Teresa thought. How could she stand there and say that with such assuredness, such faith? You know the answer to that, Teresa, a voice spoke deep within her spirit.

"Heather, I've got to go in. I'm sure they will want me to brief them. There's a crew attempting to reach them from behind the fire. They should be getting close. We'll get them out."

Heather shook her head and smiled as Teresa turned and entered the tent. She turned away, facing the mountain with its great column of blackened gray smoke and tentacles of fire. Hang on Jack, God will make a way, she thought, tears smearing the dust across her face.

Jason Stanley turned his white suburban off the main road at the Forest Service guard station just as the tanker turned ahead of him, spraying a fine mist of water over the gravel road in a constant battle to control the ever-present dust. A helicopter had just landed and the pilots were exiting the ship. Jason couldn't remember the pilot's name, but he definitely remembered what she looked like. Dark shoulder length hair and bright green eyes with a body to kill for.

"Boy, I would sure love to take a ride with her," he whispered to himself as he watched the pilot walk toward the communications tent.

Jason quickly grabbed his camera and note pad and locked his door. He had to get something, anything before the other news agencies caught wind of what was going on. Still frustrated at his boss's apparent disinterest in the story, he walked quickly across the road. He knew that he was supposed to be with the information officer, but that Indian was still back at the ICP, most likely already lining up interviews with the television networks.

Jason watched as the pilot talked briefly with another woman before entering the tent. He wasn't sure but he thought that the other woman was one of the pilot's wives. If he was really lucky, she may even be the wife of one of the men who had been killed in the crash. That would be great, he thought. A real human-interest story. An interview with the deceased spouse after she received word of her husbands demise. Now if he could just get a flight up to the scene or maybe even hitch a ride on one of the four wheelers nearby.

He spied three of the four wheelers over behind the tent, parked side by side. That would be the ticket, he thought. If he could get a ride on one of those things, he could follow the fireline to the crash site itself. Maybe there was hope yet, he thought as he crossed the road and made his way past the first tent by which the woman stood, looking up toward the column of smoke on the mountain.

"Excuse me. I am Jason Stanley of the Jackson Times," Jason introduced himself.

The woman ignored him, continuing to stare up at the smoke column. He noticed streaks across her face from where she had been crying.

Jason cleared his throat and introduced himself again.

"Excuse me. Could I talk with you a moment?"

Heather turned to face him. Her weather beaten face, although streaked with dust and tears had a strong, healthy look, her age adding a few winkles around the edges, her eyes strong and blue as the sky above, her spirit within casting a determined glow over her cheeks. Heather had not had an easy life, having endured the divorce of her parents as a young child, the abuse of a step dad during her teenage years, but she had persevered through all of it. The only bit of stability during most of her childhood had been the church bus with its grandpa driver that came by each Sunday to take her to church. Heather did not cry when her father died after the divorce. She did not attend the funeral of her step dad when he died several years after she graduated for college, but when that particular bus driver died just a few years ago, she drove across three states to be there. He had shown her love like no one else, until Jack had come into her life. They had been married for many years, had suffered through the period when they had wanted children only to find out that she was barren. They had been true soul mates. Now he was up there on the mountain. Her very life was on the mountain among the wreckage of a burning helicopter, possibly even now dying a horrible death.

Heather did not particularly like reporters, her step dad had been one and when she recognized this one, she definitely did not like him. He was a young hothead that thought being a reporter meant that he could trample over anybody around him.

"Mr. Stanley, your story is in there, " she said pointed to the tent behind her, "I really don't wish to be interviewed now."

Heather smiled and turned to walk back to her trailer where she could be alone and pray. Inside her stomach was knotted up with worry, her heart beating unnaturally fast, but strength deep within her grew stronger as she prayed. She left the reporter standing by the tent.

"But surely you can tell me how you feel. You are the pilot's wife correct?"

"Heather said that she did not wish to be bothered Mr. Stanley. I would advise that you honor her wishes."

Jason turned sharply to see who had addressed him and was taken aback by the female pilot who stood looking down at him.

"But this is news! What are you trying to hide? I know there has been a crash. I am just doing my job."

Teresa stepped closer to the younger man and he stepped back, "Leave her alone Stanley." She stated threateningly.

"Or what? I have a right to tell this story. People have a right to know what is going on."

Teresa just shook her head and pushed past him. She had given her briefing to the group inside and wanted to ensure that her ship was ready for immediate lift off as soon as the winds subsided to safe levels. They were blowing even stronger than before with gusts of up to 40 mph at times, stirring the dust from the road. A dozen empty quebees, water containers made of plastic, rolled across in front of her. She stopped one of the ground support guys who were chasing the run away containers.

"Bob can you make sure that Heather is okay? Don't let that reporter near her."

Bob eyed the reporter and then shook his head. He had grown very fond of Heather and Jack, having worked with them on and off for over five years, "Sure thing, Teresa. He won't get to her. I promise."

"Thanks, Bob. I appreciate it. Also see if you can get the brass to call Information. Tell him that he's got a rogue reporter out here and we would appreciate it if he reined him in."

"Will do," Bob answered.

Bob walked over to the trailer and peered in the screen door. Inside Heather was on her knees at the table, praying softly. He did not disturb her, but reached inside and closed the door, making sure that it was locked. He then stood by the door as a guard until the reporter turned away and disappeared into the tent. Bob then returned to his job, but continued to watch over the trailer. Heather was a good woman, he thought. She was old enough to be his mother. In fact, she reminded him of his mom some. She certainly prayed like his mother always did.

They were a strange couple. Jack was a good man and loved his wife dearly; everyone could see that. But he had never really embraced Christianity himself the way Heather did. He accepted the fact that she was a very devout believer and drew strength from her, but he always said that Christianity was for women and for men that needed a crutch to limp through life with. He believed in working hard and treating people with respect, following the Golden Rule and accepting people for who they were. Any organized religion was a foreign system to him, one that he figured he could live his life without. He had never understood that true Christianity was not a religion in the traditional sense; it was a relationship with the Creator of the universe.

CHAPTER TWENTY SEVEN

JULIET DIVISION
PRESENT DAY

The burning snag fell suddenly, the sharp snap echoing against the cliff walls the only warning. The firefighters scattered back down the road behind them, searching briefly upward to find the falling tree. Burning embers rained down over them as the giant ponderosa pine crashed below with a whoosh and thud, the blackened trunk half buried in gray ash, the top burning lively in an otherwise dead environment.

John Davis had reached the forks in the road. The wind that had a few minutes before been calm was now swirling against the face of the mountain, blowing hot embers and gray ash over them, casting them in a veil of death. The wind direction had changed with the renewed strength, which meant that hopefully the front was passing over them and soon the winds would calm again or finally die away.

Up ahead, he saw the blackened corpse of a rabbit that stood frozen in death, it's legs outstretched in flight. Davis toggled his radio and called Petrosky who remained back in the safety zone with the crews.

"Go ahead, Davis," the radio answered back.

"We've made it to the forks in the road. The wind is blowing very strong here and the mountain above us all along the ridge is filled with snags. What's the fire doing?"

Petrosky stood at the lookout position where he could still see the head of the fire as it began to gain strength across the lee side of the mountain in year old beetle killed timber. The wind had definitely shifted causing the many spots that had landed deep within the drainage to blow back up the ridgeline from the backside, threatening the safety zone once again.

"John the entire side of the drainage is now burning and with the wind shift, a new head is developing that is burning back up to the meadow. Your side of the mountain looks good."

"Copy that. The wind is so strong here that we can't climb up through the snag patch to the meadow at this point. We're going to stop a moment and figure on what we can do. Davis clear."

"Petrosky clear."

The relief column gathered around their leader as the wind continued to pelt them with ash and flying debris. Davis had to talk loudly for his men to hear him over the wind, which was growing harder as his throat rebelled against the ash and smoke. He pulled his bandana further up over his nose. Nearby was a rocky wall void of any living plant and no snags.

Davis pointed to the cleft of rock, "Lets hold up here for a bit out of the wind and see if we can ride this thing out a while."

The crew gathered by the rock that shielded them from the windstorm. They either had to wait for the wind to blow by or find another way up to the meadow. Several snags fell across the mountain above them adding their dead corpses to the carnage below. They definitely could not get through that maze until after the wind subsided. Each knelt down behind the rock wall to wait, each one thinking of the firefighters up on the hill above them.

Yellow eyes peered down from the snags high on the ridge, delighted that the strengthening wind hindered the approaching firefighters. The Watcher knew that the group would make it to the meadow eventually, but it would be too late. The new fire burning up the backside of the ridge would pass over the prey and the only thing to be found by the group below would be the charred remains of three men. Nasi smiled. His plan was working. If he could not stop the Rivergate from opening, he would attack the Gatekeepers themselves. One by one he would destroy them. He thought of the woman Nicole.

Years ago his kind had almost destroyed her, but her husband had pulled her from the abyss of self-destruction. Now Tom himself would be the key to once again opening her heart to the deception. She would be next. Let Sarat fight for his beloved gate. It was only as powerful as the Redeemed ones allowed it to be. As their numbers continued to be attacked by his kind, they would be so busy defending their own selves that they will lose interest in continuing to open the gate further. As their spirits grow less, so will the open portal, Nasi thought and smiled again. He turned back to the burning meadow covered in such black smoke that even he could not see entirely through its barriers.

"You wanted to die, Tom," Nasi remarked to the smoke that covered the place the two men had last been seen seeking protection behind their shelters, "Now you have your chance. And I'll be waiting for you when you cross over. You think the fire is hot now my friend. Just wait. You'll see."

CHAPTER TWENTY EIGHT

THE PORTAL

"Please Nicole forgive me. God what have I done? I don't wish to die! I want to live!" Tom screamed as the shadows exploded around him in a dazzling display of colors and white light so bright that he shielded his eyes from the heat.

"Mackenzie! Wake up lad! You got to wake up!" a voice shouted from beyond the swirling lights.

Tom struggled through the lights until they suddenly disappeared. For a moment he was disoriented and then remembered where he had been. Markus shook him.

"You have got to see this Mackenzie. Something has happened by the Malpais. The Blessed Mary has visited us. I have seen through to the other side!"

What was this crazy man shouting about? Tom sat up on his pallet under the shelter built of logs and tree branches and covered with pine tops.

"Markus what are you shouting about? What has happened?"

The older man paced back and forth by the shelter, "You were sleepy after dinner and wished to lie down for a nap. You are still weak, your body is unused to this place and it takes time to grow accustomed to it. It took me several days, but do not worry, with my good cooking you will be fine. Coronado always said that I was the best cook that he had ever employed. His favorite dish was…."

"Markus! Enough of that! Tell me what is wrong." Tom stood up.

What was going on? First he was eating stew and then he was in the church office. There were shadows, dreadful shadows that pulled at his spirit and then the lights had come. He looked around him. The camp was as it was before. A small fire burned cheerfully between the shelters. The pilot still lay sleeping in the other shelter. The sky was remarkably clear, the strong pungent aroma of pine needles almost burning his lungs as he took a deep breathe to clear his thoughts.

"You have to see this Mackenzie. I have seen to the other side and it is truly a terrible place. Hades is coming and we must flee. The Blessed Mary has visited me. Through the lights I saw her form and then the fire! Oh it was terrible! Walls of flames, black smoke. I have seen Hades itself!"

Markus crossed himself, continuing to pace, shaking his head, tears running down his aged face. He looked older than before. He looked terribly frightened.

"Settle down, Markus. Tell me what you have seen."

"The tunnel is by the Malpais. I was checking my snares near where I found you the other day and noticed that there was a crack in the black rock that I had never noticed before. I walked to the crack in the wall. I have found several others along the face of the lava, each of which led to hidden valleys full of green grass and water, wild game and walled structures partially hidden under the rocks as if the lava had tried to hide them. Coronado had said that there were lost cities filled with treasure, but we never found them. I think maybe they were destroyed by the lava flow. I thought that this crack may be another trail through the lava beds and tried to enter it. But when I did, the crack suddenly disappeared and there was nothing but the solid wall."

"But what of the fire Markus? You said you saw fire."

"Yes, yes. When I took a step back I saw the opening again, only it was full of a bright white light and then I saw the Blessed Virgin standing in the light and then the light disappeared. Then there were flames and smoke, swirling winds and falling trees. A strange shadow was cast over the ground like a giant bird flew over. I heard a great thumping noise. It was horrible Mackenzie. I have seen Hades itself. Oh God, please forgive me! This is a sign Mackenzie. Mary has condemned me for the life I lived. I could have saved those poor girls, Mackenzie. I watched while they were raped and killed. I could have saved them…" Markus began to cry, falling to his knees.

Tom rushed over and knelt beside the man. He looked so very, very old as if he had aged twenty years since they had eaten the stew together.

"Come now Markus. You could not have saved those girls. The soldiers would have killed you. You have asked God to forgive you. He will do that. Now come and show me what you've seen. Surely there is another explanation."

Markus wiped his eyes and looked up to Tom. He had regained his composure.

"Lad help me up. I have aged so much over the past few days and my legs are weak. You spoke before that you have come to this place from a fire. I saw a fire through the tunnel. I saw Hades itself. If you came from that place through the tunnel, then Hades itself can come through as well."

Tom helped the man to stand, "Show me the tunnel Markus. Maybe I can see what it is."

Tom still could not fathom what had happened to him. What place was this? How could a man that had lived hundreds of years before be alive here in this place now? Or what was now? Had he somehow gone back in time himself? There was much about this world that man in all of his wisdom still did not understand. Tom looked past the pines to the Malpais, a place of mystery, a place of black rock, hidden caves and tunnels, places where water lay frozen in the ground, where ancient mysteries lay hidden. He had been to the Malpais of New Mexico several years before on a fire. South of Grants New Mexico, the Malpais National Park stretched over 40, 000 acres of wilderness covered with the remains of an ancient civilization that had vanished over eight hundred years before. Could this be the very place only in a different time, a different dimension?

Tom had camped for several days in a valley of green grass and scattered pines known as The Hole in the Wall during a severe drought that caused the grass to dry up and blow away. The fire had burned through the valley and across the lava beds themselves, threatening the town of Grants and burning toward the Ring of Craters along the Continental Divide. During his tour of duty there, two hikers had gone missing along the western park boundary in a place known as the Tubes. He had been involved in a search for the hikers that had lasted several days after he had returned home. For three days he had searched a section of the lava beds where underground caves stretched for miles, where one slip could cause a man to fall hundreds of feet down into the caves. The hikers had never been found. He remembered seeing places within the Malpais where the heat waves played on the imagination, where the rock formations would change and waver. It had seemed the ancient legends came alive, and unworldly spirits haunted the rocks and caves themselves. He had heard the locals talk of places within the Malpais where mankind had no right to be, where the laws of physics seemed to not exist, a place between time and space.

Could he have somehow gone into one of those places now?

"I will point the way, Mackenzie, but I fear the fires. I fear what may be on the other side." Markus turned and faced Tom, " Mackenzie, you must somehow escape this place. It is too late for me. Somehow I have grown old here. I think that I have only been here seven days, but then again it seems that I have been here many, many years. Maybe the tunnel is a way out, but I don't understand the things that I saw and heard. A great bird flew over the fire, red water rushed down. There was a great noise and I ran."

Tom beat his hand repeatedly against his chest as he talked, "Did the bird sound like this?"

"Yes, yes. Thumping, constant thumping."

A helicopter!

"Markus, You have not seen Hell. Somehow you have seen where I've come from. There was a great fire burning and I was one of many that were fighting to put out the fire. Show me the tunnel, Markus."

"No, Mackenzie. My fear is too great! Follow the trail to the edge of the lava beds. Directly across from the great archway, you will see where the lava beds suddenly rises high above the surrounding wall. That is where I saw the opening."

Tom checked on the pilot. He still lay sleeping, with a nasty head wound that had been bandaged. He checked his pulse. He appeared to be okay, although Tom had to somehow get him out of this place and to a hospital.

"Don't worry Markus. I'll be back. I must see if what you have seen is the way back."

Markus crossed himself in prayer again, but would not walk past the edge of the pine grove.

The thick grove of ponderosa pine lay sheltered up against the cliff walls of a mesa that stretched far to the north and south. Beyond the grove of trees lay an open valley with only clumps of juniper and tall yellow grass scattered with purple sage. Tom stood just outside of the pines, looking for the place along the black wall of lava that Markus had described. Several hundred yards north, he spotted a place where the wall was noticeably higher than elsewhere. The lava had flowed across the valley from the north to within several hundred feet of the mesa at this point where for whatever reason, it had turned back leaving a wall that was 40 to 50 feet high. Across from this point, the red cliff walls rose sharply several hundred feet high to the rim of the mesa where dark green pines flourished. At a point where the mesa turned toward the east in a bowl shaped valley, an archway spanned across the face of the cliff approximately 50 feet above the valley floor.

Tom could not believe it. He had once stood at this very point looking up at the arch, but he had been standing on pavement in a parking lot. Tourists were taking pictures as he had stopped to take one himself before traveling back to Grants on the day before his flight home to North Carolina. Now, however, there was no highway, no parking areas. There was only a deserted valley covered in lush grass between the sandstone cliffs with its dramatic archway that the Spaniards thought was a gateway to Heaven and the Malpais that many of them though to be the very gates of Hell itself.

The day was warm, the air clearer than he had ever experienced, and the sky more blue then he had thought possible. He walked cautiously across the meadow to the black wall of lava. From a distance the wall seemed to be one solid form, but upon closer inspection, he found several fissures and cracks across the face of the wall, all of which were too small for a man to enter. He knew that there were several openings along the wall that allowed a person to travel several miles into the heart of the lava beds to the scattered hidden meadows including the Hole in the Wall itself. The natives had used the trails for centuries to hunt game and locate the many ice caves scattered throughout the maze. Outlaws had used the same trails to hide from the law and cattle rustlers had hidden stolen cattle within the scattered meadows. It was very easy to get lost within the Malpais because of the maze of black rock.

Tom continued to inspect the wall until he stood directly across from the archway at the point where the lava was much higher. It was here where Markus had found him several days before. Somewhere along the wall, Markus had seen an opening, a tunnel that may be the way out of this place.

Tom inspected the wall closely, but saw nothing and then a blade of grass suddenly disappeared as if it was swallowed up by the rock itself. Tom reached out to touch the rock and his hand disappeared as well. He quickly jerked his hand back, but took a step closer. He could now see a narrow crack in the wall several feet wide, but too narrow for him to enter. He took another step and suddenly in a brilliant flash of light he saw the wall open up and flames rushed toward him in a great roar. He jumped back quickly, the intense heat unbearable, but not before he thought he saw a floating image of a man in the flames.

"It is not time," a voice echoed from the wall itself. Tom fell back over the clump of Junipers as the flashing lights engulfed him.

Shadows floated within the lights, formless shapes swirled past him, dark memories of his past, fleeting guilt, failure, deception, and sin. Tom struggled to back away from the onslaught, shielding his eyes from the brilliant lights, and from shadows as well. The lights sheared his very soul with a holy dread. The shadows pulled unwanted memories up from his very being.

The shadows grew closer, taking on the appearances of hooded men with glowing red eyes, holding swords, their long cloaks splattered with sulfur and tar. They were frightful creatures, screaming and moaning, there voices intermingling to form one continuous chant. The men materialized before him, taking definite shape from the swirling shadows, lined side by side, their swords held before them. They stood motionless, their eyes piercing from under the black hoods that covered their faces in darkened shadows.

The lights disappeared, leaving only darkness surrounding the even blacker figures as if they drew strength from the darkness that covered them. Tom fell back against a cold, rock wall behind him, cowering away from the incredible guilt that flowed from the specters, as they stood, now silent. Tom looked wildly around him, desperately seeking for a place of escape, a way out from this terrible place. What had happened to him? What horrible place had he gone to?

The hooded figures began to whisper, their chanting at first barely discernable above the crackling of a fire that burned somewhere off in the distance beyond the black veil that covered them. Tom could not understand what they were saying, even as the chanting increased, but he could understand individual voices that assaulted his spirit from somewhere deep within his own mind, familiar voices that taunted him, tormented him with slanderous guilt laden words.

"You wished to die."

"You have failed. Look what a mess you have created for your family."

"You are a dead man. Even now your body has succumbed to the flames."

"All of those sermons, all the prayers, all the kids that you tried to reach out to. What good have they done you? You still failed miserably."

"You wished to die. You have failed. Look what a mess...."

"No!" Tom screamed, holding his hands over both ears, but nothing could drown out the voices that came out of the chanting, but also seemed to be separate.

"Who are you? What is this place?" he pleaded, falling on his knees before the hooded figures that stood over him. Their broadswords were clasped in their gloved hands before them, the stained points embedded in the soft dirt at their feet.

The chanting suddenly stopped and then the voices did as well.

Tom knelt in darkness, only the red eyes of the figures casting a pale glow that washed over his body. There was no sound but the faint crackle of a distant fire that oddly seemed to be very close as well. The figures stood completely still like statues and then beginning from both ends of the line the red eyes disappeared one by one until only one set remained that hovered directly over Tom as he stared upward in paralyzing fear.

The final figure took shape again and stood before him, this time holding the sword over Tom's head, the steel shining brightly from a light of its own making, the stain a brilliant crimson.

"I am your accuser and this place is your soul," the phantom proclaimed.

Tom backed away from the apparition that hovered over him, floating in a gathering mist. How could this be? The rock wall was immediately behind him. A small orange glow across the mist before him was intermittently blocked by the phantom as it wavered back and forth.

"You have failed, Tom. You wished to die. Now you have succeeded. The fires of life have finally overtaken you. You were so proud, Tom, proud of what you thought you had done. All of those kids you thought that you had saved. Where are they now Tom? You are alone. You know that don't you. While you zealously thought that you were ministering to all of those children, you forsook your own family. You have driven them to ruin. You lived a double life. Youth minister on the surface, but deep down you were a fraud. Now what have you got? You wished to die. To end it all in some vain martyrdom as if by killing yourself, you will have saved your family. You have only doomed their existence."

The specter completely overshadowed Tom, the blackness that was his soul fading away into the fire.

Flashing lights pierced the black smoke.

"Sarat, one has gotten through," the Guardian shouted. "We must drive him away!"

"No Kapar!" Sarat commanded, "The true Gatekeepers have gathered. The one true Gatekeeper that holds the key to Tom's salvation proclaimed his destiny, but Tom must overcome himself as well. Hold your weapons. Our time is very near."

The fire completely covered the meadow now, black smoke completely blocking the sun, the air itself heated with the intense heat and turning red. The flames were devouring the oxygen as it flowed past in pure energy.

CHAPTER TWENTY NINE

WILKESBORO, NC
PRESENT DAY

The First Guards stood ready before the walls of the Rivergate, their commander pacing back in forth in front of the glistening ranks of battle hardened warriors with their golden swords and bronzed breast plates, their multicolored standards fluttering in the Spirit's wind. One of the true Gatekeepers was in trouble, the Commander thought, and why the troop did not attack to help her was a troubling mystery to him. He could see the gathering dark regiment through the trees that lined the river. He could also see a Guardian and Throne Warrior even now fighting sporadically with scouts that darted in and out through the buildings.

The Watch Captain appeared next to the Commander and he saluted his superior smartly, "The warriors are ready, Captain. We can drive them away from the woman if you will but give the order."

"Patience, Commander. Our Lord is moving even now in the spirit of the woman. When she says the word, the command will be given."

Nicole began to shake inwardly with fear. She could sense that her husband was in grave danger. She did not understand how, but she had always known when Tom was in trouble. As a firefighter, he, at times, had to go into dangerous situations. When others ran, firefighters attacked. That was just the way it was. But as she turned down the last road toward the church, the fear of the letter that she held coming true was suddenly too much for her to bear and she began to cry. The tears came first from her innermost soul, and then outwardly as they streamed down her face.

"Just speak the word, Nicole. Proclaim Tom's deliverance. You are a Gatekeeper! You have that right given to you by our Lord. You can bind on earth and loose on earth. You can overcome evil with your spoken word if you will just believe in the power that is within you." Raham spoke to Nicole's spirit.

"Mom...."

Nicole's sobs continued as she pulled the vehicle over to the side of the road.

"Mom, Dad's going to be okay! We don't need to ask anyone to pray for him. We can do that ourselves!"

Nicole's breath suddenly caught, and she looked into her older son's eyes. The realization of what he had just said struck her spirit like a double-edged sword.

"Yes!" she whispered. "You are exactly right!"

"That's it Nicole. You know you have the power. Now just operate in the authority given to you as a Gatekeeper. You have a portal open within yourself. Tom needs you to use it," Raham spoke as she felt renewed strength from the growing faith. She smiled and turned to Laham beside her. The enemy had attacked, but it was too late.

"Now Commander," the Captain commanded, "Our time is now!"

The Commander ordered the First Guards unit into action as he drew his own sword and awaited further orders from the Captain. He had expected to attack the enemy that hovered near the woman's van, but her sudden prayer of faith had so empowered the two Guardians protecting her that the enemy had quickly retreated from their powerful swords. Only a few of the enemy remained as they scattered back over the hills in defeat.

The Captain pointed toward the evening sun, "She has sent prayers forward for her husband and the Lord has responded. Tom Mackenzie is the target and you must go to his assistance. Sarat has prepared the way, but they are hard pressed. Good hunting Commander. Go in the strength of the Lord!"

The First Guards disappeared suddenly in a flash of silver as the Second Guards looked from the parapets. Maybe next time, their Commander thought. He was hoping to join in the fight as well.

CHAPTER THIRTY

THE PORTAL

Tom shrank beneath the overbearing weight of the phantom as it covered him entirely, pressing down on him, the stench of death and burning flesh sickening. He flung wildly out to try and force the shadow from him, but his arms flailed harmlessly through the darkness. The guilt of failure that had driven him into depths of the lies of depression for the past three years was now pushing him toward the growing orange-red light that flickered in the blackness. The closer the shadow pushed him, the more he felt the heat. He began to cough as acrid smoke filled his lungs and panic rose up within him because he suddenly knew that the phantom that was his accuser was forcing him into the flames of life that were even now searing his soul.

Tom fought even harder. He did not wish to die! He was only a failure if he gave up. He could not do that. His family depended on him. There was hope yet to redeem his life. Finally he hit a solid target with one hand, knocking the sword from the phantom. The accuser quickly retrieved the sword and hit Tom hard across the face with the flat side of the blade, knocking him backward away from the heat.

"You will pay for that, Tom," The phantom threatened.

Tom regained his footing, and turned to run but the rock wall barred his way. He turned back to face the shadow as it gathered itself from the mist and materialized into solid form once again. Tom had no place to go, no excuses this time for his behavior, no ministry to hide behind with all of the good works so that his inner depression and disobedience could not be seen. His soul lay bare before the accuser in an empty darkness of despair and hopelessness.

"But there is hope. There is always hope. Tom you know the truth, just embrace it," a voice whispered to Tom's spirit through the blackness. Kapar could not be with Tom, but he could still encourage him.

The accuser stepped forward, holding the sword extended in front of him, until the point pushed ever so slightly into his neck just below the chin.

"Your time is near Tom. Remember you wanted this to happen," the phantom turned the blade to the side, running the cold steel across Tom's face, "Its actually for the good you know. How can you return home to your wife knowing that she knows what your plans were? Your miserable life cannot be salvaged. You have failed once again and there is no hope."

For a moment Tom stood there staring into the faceless figure before him, feeling the cold steel as it began to burn his face, yet he could feel no pain. His soul began to weaken under the accuser's weight, yet his spirit still had life within it that refused to yield. He had made terrible choices in the past, that was certain, and he and his family had had to pay for them, but it had not all been bad. God had used him as well. He could feel that. Somehow, he had been a small part of a larger plan that was still developing.

"If you only knew what you had done, what doors you had a hand in opening, you would not have thought that all that you have done was a failure," Sarat whispered from behind the veil of darkness.

Tom's spirit stirred suddenly, and the phantom stepped back. A story suddenly came to mind, a story of another who had once stood before the accuser. A story of a man destined to be the high priest of Israel who stood in the rags of his humanity, yet was given a garment of pureness and a turban of authority. Tom suddenly knew that the same could happen to him. He quoted what he could remember from the scriptures in Zechariah.

"The Lord rebukes you. Am I not a burning stick that has been pulled from the fire? The Lord rebukes you accuser. The blood of

Christ has turned my rags into pure garments. He has made me whole. I may have failed, but I am not a failure."

The whole world seemed to swirl before Tom suddenly as the phantom faded away into multicolored lights. For a moment the desert lay before him, and Markus stood to one side, yelling to him, waving excitedly, but Tom could not hear what he was saying. The glow became very bright around him, and Tom was enveloped in a sea of white light.

The Gatekeeper, Nasag watched from beyond the veil. From his vantage point between the spiritual and physical realms that intersected at the fallen portal, he could see the fight within Tom's soul as well as the one going on outside of the portal itself. The enemy had been allowed access to the portal within Tom's spirit, but Nasag would not allow access to the fallen portal itself. Sarat's plan to protect Tom from the physical fire exposed the fallen portal to attack. With the Accusers so near, Nasag stood and watched apprehensively.

If Tom failed the test, then Nasag would have to fight hard to keep the portal out of enemy hands because the Accusers would realize that they had gained access to the fallen portal through the spirit within Tom. But Tom had not failed the test. The spiritual portal within Tom's heart exploded open before Nasag and the Gatekeeper immediately fell to his knees in worship as the Holy Spirit seared His way through Tom's past failures and unbelief and intertwined in loving embrace around the man's spirit.

Kapar also knew that the Holy Spirit was working and fought with renewed strength, knowing that his charge had just experienced God in a new and powerful way. But they still had to overcome the forces that threatened Tom's life. In the midst of the physical fires that swept across the meadow, Kapar fought valiantly the spiritual forces that burned after Tom's soul.

The Gatekeeper, Nasag stood up as Tom vanished before him suddenly and then re appeared at the door to the fallen portal. Nasag knew that it was an illusion created by the portal itself and was accustomed to it. When Tom had first approached the portal opening, Nasag had warned him away, but when it was safe for him to leave, he hoped that Tom would try again. Nasag glanced back to where the battle raged and assuring himself that it was safe to do so, he opened the portal to allow Tom to see through to the other side. When the time was right, Tom would have to walk through the opening. That was the only way out. If Tom did not do that, then he would be trapped between the worlds lost in time.

Tom opened his eyes. Markus knelt over him, shaking his shoulders. He lay among the purple sage by the black wall of the Malpais.

"Mackenzie! Are you okay? You took a nasty fall, you did. First you disappeared behind the lava and just as quickly you fell backwards like something threw you! What did you see, lad? Tell me. Did you see the Blessed Virgin?"

Tom sat up as Markus backed away and stood up. The priest began to pace back and forth nervously. Tom looked across the face of the wall and spotted the crack. A strange pale light glowed from behind the opening and for a brief time, Tom saw the meadow covered in flames and then the light disappeared and only the black wall remained. He sat staring at the opening as Markus paced back and forth behind him, mumbling excitedly and praying. Tom could not explain what had happened to him. His mind tried desperately to make sense out of everything around him. Questions began flooding his mind that had no answers. Where was he? How had he gotten here? What was this place? How was he going to get back to his own reality? And most importantly of all. What had just happened to him? He shook his head. He knew that after he had entered the opening, he had somehow experienced a direct confrontation with all of the forces that was against him in the spiritual realm. All of the depression, the guilt, the failures, the lies. It was like a dream, although he knew that somehow it had not been a dream and he had overcome. For the first time in years, he felt as if everything was going to be okay. He felt that he was not a failure and that God had a purpose for his life again. Now he just needed to have the faith to go through the opening again, back to his own time, his own world, his own destiny. He had purpose again in his life!

"Tell me Mackenzie! What is beyond the opening? Is Hades indeed coming for us?" Markus asked, bringing Toms thought back to the here and now, where ever that was for the moment.

"No Markus. Hell is not coming for us. I have seen the way out of this place. A way back to where I came from. We need to get my friend and come back. I believe that when the time is right we can go through the opening back to the place where I came from. When I first entered the opening, I heard a voice say that it was not time. I don't understand what is happening, but I felt that whoever it was that warned me is on our side."

Tom stood up and dusted the sand from his pants and shirt and Markus stared at him, the man's facial expression changing from one of terror and confusion to sudden understanding.

"So Mackenzie, you have met the Accusers and you have triumphed," the priest said in a low and reassuring voice.

Tom looked up startled by the man's statement. How could he have known?

"You no longer wish to die Mackenzie, but have renewed purpose for your life." Markus shook his head in agreement. "Good, good. You have much left to do in this life lad. Like I said before. You are only a failure if you stop trying."

Markus turned and walked away, leaving Tom standing among the sage, totally perplexed by the statement. Who was that man, he thought. Or was he even a man? It didn't matter. What did matter was that Tom knew that somehow God had touched his soul and he knew that he had a purpose and that he could overcome his own past and press own toward a bright and new future. He walked after the priest who had just as quickly changed back into his old self, mumbling nervously.

Tom caught up to Markus next to the fire. Jack Darnell still lay under the shelter asleep. Tom checked on the man and was reassured when he heard him breathing normally. He shook him softly to see if he could wake him, but to no avail. Jack was unconscious, but otherwise appeared to be okay. The falling snag may have hit him, knocking him unconscious, Tom reasoned. Or maybe you both were hit on the head and this is all some kind of crazy dream. Tom laughed the thought away. Either way, he knew that he had to get himself and Jack back through that opening in the wall. He then thought of Markus. The man had been here for hundreds of years. He couldn't leave him.

"Markus come with us. I know that the opening will lead us back to where I came from," Tom asked.

"No, no! Mackenzie. That is your time, not mine. I fear the opening." Markus began pacing again.

"But you can't stay here in this place, Markus. You need to come with us. The opening is the way out. I promise you, it is the way out of this place! I know it!"

"It is your way out, lad, not mine. I will help you with your friend but I will not go with you. The opening is your journey to take. You have met the Accusers and won, therefore you can leave. I on the other hand cannot."

Tom placed his hand on the priest's shoulder and looked directly into his eyes upon hearing Markus' answer, "How do you know what I saw in the opening Markus? Who are you priest?"

The two men stared at each other for a moment and Tom could see suddenly a man that was full of wisdom and strength for just a brief moment and then just as quickly a man that was confused and scared.

Markus dropped his eyes and then closed them, breathing deeply, "I did not pass the test Mackenzie. I too faced my own Accusers when I first tried to leave this place, but what they showed me of myself terrified me."

Tom felt the man's fear, his sadness. He remembered the terror that he had first experienced, "Markus you said it yourself. A man is only a failure when he stops trying."

"It is easier to say that to someone else than to live it yourself, Mackenzie. I followed after the Cross for most of my life, but the past few years I saw much violence. I believed that what we did to the natives of this country was for their own good. Even when I began to question how we treated them in the name of the Cross, I stood by and condoned it. The men raped those poor girls, Mackenzie. I did nothing to help! Nothing."

Markus pushed away and turned toward the shelter where the pilot lay, "That is my burden lad, not yours. You have a family to return to. You have faced the Accusers and won. I must do the same. I know what I must do and I pray that before this place destroys me I will have the courage to do so. But now it is your time. The door is open now, lad. When God opens a door, you should go through it straightway. Now help me with your friend."

Tom tried to wake up Jack again, but could not, so after fashioning a stretcher from several poles and the fire shelters; they placed the pilot carefully on the stretcher. With Tom in the front and Markus behind, the two carried the stretcher to the opening, where Markus stepped back, his nervousness returning. Tom looked though the opening, but saw nothing. Had the door shut? He stepped cautiously into the opening and immediately saw the fading lights again and the meadow, now covered in smoke, but no fire. He could see a pile of rocks and green grass. To one side there appeared to be a line of pink retardant. It appeared to be safe, but he could not tell for sure. He stepped back out of the opening in the rock.

"Are you sure Markus, that you won't come with us?" Tom asked.

"I'm sure, lad. The opening is for you. You must take it. I will find my way, but not at this time." Markus answered.

Tom pulled the stretcher though the opening in the wall.

CHAPTER THIRTY ONE

JULIET DIVISION
PRESENT DAY

T hankfully the wind began to subside somewhat and change directions as the frontal passage pushed through Wyoming. Davis called to see if the helicopter could fly, but the winds were still too strong at the helibase for them to safely lift off. All across the Beaver Fire the raging firestorm began to die down, although there were still many areas that were threatened where entire sections of fireline had been overrun.

The crew emerged from their rocky shelter to a point where they could see up through the burned out forest to the ridgeline above. The fire had completely blackened the landscape. Only smoking stump holes, and snags, and fine white-gray ash that in places were over a foot deep remained. The land had been sterilized by the intensity of the fire. It would be many years before a new forest would develop on this particular mountainside. Because of the extreme slope and lack of vegetation, landslides and severe erosion were possibilities if it ever rained again. But now the area appeared to be safe as long as the crew did not venture into the snag patch.

"Okay guys, let's see if we can make it up to the top. Keep a close watch on the snags above and watch out for stump holes," Davis advised as he buckled on his gear and prepared for the hike straight up the mountain. In single file the small group began climbing up though the moon like landscape. Up above, there were several fires still burning. One was directly above them and over the ridge. A closer one was just over the lip of the crest that they reasoned must be the incinerated helicopter because of the black smoke. They were getting close and as they quietly climbed, each man wondered in his heart whether they would find survivors or just blackened corpses. Davis trembled at the thought and said a silent prayer. Even the worst firefighter knew that when the chips were down, you could still pray.

Others were praying as well, from the family van in North Carolina to the kitchen in New York as well as the trailer at the helibase and scattered firefighters across the Beaver Fire. The true Gatekeepers were unknowingly joining their prayers together and forces of light were responding.

Heather stopped praying for her husband and stood up, looking out the window and across the field. The wind was blowing less. She could see that Teresa had followed through with her word and was warming up her ship so that as soon as the permission was given she could be airborne. But that was not the reason that Heather had suddenly stopped praying. A shift had suddenly occurred and in her spirit she knew that God was intervening. She wiped the tears from her eyes and opened the front door to step outside. The little reporter was pacing back and forth in front of the tent. She was ready to give him a statement now because she knew in her heart that her husband would be okay.

The group emerged thirty minutes later, climbing the last few feet of the slope very carefully because of the many rocks that had loosened as the ground had burned around them. The ones in front turned to help the others over the ledge of rock and then all turned hesitantly to look out across the meadow.

It appeared at first that the entire meadow had burned. Then they saw the line of pink slurry and patch of green grass beyond it among a jumble of rocks, but there was no sign of any shelters. Across the far side of the opening the stricken helicopter still burned, black smoke billowing upward, the smell of burnt rubber, steel and fuel still very strong.

"IC, this is Davis," the strike team leader spoke over his radio.

All radios listened expectantly for the next message as the IC answered.

"We have made it to the meadow. We'll let you know what we find as soon as we can."

"Copy that Davis," the IC responded, "Be advised that Foxtrot Seven-Nine will be airborne shortly. Let me know if there is room to land for evac."

"Could be room, but I'm not sure. We may have to take down a few trees."

"Copy that. Do what you can, but be careful."

"Ayers you take those trees down along the edge to make more room for the helicopter. The rest of us will start searching." No one wanted to say what they were searching for. There were no shelters evident in the meadow. Had the crew not made it out of the chopper?

"You are too late," a hollow, raspy voice spoke from the treetops as the crew began their search.

Nasi flew over the helicopter as the last of the flames swept down the far side of the mountain. His forces tentatively approached as well to also see their handiwork, keeping an eye on the warriors who stood by the rocks.

"Sarat, it appears your gallant Gatekeeper has fallen. And you Kapar seem to be out of a job." Nasi taunted as he landed in the middle of the pink slurry. He searched the rocks where he had last seen Tom before the dark smoke covered him. Where were the bodies? He looked around at his troops who also were totally confused. It could not be, he reasoned. The men had fled to this very spot before diving under their shelters, but they were nowhere to be seen. Only one body lay partially burned by the rocks.

"What have you done, Sarat?" Nasi screamed as he saw the portal open behind the warriors and the shrouded figures of two men coming through it.

"It appears Nasi that you are suddenly out of a job. The Gatekeepers have responded. Rivergate forces are approaching and your time is limited." Sarat responded.

"No!" Nasi screamed and drawing his mighty sword he attacked.

Behind him his army was already being decimated by elements of the First Guards.

"You have been a thorn in my side for too long Nasi," Sarat taunted his adversary as he parried the incoming blow. Nasi was already weakened because of the surge of power that radiated over the meadow with the attack of the First Guards.

"You pushed too hard Nasi," Sarat side stepped another attack, the two swords spraying the ground with a sapphire blue light as the metal clashed. "The adversity that you have tried to place on Tom and his wife is the very thing that drove them to fully open the portals in their own lives. To a true Gatekeeper, adversity is only a means to reveal their real nature. In their weakness, my Lord is strong! By pushing them too hard Nasi, you have doomed yourself!"

Tom suddenly slipped on the rocks and fell, Jack rolling past him. The stretcher was gone. He tried to get up just as a tree limb crashed down over him, hitting him on the head and knocking him unconscious.

Sarat parried a blow with his sword and grabbed Nasi by his neck with crushing strength. He lifted the warrior up as Nasi' sword clamored down among the rocks and disappeared. All around them the air was full of warriors in mortal combat.

"Your army is finished, Nasi, You will no longer have rule over the valley. The Rivergate is fully open now. You tried to destroy it after Eden. You tried in vain time and time again to keep the true Gatekeepers from unlocking its power but you have failed. Look across time and space. See the battlements, the fluttering banners, the warriors, the stairway to heaven itself."

Nasi looked down to where the firefighter lay. Since the rebellion, he had ruled the valley. He had kept the Rivergate from opening for a time, but then that had all changed. First the Moravians had claimed the land. Then small groups of Redeemed had worshipped near the gate itself. He responded with greater power and for a time was able to keep the Redeemed weak and divided. He had infiltrated their churches with traditions of men and racism. But they had somehow overcome. This man's own mother had dared challenge his authority.

This man himself had once tried to challenge his authority. Nasi shook with hate and struggled to regain his weapon and kill the mortal who lay below him. But Sarat's hold on him was too strong.

"You have been a fool Nasi. The true portal is within the Gatekeepers themselves. The Rivergate is their base of power, but their true strength lies within them."

Sarat flung the defeated warrior out across the mountain, throwing his sword as well. It arced upward though the heavens, striking Nasi through the heart. For a moment, Nasi stood suspended in time and space, the golden blade protruding out from his chest. His yellow eyes glared with hatred as he tried in vain to pull the blade free. Sarat stared at him, looking past the eyes to a time when they had once been friends before the rebellion. Nasi had been a territorial spirit that had held sway over the region until the Redeemed had understood their power, rallied around the portal to heaven called the Rivergate and then opened their own portals between their spirits and the throne room of God. Sarat knew that it was not his sword that vanquished Nasi. It was the combined power of a unified people who stood under the protective battlements of the Rivergate and exercised their own spiritual right to proclaim freedom to the region that God had given to them. The battle for Tom had been a testing ground for the fully open Rivergate. It was a battle that had been won by just a few of the true Gatekeepers. What could they do if all of them realized the power within them, Sarat thought. A new day was beginning and Sarat smiled at the revealing of it as Nasi vanished in an explosion that rocked the very throne of the Evil One.

Sarat retrieved his sword, wiping the blade in the grass at his feet.

"First Guards Commander at your service Sarat. Are there any others that we need to vanquish this day?"

Sarat smiled, "No Commander. You have done well. Return to the Rivergate. I will be along shortly."

First Guards Commander saluted and ordered the bugles to announce victory. All across the mountain the bronze warriors assembled, their banners fluttering colorfully. Others helped the wounded so that all found their proper place in the ranks and with a great shout they disappeared just as quickly as they had come.

Kapar knelt over his charge, more proud of Tom than he had ever been. He had faced the Accuser and he had finally overcome him. The other firefighters were fast approaching and overhead a helicopter was hovering.

"You have done well, Kapar, but there is more work to be done." Sarat knelt down beside the Guardian.

"Will you be coming back with us to the Rivergate?" Kapar asked.

"For a time, but my kind are not needed there any longer. The true Gatekeepers hold power in the valley now. They have the power to bind on earth and loose on earth. They have the power now to establish the Kingdom in the valley. I will go elsewhere. There are other portals that must be opened."

Kapar saluted the Gatekeeper, "If not before then I will see you at the Victory Banquet."

Sarat stepped into the portal among the rocks where the other Gatekeeper stood and with a flash of light the portal closed. At that moment, the firefighters ran up to where the two men lay beneath their shelters.

The first thing Tom wanted to do when he regained consciousness was to call Nicole.

"Hello," Nicole answered her cell phone, still in the car driving to church.

"Nicole is that you?"

"Oh God! Tom you okay?"

"Yes love. I'm fine….. Please, …please forgive me," Tom pleaded, crying.

"It's okay Tom, just come home. Please just come home."

CHAPTER THIRTY TWO

EL MALPAIS NATIONAL PARK
GRANTS NEW MEXICO
FIVE YEARS LATER

"It looks like it's going to rain," Nicole said as she walked up behind her husband and pulled him back against her. "You having a good time?" She snuggled herself against his back, closing her eyes and thinking of how much she loved the man.

"Yes, you?'" Tom responded as he gazed out the window and across the desert to the black expanse of the lava beds.

"Wonderful."

His two youngest children were looking through the museum store finding more toys that they would soon come running up to their Dad to ask him to buy. They had grown so much these past five years he thought. Both were in school and Nathan was a sophomore at state, majoring in computer science.

"Hey dad! You've got to see this book. It's way cool." Nathan, taller than Tom by three inches, held up a large book concerning the history of the Malpais. He brought the book over as Nicole gave Tom a final hug, and left to ensure that the younger ones were not getting into too much trouble. The family had been on vacation for a week with one more to go, trying their best to see the West and visit all of the places that Tom had seen all of those years before as a wild land firefighter.

"It talks about hidden treasure in the Badlands, of places where time seems to stand still. When you were here on the fire, you found a place like that, didn't you?"

Tom shook his head as he took the book in his hand, thinking of the time he had been to this very place when he had been a Division Supervisor on the Cherry Fire. He had camped in the Badlands for several days and remembered the strange places he had encountered. There were places where men could get lost forever, places where the spirits of old seemed to rule the night. It was truly a remarkable land, full of mystery. He had only been to New Mexico once back before he had quit the Forest Service to begin a business as a Consultant Forester and also a youth minister two years earlier. Well there had been that other time, but that could only have been a dream, a bad dream that had changed his life forever. He shivered at the thought of what could have happened as he watched his wife kneel down beside her two youngest children. How he loved his family, he thought.

Tom flipped through the pages, looking at the pictures until he was suddenly struck by a particular photograph of one of the many rock drawings that the ancient inhabitants of the land had done. The picture looked oddly like a helicopter! That was strange, he thought and then he turned the page to a section about hidden treasure.

Tom took a step back as his wife returned to look down at the book as well.

There have been many tales over the years of hidden treasure within the Malpais. Although most of them are undoubtedly fiction, there are documented cases where people have found treasure hidden in the mazes within the lava beds. One such story involves a certain Markus O'Rielly who was a servant of Coronado himself. The story goes that Markus disappeared from the Spanish expedition in 1540 as they were traveling through the area and was thought to be lost within the lave beds. Several weeks later, however Markus returned to the party, explaining that he had indeed been lost. He spoke of seeing strange things in a place where time seemed to stand still and thought all was lost until a tunnel through the rock wall across from the arch led him back to his own time and place. He was thought to be crazy and kept to himself for the rest of the trip. The next year Markus was said to have returned to Spain where he later died an old man after having married and raised five children. He died a rich man, but no one knows from where the money came. Some say he found treasure while wondering the maze of the lava beds.

"What is it, honey?" Nicole asked, noticing the far away look on her husbands face. He had changed so much since the accident those many years before, changed for the good. They had finally overcome their past, secured their future, and were walking in the full blessings of the God that had always been there for them. It had not been easy. They had to pay for the past mistakes, but together they had worked their way out from under their financial bondage. They had worked through their personal problems and had begun again to follow after the ministry that God had called them to do.

"Oh, nothing really. I was just reading about hidden treasure. Hey, it looks like the rain has stopped. Do you want to ride down to the archway? I'd like to see if it has changed since the last time I was here. It is truly a beautiful place."

Tom had always known, deep within, that somehow his experience that day on the mountain had not been a dream. Now he knew for sure. Good for you, Markus, he thought. You must have finally faced your Accusers and won.

"Yeah, that would be great. Then you can take us to that restaurant you told us about in Grants."

"Come on, kids, let's go. There is a place I want to show you, a place where I once found a great treasure."

"Treasure?" the younger children asked in unison, "Okay!"

"What treasure?" Nicole asked.

"The treasure right here around me," Tom answered, waving his hand over his wife and family.

Somehow he knew that the archway had changed a great deal but somewhere along the face of the lava wall across the highway from the arch, laid a crack in the wall, a place where he had learned to overcome, and a place where his life had started all over again.

The Gatekeeper Nasag watched as the family walked by, saluting the Guardians who traveled with the family, amazed at the open portals that joined this couple and their children with the heavens. Like it had been before, in Eden. Like it was destined to be for all of those who were called to be Gatekeepers.

Although this story is fiction, some of the characters and events portrayed are based on real occurrences. Each member of the Moravian Party described in this story really did travel from Pennsylvania to western North Carolina in order to find a safe place for a new settlement. The party did survey a tract along the upper Yadkin River, traveled through the Mulberry Fields and steered clear of Native Americans that had a seasonal village along the north bank of the Yadkin River in what is now Wilkes County. They dedicated the land to God's service and although they never settled the valley, they did settle further east in the area now known as Winston-Salem. One thing is for sure, their spiritual heritage still resonates within the valley even today.

Christopher Gist was a historical figure who lived briefly on the bluffs overlooking the Yadkin and Reddies Rivers during the same period when the Moravians travelled through the valley and although history does not show him helping the Moravians, he could have. Soon after this time period he left his cabin on the Reddies and never returned, travelling to Virginia to work with George Washington.

The Wilkesboro court house and Smithey's store are real places that stand today as testimony to times gone by. The hanging tree behind the courthouse declined slowly over time until the county forester announced it dead in the mid 1990's. A young black oak said to be sired from the tree itself was planted in its place and still grows there today.

The story of the girl Eileen is based on truth. She was part of a real family that lived in the county during the depression and through the

Second World War. The small church in Traphill remained empty for 40 years after the girl said that it would do so, proving that God speaks through children just the same as he can through adults.

I have spent time fighting fire in the Malpais. The place is truly remarkable, filled with mysterious places, hidden trails, underground tunnels, archways and walls of lava. I have stood under the great archway of rock and walked alongside the lava walls. I have seen several of the cracks in the wall that lead to trails where a man can be lost forever. Strange mysteries haunt the night. North becomes south, south becomes north. I have entered a few of the trails, but did not proceed but only a few hundred feet. Are there trails to other dimensions? Who knows, but if openings to other worlds do exist, I believe the Malpais would be one place where they would be found.

Scripture says that angels are ministering spirits to those who serve the Lord. Do they fight heavenly battles in the spiritual dimension as we live our lives? Maybe they do or maybe they don't. But one thing is for sure, as a Christian, we do not have to fight the devil at all. Jesus defeated him on the cross for us. Through the finished work of the cross, the devil is no longer relevant because all power has already been stripped from him by the work on the cross itself. The only power that the devil has over our lives is the power that we give him. God wishes for each of us to understand that we ourselves are an open door to the throne of God. All we have to do is walk through the portal.